DR BAKEWELL'S WONDROUS SCHOOL OF CONFECTIONERY

by

L.T. Talbot

RB
Rossendale Books

Published by Lulu Enterprises Inc.
3101 Hillsborough Street
Suite 210
Raleigh, NC 27607-5436
United States of America

Published in paperback 2015
Category: Fiction
Copyright L. T. Talbot © 2015
ISBN : 978-1-326-44486-0

Dedication

For Mum
to whom 'thank you' will never be enough.

In my thoughts daily, in my heart forever
xxx

Contents

Chapter 1

Tea and Biscuits

D r Bakewell sat at his big, old, solid oak wooden desk, his balding round head resting in his short, stumpy fingers. "I just don't know what we're going to do, Derek" he bemoaned to the thin man sitting in the winged red-leather armchair in the corner of the room. "They're going to close the school and I don't know what we can do to stop them. This is the only school of confectionery in England and one of the best in the world. I just don't know what we can do. It's happening all over again." Clearly troubled by this recent news, he sighed heavily, feeling as though the weight of the whole school was resting on his broad, tweed shoulders.

Sitting quietly in the armchair in the corner of the room, gently sipping his tea from a white, china teacup, Professor Derek Drumgoole stroked his pointy, grey goatee for a minute, before slowly making his suggestion. He had known George Bakewell for years (longer than either of them cared to admit) and knew his friend had a hot temper and didn't like change very much. He remembered once, when they were much younger, a new teacher wanted to introduce a new method of mixing in baking class. It was so different to how George Bakewell had been taught that the poor new teacher had been sacked for not taking his subject seriously and failing to teach proper baking methods, when all he'd wanted to do was to demonstrate new ways of baking! So it was somewhat gingerly and with a little trepidation that Professor Drumgoole voiced his suggestion.

"Well, if the reason they want to close the school is because we don't have enough pupils then maybe we should do something about that."

Dr Bakewell raised his head and looked at his colleague and friend, his lips set in a thin, firm line as Professor Drumgoole, although a little unnerved by his Headmaster's stern expression, continued with his idea.

"At the moment we only take the children and relatives of the best bakers, Chefs and cake decorators in the world, yes?" Dr Bakewell silently nodded his head, already not liking the sound of this idea and feeling his pulse start to quicken slightly. "So obviously we are going to have fewer students than all other schools and academies in the country. So why not open the doors of the school to children that otherwise wouldn't be able to attend? Let's invite all children into our school and see if we can produce the next generation of world-class bakers from ordinary folk."

The slight quickening of the pulse that George Bakewell had begun to feel a few seconds earlier now took hold; his heart beating furiously with anger and frustration, his face slowly bloomed into a vivid shade of red - much like a radish - and the vein on the temple of his head was now visibly throbbing so hard that he could stand it no longer and he exploded in a rage.

"PREPOSTEROUS" he roared, jumping to his feet at once. "This is my school, I bought the property, it's my name on the door, it's my reputation at stake and I simply will not allow any Tom, Dick and Harry to attend my school, it has to maintain its standards and it will not do so by simply allowing anyone to attend just to stop the school from closing. I'd rather it close down as the best, than keep it open as average" and with a defiant, finishing nod and a thump of the desk, he sat back down in his chair and folded his arms, confident he had made his feelings quite clear. But Professor Drumgoole persisted.

"Look, George" he said softly, placing his teacup and saucer on the small table beside him, "we have to face facts - we don't have a choice here. We simply must take in more pupils. The school is starting to fall into ruin because the fees that are paid by the parents no longer cover the cost of running the school. The Council of Confectioners has spoken to the Government about it but the Government refuses to budge and has stated that all schools with falling numbers will close, regardless of whether they are specialist, private or otherwise. We are no exception." He took a moment and a deep breath before finally adding a comment that he was sure would get through Dr Bakewell's stubbornness: "I thought you opened this school to teach, I thought you were proud of your skills and wanted to teach others; to leave a lasting legacy, forever to be known as the 'Wondrous Dr Bakewell' (Professor Drumgoole knew that Dr Bakewell was a vain man and hoped this last attempt might make him rethink his refusal). It worked - Dr Bakewell sat back in his chair, took off his little round tortoiseshell glasses and nibbled the end of the bit that goes over your ear.

"That is exactly why I opened this school, as you well know" he replied stiffly. "To teach. Not to be known as wondrous of course, but to teach children how to make the most amazing, extraordinary culinary creations. I'm not agreeing just yet, but tell me what you're thinking and then, if it's sensible, then I suppose I might give it some serious consideration. I'm not promising, mind you" he added, with a raised eyebrow, "just curious."

"A summer fete and open day" continued Professor Drumgoole, "where we open the school and our grounds to the public. We could charge a small entrance fee, but once inside we will provide a delightful insight into our wonderful school, with a chance for children to try their hand at baking and sweet making, along with all the other activities and stalls you find at a summer fete."

"Lovely, Derek" responded Dr Bakewell sarcastically, "but how exactly is that supposed to bring more pupils and more importantly, pupils of the right standards to my school?"

Professor Drumgoole sighed inwardly - not only did Dr Bakewell insist on calling it his school even though it was Professor Drumgoole that ran it (and had been doing so successfully for well over ten years), but George Bakewell never seemed to let poor Professor Drumgoole finish what he was saying before he jumped in with his questions or poo-pooing of his (often quite good) ideas. Undaunted, he carried on explaining. "What I'm proposing is that during this fete, we hold a competition. The winners of the best cakes, sweets or other creations can win a scholarship at the school." Dr Bakewell opened his mouth to say something but sharp-eyed Professor Drumgoole noticed and raised his hand up, palm outwards, in a silent gesture, as if to say 'hold on, hear me out.'

"If we advertise it in the newspapers" he continued "children can practice, then bring their entry to the fete. You would be the judge of course and the children who make whichever creations you judge to be the best will be able to attend our school. This way you can ensure that you don't miss out on losing any talented future pupils, you keep control over who attends and we can get people excited about the amazing things we do here, all at the same time."

Dr Bakewell closed his eyes for a moment after his friend had finished talking and rested his head against the back of his chair, digesting everything he had just heard. Professor Drumgoole waited patiently in silence for a minute before Dr Bakewell finally opened his eyes, fixed his colleague with a steely gaze, sighed and declared "I'll think about it. Goodnight Derek".

Chapter 2

A Bakewell Breakfast

DONG! DONG! DONG! The heavy school bell rang it's first thunderous peal of the day and tolled six times, heralding the arrival of morning and an end to sleep. Morning had arrived bringing with it beautiful, bright sunshine and a fresh, spring breeze. Caroline Coleman stirred in her bed, rubbed the sleep out of her eyes, propped herself up on her elbows and yawned. 'Friday morning already' she thought, as she flopped back down onto her pillow and pulled her blue quilt over her head. Five more minutes then she'd get up, she agreed with herself. Still, at least the weekend was almost here!

When she eventually arose and had gotten herself washed and dressed, Caroline and her best friend, Verity Rose, walked down to the school dining hall, arm in arm, for breakfast. One of the best points about being a pupil at the world-famous Dr Bakewell's school, they agreed, was that the food they had was always delicious. They walked along the breakfast bar, a huge long table which ran the whole side of the dining hall, piled high and laden with food, choosing their breakfast just like a buffet. And what a choice it was too - there was everything you could think of and then some more you probably couldn't! There were boiled eggs, poached eggs and scrambled eggs; bacon, sausage, ham and cheese. There were grilled tomatoes, fresh tomatoes, chopped tomatoes and mushrooms. And sliced bread, bread buns, croissants, pancakes, waffles and muffins. And marmalade, honey, chocolate spread, strawberry jam, raspberry jam and blueberry jams. And fresh fruit, cereal, porridge and muesli along with yoghurt, milk and water and in the centre of the table there was a large silver circular fountain with ten taps sprinkled around the rim, each tap pouring a different flavour juice. Apple, cranberry, raspberry, mango, passion fruit, tropical, blackcurrant, orange, strawberry and pineapple were all served out of the fruit juice fountain. In fact, on more than one occasion, Caroline and Verity had gotten into trouble being late for class because they had spent so long choosing breakfast!

They sat down at their House table in the centre of the refectory, eating their breakfast, chatting away to each other wondering what today would bring. At the right-hand side of the refectory, mirrored opposite the breakfast bar was the teachers banquet table; Dr Bakewell and Professor Drumgoole, the most important two, sat in the centre, where they could survey the entire room and it's students, just as a King would survey his court.

This morning Professor Drumgoole and Dr Bakewell were as usual, eating in silence. This was of no surprise to any of the students, as Dr Bakewell was well known for being stuffy and old-fashioned. However, unusually, before the school bell rang again to signal the end of breakfast, Dr Bakewell stood up, walked into the centre of the hall and stood in front of Caroline and Verity's table. He coughed to clear his throat, raised his hand in the air (the signal for silence) then began to speak. This was most unusual as Dr Bakewell normally left the hall before the pupils had finished breakfast and any school notices were read out by Professor Drumgoole. In fact, several of the students often whispered amongst themselves that Dr Bakewell should really hand over his title of Headmaster to Professor Drumgoole as he was the one most involved with the pupils and they didn't really know what Dr Bakewell actually did, other than tell them what they shouldn't be doing.

"Students" he began awkwardly, "I have something rather...interesting...to tell you this morning." Quick glances flashed around the pupils, one to another, curious as to what this interesting news was; it certainly didn't sound interesting from the way he hesitated over the word. "As some of you may know, we have developed a decrease in the number of pupils attending our marvellous school and there are certain 'repairs' needed to the building." Caroline and Verity looked behind them at the cracks which had recently appeared around one of the six stone columns which supported the arched roof of the refectory. "Last night, Professor Drumgoole and myself had a long discussion and we have decided that this year, for the first time ever, we shall hold a Summer Fete."

A murmur immediately broke out amongst the students at the mention of the fete, prompting Dr Bakewell to raise his hand again. Quickly the students ceased whispering, allowing him to continue.

"We shall open our doors to all members of the public to sample our fine produce and teachings; we shall hold a competition and the ten winners of the competition will win a scholarship to attend our School of Confectionery. In the meantime, I invite everyone of you to create your most amazing, beautiful creations to be sold at the fete in order to help us raise money for the upkeep of the school. That's all." He looked around at the stunned, silent faces and turned to walk away.

"But sir" piped up a plummy-voice from the far table that was recognised instantly. It belonged to Avery Sorrel, the richest pupil in the school. "I'm sorry sir, but that seems...well, a little odd, doesn't it?" Caroline and Verity rolled their eyes and sighed, correctly expecting another rant from the outspoken Avery.

"This is supposed to be a school of the gifted, the best of the best. You can't just allow anyone in, that's not fair on the rest of us. And why should they not have to pay while we do? Sir, I have to say I think this is a mistake" he declared rather obnoxiously. Silence fell on the hall whilst both the students and teachers reeled from Avery's cheek. He was well known for being rude and a bit above himself, but to tell Dr Bakewell he was wrong was a step too far. With baited breath everyone waited for Dr Bakewell's reaction.

* * *

Very calmly and quietly, Dr Bakewell strode over to Avery, stood behind him and told him to stand up. Avery did so but looked a little sheepish, realising he had gone too far this time, regretting his words instantly.

"Mr Sorrel" he began, loudly enough for everyone to hear him, which is of course what he intended. Avery felt himself start to tremble and his cheeks flushed a beautiful shade of crimson as Dr Bakewell continued. "Do remind me when this school became 'Sorrel's School of Confectionery'?" He waited for Avery to answer, which of course he didn't; he just stayed as quiet as a church mouse, looking at the floor feeling everyone's eyes staring at him, boring into him, shame and embarrassment burning inside him.

"Head up, boy" continued Dr Bakewell, clearly annoyed. "I asked you a question. You seem to have strong opinions on the running of this school, so I would merely like to know when it became yours to run?"

All around, students now looked away from the uncomfortable conversation and atmosphere in the refectory. Yet no-one dared speak, not even Avery.

"I...I...I..." he stammered, unable to get any words out, he was so humiliated.

"When you know all the facts, Mr Sorrel, you will be able to make what is called an 'informed opinion'. In order to know all the facts, you need to become a trusted member of staff. To become a member of staff you must pass exams and have years of practical experience. To become a trusted member of staff is another matter entirely which can take furthermore years. All of which start with the studying and successful completion of Culinary Arts and Confectionery Craft at my school. As a twelve year old know-it-all who obviously knows very little - else he would have had the common sense NOT to speak out of turn in full view of the school and question his Headmaster - you are poorly equipped to fulfil any one of the above. So any opinion you have, Avery Sorrel, is of no interest to me whatsoever and you shall do well to remember your place here is as a student, nothing more. I suggest you sit down and keep your opinions to yourself for the rest of the day, unless you wish to embarrass yourself in front of your peers once more." With that, he turned his back on a very red-faced Avery and calmly walked out of the refectory to face the day on a full stomach.

Chapter 3

Honeybourne Avenue

The next morning, as newspapers reached breakfast tables all across the country, a buzz of excitement ran through families up and down the land. Mysterious, hexagon-shaped, sparkly, purple posters had appeared overnight; in shop windows, in the newspapers and magazines - even tied to lamposts. You couldn't miss them, they were everywhere; brightly coloured with beautiful golden, curly writing, announcing a Summer Fete to be organised by the one and only world-famous master baker, Dr Bakewell.

Dr Bakewell is proud to present, for the first time ever, a summer fete and open day to be held on 31st July in the beautiful historical gardens of Honeycomb Hall.

The event will commence at 10 o'clock.

We also invite every child in the country, who is over the age of 11, to enter our competition to create and bake their very own cake. The 10 winning entries will be awarded a place to attend our School of Confectionery.

Anyone wishing to attend should meet at their local Town Hall at 7pm on 1st July for further instructions.

So get your aprons on, get practising and get baking!

Murmurs of curiosity ran through the streets - everyone knew of the legendary Dr Bakewell; he used to make the most delicious, decorative and unusual cakes and sweets of all time before his bakery was closed and he opened a school. It was a school hushed in secrecy however - no-one was ever allowed to visit, no-one knew what the school looked like or where it was. You see, Dr Bakewell always made the travel arrangements to transport his pupils to and from the school, but it was very discreet. The children that attended the school were not allowed to say where the school was or how they got there, prompting people to whisper about Dr Bakewell and accuse him of being paranoid but about what, no-one knew. All the parents knew was that on the 1st September each year, when the new school term began, they would take their children to a secret location to be transported to the school. In the summer holidays the parents received a letter telling them where that location was to be and what time their children needed to be there, so the school's red, double-decker buses could collect them from that spot and take them to school. At the end of term, the red buses would drop the children off at these same points, ready to be collected and taken home. Dr Bakewell was most adamant that only the most talented people could enter his school and any visitors would distract pupils and disrupt their learning. Not even parents were allowed to visit! So, to hear the school was opening its doors to the public was very big news indeed and baking fever took the country by storm that very afternoon.

* * *

Meanwhile, in a village called Bees End, in the kitchen of number 3 Honeybourne Avenue (a modest, little terraced house), Mrs Baker was rummaging in the cupboard under the sink. She was a quiet, softly spoken, pleasant lady who originally came from Ethiopia before moving to England. She had long, dark brown hair, high cheekbones which emphasised her big, brown eyes and had still managed to keep her athletic figure despite having three children. Although she was usually very smartly dressed, this morning she was wearing her brown and green flowery pinafore with a duster pocket at the front, complete with yellow duster hanging over the edge. Saturday morning was always set aside for housework whilst her husband took their daughter Manuka to her dance lesson, but this morning Mrs Baker couldn't find any polish anywhere and it was slowing down her busy schedule. She still had to run the vacuum cleaner around the house as well as polish the furniture so she decided to send her eldest child, Vaughan, on an errand to get some more. Well, she couldn't very well go out in the street wearing her scruffs and her pinafore, could she? She went to the bottom of the stairs and called him.

"Vaughan" she shouted up the stairs, "will you pop to the shop for me, please? I need some polish so I can finish off the housework". She heard a door open and saw Vaughan's feet appear at the top of the stairs. To be exact, what she actually saw were two grey socks, with her son's feet inside.

"Okay Mum" he answered, "I'll be as quick as I can". Down the stairs ran Vaughan, a small, skinny boy of twelve with short hair of darkest brown, equally dark treacle-brown eyes and warm, caramel colour skin. When he reached the bottom step he sat down and pulled on his old, tatty trainers which matched perfectly with his faded blue jeans and old grey jumper. Mrs Baker gave Vaughan some money for the polish and smiled at him as the door closed behind him on his way out. He was such a good boy, she thought, always willing to help. She was very proud of her children.

* * *

Vaughan had lived at number 3 Honeybourne Avenue, Bees End since he was three, with his mother Gill, his father Melvyn and his younger sister Manuka, who was seven. They moved there just after his little sister, Lucille, died when only a baby and Vaughan was two. They liked living in Bees End; it was a typical little village where everyone knew everyone and it was a friendly place. Mr Baker was a small, thin, man with pale skin, mousey brown hair and a little tuft of a moustache which just hid his upper lip from view. He worked in The Hive, the local honey factory in the next town, a larger place called Honey Wood. 'Couldn't have given the place a better name!' he joked with his colleagues at the factory. His job was to make sure that all the honey that was sent to the shops was pure and of good quality. He always said the best part of his job was when he was sent overseas to research honey; he spent three months bee-keeping in Ethiopia where he met the lady who was to become his wife. He didn't earn very much money but he was happy - he said finding Mrs Baker was better than any amount of money he could ever have been paid - plus he was given lots of honey products to take home to test out each month!

Mrs Baker was a housewife who very much enjoyed being at home. She used to be a professional athlete but she had to stop running when she had her children. She was devoted to her family and when Vaughan and Manuka were at school she would experiment with the free honey that her husband brought home at the end of each month. They used honey for first-aid, solid beeswax honey for polish (although she had just finished the last of her supply recently and hence sent Vaughan on his errand), and they used honey in tea instead of sugar. In fact she often joked that the Baker family owed their livelihood to bees and if it weren't for the bees in Bees End and Honey Wood, it would be little short of a disaster! Consequently, when she wasn't experimenting in the house or doing housework, she would most likely be found in the kitchen baking cakes or in the garden, planting and tending to a mass of bright, colourful flowers to keep the bees happy and honey sweet!

* * *

As Vaughan was standing at the till of the corner shop waiting to pay for the polish, something in the shop window caught his eye.

"What's that, Mr Singh?" he asked the shopkeeper, pointing to the poster.

"Oh that poster?" replied Mr Singh, "Yes, that was stuck to the window this morning before I had even opened up the shop. I don't know who put it there but its very eye-catching, isn't it, all sparkly and such an unusual shape. Go out the front and you'll be able to read it - it seems the famous Dr Bakewell is going to have a summer fete at his School of Confectionery and everyone is invited. Have you heard of Dr Bakewell then Vaughan?" Mr Singh didn't get an answer - by the time he had said that there was going to be a fete, Vaughan left the shop so quickly to read the poster he forgot his change! Mr Singh walked around the till to the front door just as Vaughan started to run home.

"VAUGHAN!" Mr Singh leant out of the door and hollered down the road after him. "YOU - FORGOT - YOUR - CHANGE!"

But it was no use. Vaughan had read the poster and was now very possibly the most excited child in England - if not the most excited then certainly one of the most! He ran home as quickly as he could and could barely speak by the time he got home, he was so out of breath! For Vaughan had loved baking and cooking all his life. Thanks to his Mum, Vaughan had grown up helping her mix cake batter and decorate all sorts of cakes; it was their special time together and he loved nothing more. He knew that the school's Summer Fete was his big chance and he had to get himself into that school.

"Mum, Mum" he panted as he flung open the front door and entered his home.

"Vaughan, whatever's the matter" asked Mrs Baker, quickly appearing in the hallway.

"Dr....Bakewell....fete....school...." Vaughan gasped, propping himself up against the staircase. Mrs Baker sat him down on the stairs and fetched Vaughan a drink of water, while he slowly got his breath back. He took a sip of water and looked at his Mum.

"Thanks Mum", he smiled, his breathing returning to normal.

"You frightened the life out of me there for a minute", Mrs Baker scolded him, "now, what's all this about Dr Bakewell?"

"He's having a school fete on 31st July" explained Vaughan "everyone's invited to go. It's the first time anyone has ever been able to visit the school and guess what Mum, guess what the best part is?" She smiled at him, realising why he was so excited. She knew that Dr Bakewell was a hero of Vaughan's. If he was having a fete then they'd certainly take Vaughan, she knew it would make his summer.

"Well, that is a turn up for the books" Mrs Baker agreed "and what's the best part?"

"He's having a competition. Any child over the age of 11 is invited to bake and create their own cake and enter it in the competition. There will be ten winners and you'll never guess what the prize is!"

Mrs Baker was genuinely curious herself now - she'd never let onto Vaughan as she knew he admired Dr Bakewell, but she'd heard from a few people that he was really a bit of a sourpuss and a snob. Wondering what he would offer as a prize, she nudged Vaughan to continue. "Go on then, what's the prize?"

"All ten winners" beamed Vaughan "win a scholarship to study at his school! Imagine, ten people like me able to attend Dr Bakewell's School of Confectionery!" Looking up at the ceiling, his eyes glazed over as he began daydreaming about going to Dr Bakewell's school. Mrs Baker's heart sank however, when she heard this. There would surely be thousands of people entering that competition and only ten places available? How on earth would Vaughan cope if he didn't win? He was good at baking she knew, but there'd be a lot of competition for such a prize. What would his chance be? There was only one thing to do, she thought to herself.

"Come on then" she said, standing up and smoothing down her pinafore. "There's no time to waste, is there?" Confused, Vaughan looked up at her.

"Come on...where?" he enquired.

"To the library of course, then the shops" she replied, "we need to brush up your knowledge, research recipes and get you plenty of ingredients so you can start baking." Vaughan looked up and smiled at her - she really understood how important this was to him. "But Mum, don't you want to get changed first" he suggested, reminding her that she was still in her cleaning clothes, complete with duster in her pocket. She bent down, put her arm round Vaughan's shoulders and whispered into his ear:

"On any ordinary day, then yes..." she confirmed "but this is no ordinary day!" With that, she quickly brushed her hair, took the duster out of her pocket and threw it on the telephone, picked up her handbag, and walked out the door - still wearing her pinafore! "Well? Come on then - you have a competition to win!"

* * *

Vaughan Baker had almost finished his first year of Secondary School at Honey Wood Comprehensive, but he didn't really like his school. The teachers were nice but there were some boys in his class who teased him because his favourite lesson was cooking. They would say that cooking was for girls and call him girly names (Dawn, most often because it rhymed with Vaughan); he stood up to them one day and told them very loudly that a lot of the famous chefs and bakers were actually men so they should get their facts right first otherwise they just show themselves up. Naturally, the bullies didn't like this because Vaughan had had a point and had made them look stupid in front of the class; they also didn't like the fact that Vaughan had stood up to them. They only liked it when they thought they could upset him and he didn't answer back. So

Vaughan was quite looking forward to being able to go to a school where you could learn to bake properly and everyone there was good at baking. That would show those bullies, wouldn't it?!

Together Mrs Baker and Vaughan went to Honey Wood library and took out as many recipe books as they were allowed, to get ideas and start practising. Vaughan also found some of Dr Bakewell's own books he'd written: 'Dr Bakewell's Christmas Creations'; 'Dr Bakewell's Cakes for the Macabre'; 'Dr Bakewell's Birthday Parties' and 'Dr Bakewell's Hallowe'en Horrors'. He found these particularly useful as it gave an insight into Dr Bakewell himself and gave creative suggestions Vaughan doubted he would have thought of on his own. He read about different flavours that had been used in recipes before - some sounded very strange indeed - like strawberry and white chocolate or chocolate and chilli; he'd even found a recipe for courgette cake! Imagine that, a cake made out of vegetables! Yes, he would have fun experimenting in the kitchen, of that he was sure but Vaughan knew that he would have to create something really marvellous if there were only ten places on offer. So with the image of attending that school firmly in his mind, he set to work, concentrating as hard as he possibly could, to come up with the best cake ever created.

Chapter 4

Chocolate Chess

P reparations for the grand summer fete were also taking place at Honeycomb Hall, otherwise known as Dr Bakewell's school. Madame Rougerie, the Pastry Chef and Head of Student Kitchens, was at her wit's end with children wanting to spend all their spare time in the kitchens practising and creating. Cuthbert Flowerdew, the Head Gardener, had been tasked with making sure the school's gardens were immaculate and all the trees, shrubs, flowers were pruned and lawns mown and swept; there wasn't 'to be a dead leaf or twig in sight' (to use Dr Bakewell's exact words). All in all, every teacher and assistant at the school was working extra hard to both help the pupils and also make sure Dr Bakewell wasn't let down. Everyone knew that deep down the fete was really the idea of Professor Drumgoole and Dr Bakewell still wasn't convinced it would work, but Professor Drumgoole was so well-liked and respected that they didn't want his idea to flop. Of course, the other reason was that the school had started to fall into disrepair and the teachers knew that if things didn't change soon, the school could close forever, so the pressure was on everyone to make this fete a huge success.

Meanwhile, back at Honeybourne Avenue, Vaughan was pouring through all the books they'd borrowed from the library, looking for ideas. He knew that because this was a competition for children, the rules stated that they could copy a recipe or cake from another book (the only rule was that the parents had to sign a form to say that the entry was made completely by their child and that no help was given) but Vaughan didn't want to risk making the same cake as someone else. So, he decided he must create his own cake.

The only trouble was, what kind of cake should he make, that would be good enough to win a scholarship?

After watching Vaughan sitting at the dining table flicking through books for almost two hours, Mr Baker had decided enough was enough and Vaughan should take a break. Off he went, out of the room and came back five minutes later with a square wooden box under his arm.

"Right Vaughan" Mr Baker said as he closed the door of the dining room behind him, "you need a break. Now." he added as Vaughan began to protest. "Nothing clears your mind like a good game of chess" and he swiftly moved the books to the side of the table with a sweep of his arm, sat on the chair opposite his son and placed the square wooden box on the table between them. Vaughan took out the old wooden chessboard along with the ebony and ashwood figurines from the box and placed them on their squares, ready to start.

"White or black?" he asked his father.

"Ebony!" stated Mr Baker as they both laughed. So playing as white, Vaughan moved his ashwood pawn into position and the game began.

* * *

"Chess certainly is your game, Vaughan" Mr Baker stated, as Vaughan took his father's knight and added it to the pawns, bishop and rook that he had already taken from his Dad. "I bet you could give that Dr Bakewell a run for his money if you got into that school you know" he carried on, "I hear he's a big fan of chess. Always good to have something in common, isn't it?" And that was it. Like a lightbulb switching on in his head, Vaughan instantly knew what he should bake. Of course - in the Dr Bakewell books he'd read at the library it mentioned that Dr Bakewell was a keen chess player, so what better to create than his very own, edible chessboard? He'd never seen one anywhere before so it would be truly unique and Dr Bakewell would surely notice it.

"Sorry Dad" Vaughan apologised as he swiftly rose to his feet, rocking the table as he did so and knocking the remaining chess pieces over, "but I know what I'm going to bake and I need to do it now while it's in my head" and he rushed straight into the kitchen and shut the door, leaving his Dad staring after him smiling.

"Well, what do you know!" Mr Baker mused to himself, rubbing his finger along his moustache!

Half an hour later the kitchen door was still shut and now Vaughan's little sister, Manuka, was pressing her ear against the door, giggling. Most of the time all that she could hear were clinking and clunking noises; the whirring of an electric mixer and the chinks of stirring spoons but occasionally these sounds were interrupted by choruses of 'bit more...bit more...whoops, not that much!' and 'almost there....not yet....yep, there you go!' as Vaughan was baking, which made her giggle.

It was a good job that the door was closed because if Mrs Baker could have seen the state of the kitchen she'd have had a fit. To use one of her phrases, she would have said it 'looked like a bomb had hit it.' There were broken eggshells, flour and spilled sugar on the kitchen table, the remains of melted chocolate in bowls left on the windowsill, blobs of cake mixture splattered all over the walls and dirty spoons, knives and mixing bowls piled high in the sink. Vaughan himself wasn't much tidier, he had flour and cocoa all over his apron, cake mixture splashed up his arms, chocolate smeared over his face and his hair was dusted in white flour! But he didn't care - he was inspired and he was going to make this practice cake perfect no matter how messy it was!

One and a half hours later, the kitchen door opened. Fortunately Manuka had long since given up listening at the door and was now watching a film on television with her parents. Vaughan proudly walked into the living room with his cake in his hands and coughed, to get their attention.

All three of them turned around to see a dishevelled Vaughan, covered from head to foot in ingredients, beaming proudly.

"This is it" he announced as he placed the cake on the dining room table behind them "this is my entry. Almost - I need to get a couple of decorations to finish it off first. What do you think?" Mr and Mrs Baker peered at the cake and back at Vaughan.

"I think it's perfect son" said Mr Baker, getting it straight away. "Good idea and very well done." Mrs Baker however wasn't quite sure what it was.

"It's very square dear" she commented cautiously, "but I don't really see what it's meant to be. Is it a pattern cake?" she asked politely. Vaughan smiled and laughed to himself, he knew his Mum wouldn't get it until the final decorations were in place.

"It's a chessboard, Mum" he explained "a chocolate chessboard. I need to work out how to make the pieces to finish it off but the cake itself is done. The dark squares are made with dark chocolate and the light squares are made with white chocolate. What do you think, will you try it to see how it tastes?"

"Of course we will, love" she agreed "and I have an idea how you can make the playing pieces you need for the real cake entry next week. Well done Vaughan, it's a brilliant idea and I'm sure Dr Bakewell will love it!" With that, she went to the kitchen to fetch plates, cut and served everyone a slice of cake each as they sat around the table and gobbled down what they all agreed, was a very inventive, tasty cake indeed.

Chapter 5

Concrete Icing

As July arrived, the weather became warmer, the school holidays were fast approaching and the grand summer fete was only weeks away.

Vaughan woke bright and early on July 30th, the day before the summer fete. Mr and Mrs Baker, Vaughan and Manuka had all attended the Honey Wood Town Hall meeting on 1st July as instructed by Dr Bakewell's poster. At the meeting they had been informed that they would need to be at Castleton Town Hall for eight o'clock on the morning of the fete, to be able to get to the school on time. Dr Bakewell, it was said, was a stickler for time and as the fete would open at ten o'clock, he would expect everybody to be there ready and waiting. He did not like lateness. So (on Professor Drumgoole's advice), he would organise the transport from Castleton Town Hall to the school himself. This way no-one would be late and miss out (and although Dr Bakewell didn't say this out loud, it also meant he wouldn't have hundreds of cars rumbling around his school grounds churning up his precious gardens). Because of this - and because Castleton was quite a long way away - the Bakers had decided to get a train to Castleton the day before, so they could be sure they wouldn't be late and miss the transport to the school.

On their long train journey from Honey Wood to Castleton, they discussed what they thought the school would look like, how well Vaughan's cake looked and whether Dr Bakewell would like it. They wondered what Dr Bakewell himself would look like and pondered how they would get from Castleton Town Hall to the school.

By July 30th however, Dr Bakewell was quite unsettled and was having second thoughts about the open day. He summoned Professor Drumgoole to his office for a private discussion over tea and biscuits.

"But everyone will know where the school is" he mithered to Professor Drumgoole. "Once they know where our school is, the mystery goes. Once the mystery goes then everything else will follow soon after - people will lose interest, copycat schools will spring up everywhere, our recipes will be copied... people won't be so curious anymore, we'll be like every other school. We'll lose our reputation, oh my oh my, this is not a good idea Derek, is it too late to cancel?"

"Oh for heaven's sake George, will you calm down?" responded Professor Drumgoole, who was becoming quite annoyed with Dr Bakewell. "Listen to yourself will you? I'll tell you what will happen shall I? Yes, everyone will know where the school is. And? What harm will that do? Absolutely none at all. So 'the mystery goes' you say - only the mystery about where we are and what the school looks like. Our recipes, our experiments, our plans, our teachings, none of that can be taken away from us. Our cakes and creations will still be world-class as they are now. And so what if copycat schools suddenly spring up all over the country? None of them will have your name to them, will they? And if they do open up, isn't that a good thing? That more children can learn the arts of baking and confectionery making? The more the merrier I say and let's make the world a sweeter place. After all -that's what our school motto says, does it not?"

His lips twitched into the tiniest smile as he tried to lighten Dr Bakewell's mood. It didn't work however; Dr Bakewell just rolled his eyes, humphed at Professor Drumgoole and sat down in his big leather chair.

* * *

July 31st arrived at last. Dr Bakewell woke up with a feeling of dread, wishing he could stay in bed all day instead and that this fete idea had just been a nightmare. Any minute now he would open his eyes and it would be the last day of school as usual with nothing special about it at all. Professor Drumgoole on the other hand, awoke with a feeling of nervousness and excitement. He was very much looking forward to today and he knew the pupils were too - they were looking forward to being able to show-off a little, to have a fun last day of term - the music, the stalls and generally enjoying themselves. He was also nervous though because he knew that if the fete wasn't a success, Dr Bakewell wouldn't be very pleased with him and this fete was his chance of trying to save the school from either closing or falling down. He got out of bed and wandered to his window, looking at its stone frame. Running along the edge was a wonky white line which he traced with his finger and smiled. This was one of Dr Bakewell's repairs to the school - last winter they had noticed several cracks appearing in some of the bricks and stonework. Naturally, Dr Bakewell was keen to keep out any outsiders, so it was 'out of the question' to 'hire a builder to carry out such small repairs'. And anyway, 'they cost a fortune' Professor Drumgoole remembered Dr Bakewell saying, when they spotted the cracks. Being a clever man and also an ingenious baker, Dr Bakewell created his own remedy - concrete icing! He had spent a few weeks perfecting the icing so it set absolutely rock hard, then he made a batch of his concrete icing, poured it into his piping bag and piped the icing into the crack! It did the job though, even if you could trace the line with your fingers and have an unexplained urge to lick the seam!

Chapter 6

The Red Buses

As the alarm clock rang it's shrill sound, piercing his dreams and crudely ending his sleep, Vaughan flung his arm out from under the thick flowery duvet of his bed-and-breakfast bed, switched it off and jumped out of his bed quicker than he ever had before. He and his family had spent the night in a cosy little bed and breakfast in Castleton, only a ten minute walk from the town hall. He and Manuka had shared one room while Mr and Mrs Baker had been given the room next door. They both got themselves washed and dressed before going downstairs where they met their parents for breakfast.

"Morning Bakers" chirped Mr Baker to his children happily, winking at Vaughan who, this morning, felt incredibly nervous.

"Come on, sit down, we need a hearty breakfast on such a big day as this, don't we?" Vaughan hadn't missed his Dad's little joke when he emphasised the word 'baker'. He just hoped he would be a real baker, he'd put so much effort and concentration into his cake and his parents had been so supportive, he didn't want to disappoint them. Looking at the full English breakfast laid out on his plate, he suddenly didn't feel very hungry anymore. His stomach was gurgling and churning already and he hadn't even arrived at the school yet!

"I'm not that hungry, actually Dad" Vaughan replied, pushing his plate away from him, "I think I'll just have some fruit juice".

"I know you're nervous Vaughan" his Mum piped up "but you really have to eat something. Breakfast is the most important meal of the day and we don't know how long it'll be before we get to the school or when we'll next be able to eat. Have a bit of toast at least - that'll stop the butterflies in your belly!" she smiled knowingly.

Vaughan smiled shyly back - his mother had an uncanny knack of knowing how he was feeling. It was quite reassuring at times like this although it could also be a little unnerving sometimes. He did as his parents advised and managed to eat one piece of toast and have a drink of orange juice. His Mum was right, he did feel a little better for it. Once breakfast was finished, they headed back to their rooms to collect their luggage and the all-important cake. Mr Baker had brought a large rucksack big enough to fit everything in, so they only had one bag to worry about. Mrs Baker and Vaughan took turns to carry the cake which was safely hidden from sight in a large, white cardboard box that Mr Baker had brought home from work. With everything ready to go, they thanked the owners of the B&B, said goodbye and walked out into glorious bright sunshine, ready to go and meet the world famous Dr Bakewell.

* * *

Castleton Town Hall was just how Vaughan expected it to look. It wasn't particularly large; it was an old, rectangular pale yellow wooden building with heavy, old wooden front doors. Above the doors were metal, black capital letters confirming that this building was indeed 'Castleton Town Hall'; above the name hung a very large, round black and white clock. Vaughan looked at the time on the clock and found it was a quarter to eight.

"Plenty of time yet people" declared Mr Baker, so they sat down on an empty wooden bench near the doors, Mrs Baker holding the cake box safely in her hands whilst resting it on her lap. As they waited, they passed the time 'people spotting' and commenting on the cakes they could just see, through the varying sorts of plastic boxes they were being carried in. There were more people there than Vaughan had expected, which didn't help his anxiety. For some reason, he had expected only about twenty people but he realised now how foolish that he had been - there were more like one hundred people there.

"Just look at all these people carrying cakes" whispered Manuka "I wonder if anyone here will win?" Vaughan looked at his feet and swallowed - he'd thought the very same thing.

"I'm sure one of these young bakers will win." Mr Baker said confidently, "Our Vaughan of course!"
Manuka chuckled with her father as he ruffled her hair, before telling him off for making her hair a mess.

Just as Manuka had finished smoothing her hair back into place, rumbles could be heard in the distance. All four Bakers stood up and leant forward, peering into the distance, trying to get a better view of what was coming down the road. Within seconds two double-decker red buses appeared and pulled up outside the Town Hall. These buses had no doors - they had a corner missing from the back, where two steps and a pole were fitted to allow people to alight the bus. Standing on the top step, holding onto the black balance pole for support, was a thin, elderly man dressed in a beautifully tailored suit, pillar-box red from head to foot (apart from his lapels, pockets and cuffs which were lined in black and his shoes which were mirror-shiny black). He stepped down onto the pavement and ushered everyone into the waiting buses.

"All aboard for the journey of a lifetime" he shouted "all aboard for Dr Bakewell's Summer Fete. One bus as a time please." With that, the waiting families filed into the buses, filling the first bus completely before that drove off and the second bus allowed people on. Sitting down in the first four seats of the bus, the Bakers wriggled to get comfortable.

"I'm sure you'll do well love" Mrs Baker tried to reassure Vaughan "but if for any reason you don't, then don't worry too much - you can always try next year."

Next year - Vaughan hadn't thought of that! Of course he could, this competition was going to happen every year from now on, so he could try every year. But then again, he didn't want to spend another year at Honey Wood Comprehensive, being laughed at. Best not think about it, he told himself as the doors of the bus shut and the driver started the engine.

"Yeah" he mumbled, looking up at his Mum "Yeah, I could always try next year."

Chapter 7

Honeycomb Hall

After what felt like hours, Vaughan noticed that the buses were now bouncing their way down some rather narrow, country lanes. He hoped they wouldn't meet any traffic coming the other way, because the buses filled the entire width of the lane - a couple of times the bracken of the hedges had scraped the bus windows, so narrow were some of the lanes they drove through! He had no idea where they were and as all he could see out of the window were the hedges which lined the lanes, he couldn't even make a guess.

Eventually the bus slowed down and turned left, into the wide, gated entrance of a private, gravelled drive. As they drove between the two small, stone lodging houses which stood on either side of black, wrought-iron gates, the gates opened wide allowing the buses to trundle onto the perfectly straight driveway which lay before them, which was lined each side with perfectly trimmed triangular green trees. Vaughan immediately imagined these trees decorated with fairy lights and baubles, for they looked for all the world like perfectly groomed Christmas trees.

At the far end of the drive, Vaughan could just make out a rectangular building on the horizon, with three tall towers; one in the middle, one on the right and one on the left, the middle one being the thinnest, but tallest. Counting the trees as they drove past, as he reached twenty, the last one, the bus stopped and the elderly, red-suited conductor stood in the aisle and addressed the passengers.

"Ladies, gentlemen and children" he declared "Welcome to Honeycomb Hall!"

Everyone gathered up their families and their belongings and carefully stepped down out of the bus. It was only then they realised how many buses there were in total. Dr Bakewell had obviously arranged several meeting places, for there were twenty red buses in total, all lined up in front of the building in two rows of ten. Noticing the way they had parked, Vaughan decided they looked like soldiers, all in line, one behind the other and side by side. When all twenty buses had been dismounted, off they trundled back down the long driveway, like ladybirds crawling down a flower stem, leaving everyone behind them staring at the most beautiful, imposing building they had ever seen.

* * *

The rectangular building Vaughan had spotted appeared to be a mansion or stately home, not like any school he had ever seen. No wonder nobody had realised it was here, he thought, all tucked away like this. The name plaque on one of the little stone houses by the gate merely stated that this building was 'Honeycomb Hall'; there was nothing to suggest that this was even a school, let alone a world-famous confectionery school. There were no giant candy canes or statues of cakes in the grounds, as he had half expected there to be. He supposed even local people didn't realise it was here and must have thought it was just a mansion that belonged to a very rich, private family.

On either side of the gravel driveway were twenty cone-shaped trees (Vaughan knew this for a fact because he had counted them) with vast amounts of grass either side. Where they now stood was in the centre of the drive in the large space the buses had vacated just a few moments earlier, directly facing the school of imposing red brick.

The tallest, centre tower that Vaughan had seen from half way down the drive, he now realised was a stone clock tower, which was showing the time as one minute to ten. 'The event will commence at ten o'clock' he remembered as he looked at the clock face, picturing the sparkly poster in his mind's eye, his excitement building more and more. In between the two smaller towers on either side of the school, the wall grew upwards and formed three rounded triangles of brick, somehow blending the front wall of the school up into the roof; in the centre of each triangle was a white, square-paned window.

Back at ground level, in the centre of the building, right underneath the stone clock tower and the middle triangle, was a huge arched doorway, complete with an antique-looking, heavy, black panelled door. The door was framed by ivy which although only about a metre high, Vaughan guessed, covered the entire width of the school; obviously having nowhere else to go after covering the whole width of the school, it had started to creep its way upwards around the door and ground floor windows. For some reason, looking at this door made Vaughan feel nervous. It was very sombre looking and Vaughan felt a little intimidated by the sheer size and beauty of Honeycomb Hall.

"Ooh, look at it" gushed Manuka, "it's so beautiful! I want to live here!"

"Yes, it certainly is" agreed Mr and Mrs Baker together. "Let's just see how..."

But Mr Baker was cut off mid-sentence by the thunderous ringing of a large, heavy bell. Everyone looked up and saw the massive gold bell above the clock tower swinging to and fro, declaring that it was now ten o'clock. As it rang it's tenth and final 'dong' the black door opened and out into the dazzling sunlight stepped two, rather dapper, men.

"Ladies and gentlemen, children and future students" began the thinner man, walking forwards onto the driveway. Vaughan noticed how smart he looked in his grey suit, cream-colour bow-tie, toffee-colour waistcoat and matching grey, neatly clipped beard which hugged his chin.

"Thank you all for coming here today. I trust you have had a pleasant journey and it seems we have also been blessed with wonderful weather for a what we hope will be a wonderful day. My name is Professor Drumgoole and I take great pleasure in introducing you to a man you all know by name. Today, you will also come to know him by sight and for some of you, you will soon come to know him as your Headmaster. Ladies, gentleman and children - I present the one and only, Dr George Bakewell!"

Rapturous applause and beaming smiles all round welcomed Dr Bakewell enthusiastically as the shorter, very smart man also stepped forwards off the front steps to stand alongside his colleague. You certainly couldn't miss Dr Bakewell. He wore a toffee-colour trouser suit and black bowler hat, a pair of circular tortoiseshell glasses balancing on his snub nose. Underneath his cream-colour bow-tie, a gold pocket-watch draped importantly across his brown-and-cream striped waistcoat, making him look like a cross between a bank manager and a mint humbug. Dr Bakewell was a stout, rounded man with a horseshoe of greying ginger hair circling his balding head (which was today hidden underneath the bowler hat) and covering his top lip, which clashed slightly with his toffee clothing. Vaughan considered them for a moment and decided they looked completely the opposite of each other. Apart from their matching bow-ties, their outfits and body shapes made them look like negatives of each other!

"Thank you, Professor" smiled Dr Bakewell at Professor Drumgoole "for such an introduction." Turning to face his eager audience he continued with his own welcome.

"May I also personally thank each and every one of you, for attending our open day today and for taking an interest in our school. I am Dr Bakewell, as I expect you have realised" (some quiet, polite chuckles came from the parents in recognition of his joke), "and this (he swung his right arm out and around him, narrowly missing Professor Drumgoole's elbow as he did so, to indicate the mansion behind him) is Honeycomb Hall - otherwise known as 'Dr Bakewell's School of Confectionery.' I must warn you - it is not a school for the half-hearted. I expect my students to put in one hundred percent effort at all times. Lateness will not be tolerated. Laziness will not be tolerated. Bullying will not be tolerated. But our students leave here as the cream of the crop - the best of the best, so to speak - and for some of you, you will be amongst those considered the best of the best.

Today, you will have access to our grounds, meet our teachers and students, try some sample lessons and of course, take part in various activities and competitions. But most of all, we hope each and every one of you has a day to remember, a lot of fun and I sincerely hope we live up to your expectations of us. And with that, I bid you welcome into our school. For those children wishing to enter a cake into our competition, please take your cake and stand over by Professor Drumgoole over there" (for Professor Drumgoole had moved away after almost being whacked by Dr Bakewell earlier and was now standing at the far right side of the school in front of a white marquee) "and the remainder of you are now welcome to enter our gardens. I thank you all once again and wish you a very, pleasant day."

Dr Bakewell turned his back on his audience and walked back towards the heavy black door, twisted the iron door handle and went back inside as the door swung shut, pointing out very clearly that with the introductions and welcome over, he wasn't particularly interested in the remainder of the day's events, damping down some of the crowds excitement and leaving them a little disappointed and unsure of what to expect next.

Chapter 8

The Summer Fete

Vaughan took his cake off his mother and dutifully went to the marquee to register his entry with Professor Drumgoole. There was such a variety Vaughan wondered how they would be judged; there were small cupcakes with butterflies on, brightly coloured cakes, animal shaped cakes, cakes that looked like wedding cakes, surprisingly a couple of Christmas cakes (even though it was only July), a novelty cake that looked like a suitcase and Vaughan was very pleased to see that his chessboard cake was the only one there (he had been a little worried as the previous night he had dreamt that a lot of children had had the same idea and all of the entries were chessboard cakes and all of which were much better than Vaughan's)! After all entries had been logged, recorded and put on display by some of the sixth-formers, Professor Drumgoole gathered everyone together in front of the now very full and colourful, marquee.

Fully aware that Dr Bakewell's manner earlier had somewhat quashed the children's eagerness, he decided to lift their spirits and gee everyone up again otherwise today would all have been in vain. George Bakewell really was difficult at times, he thought.

"Thank you again children, for such enthusiastic entries" he cheerfully announced to the crowd. "Never have I seen such a variety of cakes and I am very curious to see which of you will be joining us as students and I look forward to getting to know you better." Vaughan looked up at his father, as he nudged his elbow and winked at him. "Please make sure you are at the stage for two o'clock. It is most important." Professor Drumgoole added, with a mysterious smile. "And now everyone, I bid you welcome to our fete and wish you a marvellous day!"

"Where's the stage, Dad?" Vaughan whispered to Mr Baker, worried he didn't know where to go and he might miss out or get into trouble, as it was important.

"Shhh" Mr Baker replied in a whisper, "I don't know, he didn't say. Maybe he'll show us once we get into the gardens?"
Professor Drumgoole led the now re-excited crowd past the marquee and into the grounds and gardens of Honeycomb Hall, as the various songs about sweets and cakes blared out of loudspeakers. Vaughan listened to some of the candy-themed lyrics playing in various tents as he passed them, walking through the grounds: '.....a cup of sweetness and a handful of sugar....;.....candy is the sweetest thing in the world, but still not as sweet as my beautiful girl....;.....no-one can mix up things like you do, tasty little sweets that you just wanna chew....; he bakes, he bakes, those delicious cakes, those cakes...' and watched as Professor Drumgoole walked in front of them and disappeared off into the distance with a decidedly dance-like swing to his walk, his hips and hands swaying rhythmically to and fro. Squinting to get a better look, Vaughan could have sworn he saw the Professor clicking his fingers in time to the music as he shimmied his way around a hedge and disappeared out of sight.

* * *

Walking around the gardens carrying silver trays of nibbles which they were offering to the visitors, Caroline and Verity were getting tired. Although they were enjoying their unusual last day of term, it was a hot day and spending all day outside in the sun wearing full school uniform was starting to tire them out. Not only that but they wanted to have some fun on the rides and stalls too!

As their paths crossed they stopped to speak at one of the little tables dotted around the grounds. "How're you finding it?" Caroline asked Verity.

"It's okay - I quite like seeing all the visitors and acting as the hostess but my feet are killing me. I could do with a drink and a rest for a bit. How about you?" Verity replied.

"Pretty much the same" Caroline answered. "Tell you what, I'll go and find Drumgoole and ask if we can have a break. Wait here" she said, putting her tray down on the table as Verity sat down on a chair and sighed with relief.

As she sat waiting for Caroline to return, two young girls approached her looking lost.

"Excuse me" said the girl in front, "could you tell me where the Orchard is please? We've lost our Mum and she told us if we got lost we should go to the Orchard and she'll come and find us there."

Verity smiled at the girls, who looked remarkably similar. "Yes, I can. It's about five minutes walk away from here but it's difficult to tell you how to get there. Tell you what, if you can wait a few minutes until my friend comes back, we can take you ourselves so you won't get lost."

"Oh that's very kind of you, thank you." said the girl. Taking a seat each around the table, the girls introduced themselves.

"I'm Verity" Verity told them "and my friend's name - the one I'm waiting for - is Caroline. What are your names?"

"I'm Poppy Quenell" said the girl "and this is my sister."

"I'm Daisy Quenell" the second girl stepped forward shyly and introduced herself.

"Well, you can tell you're sisters" Verity smiled "you look exactly the same. Have you entered the competition?"

"Yes, we both have" answered Poppy. "We're twins, so we're really hoping that we can stay together. Either for both of us to win a place or neither of us. We'd hate to be apart in different schools, it's bad enough being in different classes and years."

"Different - years?" Verity repeated, confused. "I thought you just said you were twins? How can you be in different years if you're twins?"

"It's really weird, but it's because we have different birthdays" Poppy continued.

"Eh? How can you be twins if you have different birthdays? And how can you be the same age but be in different school years?" asked Verity cautiously, starting to think that these girls were teasing her.

"It's because of the days and times we were born" Daisy joined in. "I'm the eldest - I was born at a quarter to midnight on 31st August."

"And I was born twenty-five minutes later - at ten minutes past midnight, which makes my birthday the 1st September." said Poppy.

"And because the school year starts on 1st September, Poppy falls into the year below me. I'm always the youngest in my year and Poppy's always the oldest in her year."

"That's the strangest thing I've ever heard!" said Verity, "twins that don't share a birthday, a class or even the same year at school! I bet you're the only twins in England like that!" she laughed with them, just as Caroline appeared and joined them.

Verity introduced the girls to Caroline and told her all about their unusual birthday story. Caroline agreed that it would be better for Poppy and Daisy to follow them to the Orchard and as Professor Drumgoole had kindly told them they could finish their duties and enjoy the rest of the day, they were free to show them around if they wanted to. So with big smiles all around, Caroline and Verity lead the girls to the orchard, telling them all about the school as they went, with Poppy and Daisy getting more excited all the time.

Vaughan and Manuka also progressed further into the grounds themselves, anxious not to lose their parents there was so much going on. The atmosphere was electric, everyone was buzzing with the sense of anticipation and excitement. Manuka's mouth fell open in delight as they walked past brightly coloured table after table, each laden with bowls of sweets ranging from tiny little brightly coloured pea-sized sweets to gigantic gobstoppers and cakes, enticing them closer. There was red, yellow, blue, turquoise, white, brown, pink, green, red, purple, navy, lilac, peach, lemon, orange - any colour you had ever seen adorned the tables. As they stopped and drooled at the confectionery before them, they read the black labels neatly standing in front of each bowl, expertly written in golden, swirly writing. Traditional Rhubarb and Custard; Chilli and Ginger Bombs; Cinnamon and Cider Cuplets (Adults only); Coconut Bubble Gum; Meringue Toadstools; Marzipan Fruits; Fudgeberry Delights; Honeywhizz Fizzers; Oswald Ogres; Wistan Whispers; Swithun Sweetpeas - the names of these unheard of sweets just kept on coming and Manuka and Vaughan tried so many they started to feel a bit sick! Cake stands holding mini-cakes towered above the bowls of sweets, large cakes decorated with ribbons and in the centre of each table, standing tall and proud, were chocolate sculptures of castles, horses, flowers - there was even a sculpture of Dr Bakewell on one table! There was so much colour and so much to see, they could have spent fifteen minutes looking at everything on the table!

There were signs everywhere pointing the way to different areas; they passed signs to the Vegetable Patch, the Orchard, the All-Year Kitchen Corner and various teaching tents on their way to find the stage. Music wafted out of the teaching tents, dancing through the air and singing in the ears of whomever passed by and the Baker's soon found the stage they were to meet at later that day. As soon as they saw it they wondered how they could have worried about finding it - it would have been impossible to miss! There were lots of white fold-up chairs lined up in front of the stage for the visitors; the stage itself had been set up with big speakers each side, a red-and-white striped canopy 'roof' with matching red-and-white candy canes in front of the speakers and a backdrop of various sized and coloured lollipops, although at the moment the stage itself was calm and quiet, empty of any people.

There were several more smaller, white tents with teachers giving mini-lessons in various subjects to the visitors; a bright red and yellow helter-skelter, a coconut shy, a hook-a-duck stall, a merry-go-round, a candyfloss stall, a tombola, the sweet-laden tables, a castle shaped bouncy castle, an old fashioned 'cake-walk' ride, giant wooden swings and lots of students milling about wearing smart, caramel-colour uniforms, carrying trays of drinks and biscuits which they offered to the visitors. It was, Vaughan decided, a cross between a funfair and a school fete and so far he was loving every minute of it! Trying very hard not to think about his cake (which he was beginning to worry was very bland and boring and nothing at all like the school's cakes on show) and how the judges decision could affect his whole future, Vaughan inhaled the fresh, sweet air, closed his eyes and breathed out slowly. There was nothing more he could do now but enjoy the fete. The fete of destiny, he thought to himself, Dr Bakewell's fete - his own fate.

"Come on" he called out to his family, "race you to the cake-walk!" All four of the Bakers scurried across the field, paid their fare and giggled and squealed as they each tried - with a great deal of difficulty - to cross the ceaselessly moving wooden bridges; wobbling, stumbling and laughing as the cake-walk threw them off balance, toppling them backwards and forwards, with each step they took.

Chapter 9

And The Winners Are...

As they stumbled off the cake-walk, they each chose a teaching tent where the four of them could try their hand at a new skill together. Mr Baker chose the ice-cream parlour tent, learning how to mix the flavours and creating his own (which incidentally, tasted awful and all four of them discreetly threw their ice-creams into the bin outside the tent); Mrs Baker chose Sugarcraft; Manuka tried her hand at making candyfloss and Vaughan chose traditional sweet-making, trying his hand at making an old-fashioned herbal cough sweet with a Dr Muller-Weiss. This passed a great deal of time and they'd had so much fun that none of them realised it was now a quarter to two - and they had to be at the stage at two o'clock. After Dr Bakewell's little speech earlier, they were in no doubt that they daren't be late - they wouldn't be surprised if Dr Bakewell disqualified latecomers from the competition. So they ran as fast as they could, hand in hand so they didn't lose one another (Manuka held her Dad's hand with her left hand, her right gripped tightly to the stick of her hand-made, pink candyfloss so she didn't lose that either), to the brightest, most colourful, stage they had ever seen.

There was a crowd gathering by now and although there still wasn't anyone actually on the stage, all the music from the teaching tents had now stopped playing and the only music that could be heard was coming from the giant candy-cane speakers on the stage itself.

As the school bell swung and pealed twice, a ring which could be heard all over the grounds, the music coming from the speakers on stage suddenly stopped; bright red spotlights appeared lighting up the stage and out into the centre walked Professor Drumgoole.

"I'm glad to see you all made it on time" he said to the seated audience below. "We have come to a decision and have chosen our final ten successful entries. Before we announce the winners and call you up onto the stage, we have organised some entertainment for you. Would you please give a warm welcome to Miss Cherry Bakewell."

Professor Drumgoole started everyone clapping and as he departed the stage, the music struck up and in his place walked a tiny young lady of about twenty-five, the high-heels of her shiny red shoes tapping the floor rhythmically as she quickly tottered across the stage. She had long, white-blonde hair, cherry red lips and wore an impossibly spotless, white dress which clung neatly to her curvy silhouette. She smiled and cheerfully waved at her audience, raised her microphone, opened her mouth to sing and stunned everyone watching her into silence, immediately.

* * *

The voice that belted out of tiny Cherry Bakewell was incredible; loud, strong and so powerful it cut straight to the hearts of her audience, giving them goosebumps and making the hairs on the back of their necks stand up. Her first song was a song Vaughan hadn't heard before, about popcorn, but it was so catchy and lively you couldn't sit still - her audience couldn't help but move in time to her music as she performed; people were tapping their feet, clapping, jigging their shoulders, swaying and rocking as they sat in their chairs. In fact, the Bakers were enjoying her performance so much, that whilst Cherry was singing and performing they completely forgot their nerves and Vaughan was so caught up in the moment that he briefly forgot that today was the day that could change his life.

Cherry sang two candy-themed songs, the first about popcorn and the second one was another lively song, about a

Gingerbread Man, which she encouraged the warmed-up crowd to sing with her by singing 'Uh-huh' after each line. When she had finished singing, the audience instantly broke out into rapturous applause and rose to its feet to give her a standing ovation, after which she bowed graciously and spoke to her audience.

"Thank you, thank you" she began, in a startlingly quiet, sweet voice, quite opposite to her singing voice. "It's wonderful to be here and I have to say I have seen some of the entries in this competition. They are all incredibly good and I'm sure that the ten of you that have been awarded a place here at this fabulous school will turn out to be fantastic bakers. Now without any further delay, I believe we are ready?" she looked off-stage to her right where Dr Bakewell and Professor Drumgoole were waiting in the wings. Having receiving confirmation that the men were ready to announce the winners, she turned her attention back to the eager, expectant crowd.

"Ladies, gentlemen, boys and girls...I give you the one and only Dr Bakewell!"

* * *

The seated crowd clapped as Dr Bakewell walked out onto the red and white stage, quickly followed by Professor Drumgoole who was pushing a tea trolley which had been mysteriously covered with a white cloth. Dr Bakewell smoothed the front of his suit jacket down over his stomach and smiled as he took the microphone from Cherry.

"Ah good" he began "Well, as it's now two o'clock, I shan't waste any of your time. I have now decided which children have won a scholarship here at our school. Professor Drumgoole here, shall reveal the winning entries as I announce the winning students' names. If your name is called, please come up onto the stage and collect your entry from the Professor before returning to your seat. Although we must choose only ten winners, I would like to say to everyone that entered, all the entries were remarkably good and it genuinely was difficult to choose just ten. On behalf of Professor Drumgoole and myself I would like to congratulate each and every one of you on a job well done. Well done indeed. And now, without further ado, I give you our winning students."

Vaughan took a deep breath and waited - the whole world seemed to have stopped as he waited to hear the names of the winners be announced, desperately hoping that his would be among them.

"First of all, we have the baker of these beautiful butterfly fairy cakes - Emi Kemura." Clapping started immediately as a small, Japanese girl stood up and nervously approached the stage. Trembling as she walked up the white wooden steps at the front of the stage, she shook Dr Bakewell's hand as he smiled, congratulated her and whispered something in her ear. Emi nodded, turned and walked behind to Professor Drumgoole who quickly whipped off a white sheet revealing a plate of colourful cakes beneath. Emi picked up her fairy cakes, returned to stand by Dr Bakewell and tilted the plate to show the crowd her entry, who clapped her once more.

"Miss Kemura has given the traditional butterfly cake a twist and for that she is commended." Vaughan peered forwards and noticed all sorts of colours. It seemed that Emi had decorated the 'wings' of the butterfly cakes with brightly-coloured icing and coloured sprinkles, so much so that they looked as though real butterflies had flown in and landed on top of each cake. After a few seconds of proudly displaying her cakes to everyone, Emi returned back to her seat and the clapping died down as the next winner was announced.

"Oliver Eddington" called Dr Bakewell, scanning the crowd as a rather chubby, blond haired boy who looked to be about the same age as Vaughan stood up and made his way slowly to the stage. "Mr Eddington here is the creator of these delicious chocolate-orange chocolates. Delicious, Mr Eddington, well done boy, well done." mused Dr Bakewell as Oliver also retrieved his plate of chocolates from Professor Drumgoole and showed them off to an enthusiastic audience, before also returning to his seat. The more names that were called, the more nervous Vaughan became. All he heard were names and types of cakes. He hadn't seen any other chessboards in the tent when he registered, but that didn't mean someone else hadn't entered a better one after him.

"Florence Fitzgerald... castle cake... Georgia Flavell... bouquet of flowers... Malachi Kingston........." soon, they all became a blur of names, as Vaughan counted down how many places were available. With each name being called he started to feel sick, with each name that was called his chances of winning a place were getting less and less.

"Poppy Quenell......" Dr Bakewell continued as Vaughan curled up one more of his ten fingers, showing that only four places remained,

"Gregory Southall....." (three places, Vaughan thought), "Daisy Quenell..." (two places....),

"Vaughan Baker, for such a simple yet effective chessboard - my favourite game" he added to a chuckling crowd as Vaughan curled up another finger (just one place left now)

"Vaughan Baker?" Dr Bakewell repeated as Vaughan noticed his mother pushing him up out of his seat. What? he thought, what's she doing?

"VAUGHAN - BAKER!" repeated Dr Bakewell a little louder, craning his neck to see the missing boy. Oh my God! thought Vaughan - it's me! He's really calling my name! Almost tripping over himself he couldn't get out of the chair quick enough, Vaughan stumbled out of his row of seats and hurried up the steps to greet Dr Bakewell. He didn't look very impressed but Vaughan didn't care - he'd won a place! Dr Bakewell - the Dr Bakewell thought his baking was good enough to win him a place at this school! So what if he was the only one who'd had to be called three times - he'd won a place at Dr Bakewell's school! His head swimming with happiness, Vaughan took his chessboard off smiling Professor Drumgoole and returned to Dr Bakewell, grinning from ear to ear.

"Very ingenious, Vaughan" said Dr Bakewell "what gave you the idea?"

Lost for words, Vaughan stared up dreamily into the expectant face of Dr Bakewell, who was clearly interested in his answer.

"I was playing chess when it just came to me" mumbled Vaughan, thinking his answer probably made him sound stupid.

"Very clever" Dr Bakewell answered thoughtfully, nodding his approval. "It takes real talent to create your own cake with no guide to follow. Impressive Vaughan, very impressive. You may now go back to your seat." As Vaughan stepped down off the stage and floated on air back to his chair, still grinning, he just about heard through his dreamy haze, the name of the tenth and final winner announced:

"Finally, our last scholarship place is awarded to Miss Orla O' Brien for these inventive potato muffins!" Vaughan had no idea who Orla O'Brien was or what she'd made. He just sat there, deaf to everything and everyone around him, staring up at the building that in just over a month's time would become his school, his second home and the start of his new life.

Chapter 10

Dr Bakewell's School of Confectionery

Vaughan stood at the end of the driveway, in the same spot he'd stood in just over a month before with his parents, staring at the heavy black wooden door in front of him. He'd seen nothing of what lay behind that door at the Summer Fete, for once Dr Bakewell had retreated back inside, it had slammed shut and remained that way all day. He couldn't begin to imagine what it was like inside this magnificent building.

The other nineteen children that waited patiently with Vaughan all looked as nervous as he. Some, like Vaughan stood in silence watching the others whilst some were talking to others and introducing themselves. The other nine scholarship winners he remembered from the summer fete, recognising Poppy and Daisy Quenell immediately, giving them a shy, awkward smile, which they returned equally shyly. There was a skinny boy of similar age to Vaughan with jet black hair and striking blue eyes who was telling everyone his name was Gregory; a slim brown haired girl with glasses who kept fidgeting with her uniform, straightening her blazer and tugging her skirt, who he recognised as Orla O'Brien; an older girl of about thirteen with chubby cheeks and a very ill-timed cold (she frequently sneezed and constantly had a tissue in her hand), who introduced herself to the twins as Georgia; Malachi Kingston, a West Indian boy with a huge, beaming smile who also looked about ten or eleven; a rather chubby blond haired boy of about twelve who was the only one to look remotely confident - Vaughan remembered his name was Oliver - he was the one who'd made some sort of chocolates that Dr Bakewell had liked; he noticed Emi Kemura, the very petite Japanese girl who'd made the butterfly cakes - she was still trembling and looking at all the other children very intently and finally there was Florence Fitzgerald, a tall, freckly, ginger haired girl with very curly hair that was doing it's best to escape the plait it had been neatly tied away in. He hadn't seen the other ten children before and correctly presumed they must be this year's non-scholarship first-years. All in all, quite a mix, Vaughan mused.

Then the bell tolled. Eight times. And the heavy, black door slowly creaked open and out of the shadows stepped a tall but frail-looking old lady, who silently closed the door behind her as she stood before the children and surveyed their anxious faces.

"Welcome, children, welcome" she smiled at them, her voice sounding as frail as she looked.

"My name is Mrs Hilderstone and I am the Housekeeper of Honeycomb Hall. And I must say, you all look very smart indeed, very smart" she observed with an approving nod and friendly smile which was reflected in her crinkled, steely-grey eyes. There was something about Mrs Hilderstone that you immediately warmed to; she had silvery white hair which was loosely tied at the nape of her neck in a bun, a few straggly wisps falling down around her forehead and eyes. She wore a long, charcoal grey skirt which lightly dusted the floor as she walked; a black high-necked blouse with a red jewelled brooch pinned where the white lacy collar met at the front; over the front of her long skirt she had a spotless white apron, over which hung her loosely clasped hands and a huge ring of keys, bigger than any keyring Vaughan had ever seen in his life. There must have been at least twenty keys of all sizes on that keyring. If ever there was a typical image of an old-fashioned housekeeper, Mrs Hilderstone was it.

"Now if you would all kindly leave your luggage over there on the grass" (she pointed to the side of the school where two months earlier the competition marquee had stood) "and follow me, you may now enter your new school." She took hold of the door handle, turned it, opened the door wide and stepped inside.

* * *

Stepping over the threshold, Vaughan gasped in awe as the butterflies in his stomach awoke and flitted around, tickling his insides, making him feel sick with excitement and nerves. The first word that sprang to Vaughan's mind was 'wood'. Everywhere he looked, all he could see was beautifully polished, red cherry-wood. The floorboards were wooden (although a lot of the floor was hidden under a patterned red rug); the walls were panelled and the staircase to the right of him was also cherrywood - looking warm, inviting and majestic all at once. As Vaughan and the others stared around the hallway surveying their new environment, pupils descended down the staircase staring inquisitively at the newcomers as they passed.

A decorative grandfather clock stood against a panelled wall just to the left of the staircase, directly in front of Vaughan and the heavy black door behind him. There was something odd about the clock, Vaughan noticed, though there was no time to inspect it now. Mrs Hilderstone swiftly moved in front of the clock blocking it from view and addressed the newcomers, whose heads were rotating as they examined the unfamiliar surroundings, spellbound by its beauty.

"Ah-hem" Mrs Hilderstone coughed politely, breaking the spell and gaining their attention. "You are presently standing - as you have likely deduced - in the hallway. I shall give you a brief tour of the school, following which you will be introduced formally to Professor Drumgoole and Doctor Bakewell. Your luggage will be taken to your dormitories by our butler, Mr Soames..."

Suddenly from out of the shadows a very smart, elderly man stepped forwards, wearing a jet black suit with tiny white collar standing up around his neck, drawing attention to his jet-black tie. He seemed rather young for an elderly man, Vaughan considered.

Had he not had a shock of thick, pure, white hair he could have easily passed for a much younger man. He had no stoop, he stood bolt upright; he had thick set, broad shoulders; no sign of any wrinkles on his clean-shaven face. Mr Soames acknowledged the children with a silent nod before walking past them and going outside, to where the children had been instructed to leave their luggage.

"...so there is no need to worry about your personal belongings." continued Mrs Hilderstone. "I presume you all labelled your cases with your names, as requested?" Answered with some mumbled 'yes miss'-es and nods of heads, she carried on. "Right then - follow me."

As she turned her back on the children and proceeded to glide down the picture-lined corridor in front of her, she unexpectedly stopped and looked back at the anxious children over her shoulder.

"And children," she softly whispered, her steely-grey eyes twinkling delightfully, "you are allowed to smile!" She smiled warmly at them and the kindness in her face somehow melted away their fears and nerves; the new students of Dr Bakewell's School of Confectionery breathed a sigh of relief; chuckled and smiled warmly back in response as they continued to follow Mrs Hilderstone, their earlier anxiousness now replaced with eagerness and excitement.

Chapter 11

Condita Orbis Terrarum a Dulcis Locus

Down the hallway they proceeded, trying their best not to bump into the endless stream of students bustling through the corridor in the opposite direction. Looking from left to right, Vaughan could barely register the rooms Mrs Hilderstone pointed out as they passed, although he did spot two ginormous mouse-holes in one of the corridors they walked through.

"Kitchens...toilets down there...scullery....storage yard...here we are - the Sun Room" Mrs Hilderstone stopped and opened two panelled wooden doors. As soon as they opened, sunlight flooded through the doors so brightly that Vaughan and the others flinched and quickly closed their eyes to protect them from the unexpected brightness. Noticing the sudden flinching and closing of eyes Mrs Hilderstone looked at the new students and chuckled. "What did you expect?" she asked, sounding slightly amused, "it is called the Sun Room!"

Walking inside they could see why. Rays of sunlight were streaming in through the huge white windows so brightly that dust particles could clearly be seen floating around in the air. Once their eyes had adjusted, Vaughan and the others looked around the unexpectedly sunny room at the yellow walls, orange and yellow winged armchairs, lush green plants that were dotted here and there in bright yellow plant pots and at the big, sun-shaped, gold mirror that hung over a clean, white fireplace. It was such a difference to the dark wooden interior it was hard to believe it was part of the same building.

As they entered the room Mrs Hilderstone walked in front of them and led them around the corner of the L-shaped room to where two familiar men stood, waiting to greet them. "Doctor, Professor" she nodded to each in turn "may I introduce you to your new students." She took a step to the side, revealing a line of twenty, rather nervous students, standing silently in front of the school's most important teachers. Professor Drumgoole - unsurprisingly - smiled and spoke first.

"Welcome, my dear children. It is lovely to see you all here and may I congratulate our scholarship winners one more time. I look forward to getting to know you all better and trust you will benefit greatly from studying with us and learning from the greatest, master baker of all time - Dr Bakewell."

Dr Bakewell stood up and addressed the children himself. Remembering his first speech, Vaughan wasn't sure what to expect, but certainly didn't expect the greeting they got.

"Yes, yes, welcome to our school. And I also wish to congratulate each one of you myself too. Scholarships and non-scholarships. I say, I was most impressed with the competition entries, most impressed indeed. I truly did not expect the standard of entries to be so high and you twenty here, are the best of the best. Children of the best bakers and also winners of the competition. I am quite excited to see, with our teaching and your studying, just how good and creative you will become. So - now you know who I am, please tell me who you are and your ages." Walking down the line, Dr Bakewell shook each child's hand in turn, welcoming them to the school. "Daisy Quenell, thirteen, sir..."; "Poppy Quenell, sir...thirteen today, sir"; "Sherry Wilson, age eleven doctor..."; "Vaughan Baker, age twelve sir..."; "Florence Fitzgerald, doctor...twelve"; "David Pembleton, eleven years old sir..."; "Nicholas Patten, doctor...I'm also eleven"; "Emi Kemura, I'm twelve, sir..."; "Rebekah Johnson, doctor...I'm eleven"; "Gregory Southall, sir...I'm eleven"; "Oliver Eddington, twelve years old, doctor..."; "Alison Burke, sir...eleven"; "Stefan Gentry, doctor...I'm eleven too"; "Curtis Smith, doctor...also eleven"; "Amy Middleton, sir...eleven"; "Georgia Flavell, doctor...I'm thirteen"; "Sarah Bergman, sir...eleven years old"; "Orla O'Brien, I'm twelve, sir..."; "Malachi Kingston, eleven, doctor..."; "Michael Morris, eleven years old sir". One by one the students introduced themselves and each was given a warm smile and an individual 'welcome' from Dr Bakewell. Dr Bakewell walked back to Professor Drumgoole who handed him something that Vaughan couldn't quite tell what it was. Taking the object from Professor Drumgoole, Dr Bakewell stood upright in front of the children, raised his chin and declared "Condita orbis terrarum a dulcis locus."

Looking from one to another, the puzzled children stayed silent; not knowing what to say they assumed this was the best thing to do. Seeing the bewildered looks on their faces, Dr Bakewell explained. "Our school motto. Condita orbis terrarum a dulcis locus. Latin - fine language." Looking at their still puzzled faces, he sniffed, haughtily. "Consider this your first homework. Find out what it means. Meanwhile - each of you will be placed into one of three houses. Follow me into the Refectory where you shall select your house and join your fellow housemates for breakfast." Dr Bakewell led the way back through the Sun Room, returning to the dark hallway, through the maze of wooden corridors and stopped outside a very large, closed door. "And this" he announced "is the Refectory." He flung the massive doors wide open as once again the children stared open-mouthed, as the dining room that lay behind the doors was revealed.

* * *

A grand room, divided into three by two rows of tall stone columns, the refectory looked beautiful and majestic. Decorated elegantly in cream and gold, Vaughan felt as though he'd stepped foot inside a royal palace, more than a mere school dining room. At the far side of the room opposite the refectory doors, was a small flight of steps which led to a narrow stage, upon which stood a huge, gold gong, positioned just so that it was framed by the stone columns, giving it an air of great importance. In the middle section of the room, in between the two rows of columns, were six horizontal tables with children seated either side of each table, talking excitedly. In the narrower section to the left of the columns, standing against the wall and running the whole length of the hall, was a banquet table laden with food. On the opposite side of the room, almost hidden behind the right hand row of columns, was a matching long table also laden with food, but behind this table sat all the teachers.

Dr Bakewell marched importantly through the hall as the new students followed nervously behind in single file. As they shuffled through the room, staring at the floor, the loud excited chatter which had filled the hall only minutes earlier soon quietened down to a curious murmur. Vaughan could feel every pair of eyes in the room staring at them and heard the odd whisper as they passed, ("wonder if they'll be any good, though....."; "I don't think this is right at all........";"good for them, I say....";"can't believe Bakewell's let in 'normal' kids....") his butterflies flitting around wildly in his stomach trying to escape, as he and the others stood in front of the Teachers' Table facing them, wondering what was about to happen next.

Chapter 12

Saints of Honeycomb

D r Bakewell took his seat in the centre of the teachers table and rose to his feet, obviously about to make a speech.

"Students" he began "welcome back to a new year at Honeycomb Hall. Today is an historic day for our school. For today, we welcome twenty new students, ten of which are the successful winners of our fete competition. They have proven themselves to be talented, to be worthy of studying confectionery at our school. Boys and girls, a round of applause please as I give you our new students."

Professor Drumgoole, who was seated next to Dr Bakewell in front of the children, gestured to them to turn around and face the school. As they did so and faced a sea of caramel uniforms, a round of applause followed as instructed. Vaughan could feel his face getting hotter and hotter as he became very embarrassed and he wished they could have just slipped in quietly, with no fuss.

Dr Bakewell took from his pocket the object that Professor Drumgoole had given to him in the Sun Room. As he walked along the row of new students, he distributed a hexagon-shaped piece of fabric to each child. Vaughan took his and turned it over, revealing a school badge for their blazers. Immediately behind Dr Bakewell followed Professor Drumgoole, issuing each child with a corresponding school tie. Vaughan's badge displayed a silver beehive against a blue background with three bees swirling around the hive. Peering over the shoulder of Florence Fitzgerald, who was standing on his left, he noticed her badge was identical but for the colour of the background (which was brown) and the beehive (which was orange). The tie Professor Drumgoole had handed him had the same blue and silver stripes on a yellow background. He correctly deduced that the colours of the badges and ties dictated what house you had been placed in - clearly his house colours were blue and silver. Looking up at the pupils seated in front of him, he noticed that everyone with the same colour ties and badges were sitting together. Clearly, each house had their own tables for their own members. Once all twenty new starters had been given both tie and badge, Dr Bakewell reappeared at their side and addressed the school as one.

"The colours on your badges and ties are your house colours and show to which house you belong. Those of you with cream and green - you have been awarded a place in the house of Saint Wistan. Wistonians - please welcome your new housemates!" Suddenly, the two tables at the back of the hall, furthest away from the Refectory doors erupted in cheers as all the students seated around them rose to their feet and clapped. Dr Bakewell nodded and moved his hand towards the far end of the hall, indicating that the seven new members of St Wistan should take their seats at their tables. Vaughan noticed two boys at the St Wistan table who weren't smiling or clapping very enthusiastically when the four scholarship children - Poppy, Daisy, Oliver and Georgia - joined their tables; he also noticed that the Quenell twins took the long walk to their seats holding hands, looking very relieved at being housed together and he smiled inwardly, pleased they'd been housed together.

"Step forward those of you who hold the colours blue and silver."

Vaughan stepped forwards, along with Emi Kemura, Orla O'Brien and the other three new starters, David Pembleton, Nicholas Patten and Amy Middleton.

"You six now belong to the House of Saint Oswald. Please take your seats at your house table."

The tables in the centre were the next ones to jump to their feet, clapping loudly and welcoming all six of them. Vaughan took his seat where the students had shuffled up to make space for him, Emi, Orla, David, Nicholas and Amy, watching to see if anyone on his table looked unhappy like the boys on St Wistan's table. He was glad to see no-one on his table did.

"And finally, you seven, who hold the Autumnal colours of orange and brown, are now members of the House of Saint Swithun." The last tables, the tables right in front of the Refectory doors took their turn to stand and applaud, as Gregory Southall, Malachi Kingston, Florence Fitzgerald, Sherry Wilson, Stefan Gentry, Sarah Bergman and Michael Morris joined them, amidst pats on the back and shuffling of chairs. The newcomers were welcomed into their new houses and just had time to introduce themselves to their fellow housemates before Dr Bakewell began his start-of-term speech.

"Students, students, it is now time for the frivolity of summer to come to an end and hard-work and preparation begin. For our new scholarship students, you will have much to catch up on - particularly those of you aged twelve or over as you will have at least a year's catching up to do."

Dr Bakewell really wasn't the best at encouraging children, Vaughan thought to himself. Every speech he'd heard so far was full of expectation and warning of hard work; he wasn't turning out to be the jolly, lively man he had imagined before the school fete. But he realised Dr Bakewell had a point; most of the new starters were eleven years of age and were starting off in the first year. But he, along with a few other scholarship winners, was twelve coming thirteen and therefore was having to join the second-years. This was intimidating enough; he wondered what it would be like for those older than he, like Georgia Flavell and Daisy Quenell, who, at thirteen, were having to join as third-years.

"You will find your lessons unusual; we encourage the inventive, the creative. But the golden rule of baking is that one must always follow instructions exactly as they are given. This is what separates baking from cooking and is the most elementary of rules, from which you begin. This school tolerates no rule-breaking or bending and as such we produce some of the finest bakers and confectioners in the world. Put your minds, hearts and effort into it and in a few years time, you may well be considered one of those deemed best in the world." Vaughan and a few others breathed in deeply and puffed out their chests at these words - that was exactly what Vaughan wanted to be and now he was here, studying under the one and only Dr Bakewell, he knew he was one step closer, even if his Headmaster wasn't quite what he'd expected.

"New students, once we have finished breakfast, your House Prefects will take you to your dormitories where you will be reunited with your luggage. Existing students, you will commence classes as dictated on your timetables. Please see your Heads of House immediately after breakfast for your respective timetables. I trust you will all put one hundred percent effort into your schoolwork - as always - and wish you all a pleasant day and a good year." He walked behind him and took his seat in the centre of the teachers banquet table. Mrs Hilderstone appeared from somewhere on the right and banged a huge gold gong which Vaughan hadn't spotted before. Obviously this was the signal that the children could start breakfast for there was a sudden flurry as everyone except the teachers ran to the long tables against the left wall, which were laden with foods of all kind. Not wanting to get in anyone's way, Vaughan collected a plate and quickly grabbed the first food he could see - toast - and scurried back to his seat, more interested in watching what everyone else did, than eating. Besides, he was more nervous now than ever before and the last thing he felt like doing was eating.

Chapter 13

House of St Oswald

As soon as breakfast had finished almost all the students scurried off out of the hall, to collect their timetables and commence their lessons. Only Vaughan, the other nineteen new students, Professor Drumgoole and three older students remained. Gathering everyone together on the centre table, Professor Drumgoole sat down with them and explained.

"Children, each House has it's own Prefect who is responsible for their House and its members. These students here are your House Prefects. Prefect of St Wistan is Jeremy Jones." The tall, thin, curly-haired boy with freckles smiled and nodded in acknowledgement to Vaughan and the others.

"Prefect of St Swithun is Elouise Philips" continued Professor Drumgoole as Elouise smiled and waved hello, "and finally, Theo Banks is the Prefect of St Oswald."
Theo also smiled and said a cheery 'hello.'
"If you have any questions, concerns or need any help, you go to your House Prefect first. If there are any problems which need to go to a teacher, the House Prefect will speak to the House Master. House Master for St Wistan is Chef Goodbun the Artisan Baker; House Master for St Swithun is Professor Peach, our Professor of Natural Foods and House Master for St Oswald is Doctor Crose, Doctor of Edible Arts. Your House Prefects will now take you to your dormitories where you will meet your respective House Masters and receive your timetables. Any questions? No? Well then, Prefects, over to you." With that Professor Drumgoole rose and walked back to the hall door and out into the corridor, leaving the students in the hands of their prefects.

"Ok everyone" Elouise began, " all of you follow your Prefects. We'll leave the hall together but then we'll go in different directions so make sure you're following the right person. Everyone clear? Right then, let's be off." Elouise herded Florence, Gregory, Malachi, Sherry, Stefan, Sarah and Michael together and led them out of the hall first. Jeremy followed suit next and marched out of the hall with Poppy, Daisy, Georgia, Oliver, Rebekah, Alison and Curtis, who were almost running behind after him to keep up and finally Theo led Vaughan, Emi, Orla, David, Nicholas and Amy out of the hall.

Across the grand hallway they walked and ascended up the wooden staircase to the first floor. Once they reached the landing they turned right and Theo opened a small, wooden door that lay right in front of them. Vaughan couldn't see anything behind the door, it looked pitch black, almost like a store cupboard. Theo went in first, called the others in and closed the door behind them. Once inside, Vaughan was able to see by the chink of light coming in through a small lead-paned window, a black spiral staircase winding its way upwards into pitch blackness and out of sight. There was nothing else in this tiny, square room except the iron staircase. As Theo put his foot on the first step and began to climb he beckoned the others to follow. It was very dark in this stairwell and Vaughan noticed there were no lights at all, only the small shaft of light coming in through the narrow window. The staircase was so narrow and tightly circled, he wondered what would happen if they met anyone coming down.

Up and round, up and round they climbed in total darkness until eventually they could see light above them; one step after another they took until finally their heads popped up above a floor and they had reached another landing. One by one, Vaughan, Emi, Orla, David, Nicholas and Amy stepped off the staircase and onto the landing which also contained one leaded window and one door but this landing also contained a suit of armour. Guarding the corridor, the knight clutched a fierce looking halberd in his right hand and stood facing a huge coat of arms hung on the opposite wall. Walking past the armour (quietly saying 'Morning Ozzy' as he passed) Theo led the way to the door at the end of the short landing. Flinging it open he stood back and grinned as the children's eyes focused on what lay behind it. As they peered beyond the door, their jaws dropped, mouths agape as they gasped in wonderment.

* * *

As the door swung open, it immediately revealed a huge, white fireplace, very similar to the one they'd seen earlier in the Sun Room, only about three times as big. In the fireplace was a pile of logs with a small fire crackling away, giving off both a beautiful glow and an added warmth to the room; above the fire, on the silver chimney breast hung the same coat of arms they had just passed on the landing. As they entered further in, they found themselves in a very comfortable, homely-looking room indeed. It became obvious to Vaughan that this room belonged to the House of St Oswald, as it was decorated entirely in shades of blue, silver and white. The carpet was a deep royal blue; right in front of the crackling fire was a long, thin, white coffee table which stood on a pale-blue and white Chinese-style rug. Either side of the rug, framing the fireplace, were two plump, soft settees; one was pale-blue with dark blue and white cushions, the other was dark blue with pale-blue and white cushions. Theo sat down on the dark blue settee and told the others to sit down too. Vaughan, David and Nicholas sat next to Theo while Amy, Emi and Orla perched together on the pale-blue settee opposite.

"This is our Common Room" confirmed Theo. "Whenever we aren't in lessons, studying or eating, this is where we are. It's pretty much our living room, where we can relax, play games or just chat and hang out. No-one else is allowed in here other than Dr Bakewell, Professor Drumgoole, Dr Crose and Mrs Hilderstone.

It's the same for the other common rooms of course. Only members of the House can enter."

"What's the shield for - up there?" asked Amy, pointing to the chimney breast.

"That is the shield of Saint Oswald" Theo explained. "And that armour on the landing - that was his armour. We call him 'Ozzy' and it's tradition that the first time you pass him in the morning you should say 'hello' and as you pass him to go to bed, you should say 'goodnight' to him."

"But haven't you already passed him once this morning, Theo?" enquired Emi.

Theo looked at Emi and leant forward, speaking very quietly. "I had" he nodded "but you hadn't, had you? I was saying 'morning' on your behalf. You don't want to upset him now, do you?"

Vaughan didn't know quite what to make of this and noticed Emi looked suddenly uncomfortable, so he decided to change the subject.

"Do the other Houses have shields and suits of armour too?" asked Vaughan.

"I wouldn't know" Theo replied in his normal voice, shuffling himself back onto his seat, "we're not allowed in any other House Quarters. I expect so but I've never seen them myself."

"Well, I can confirm that they do." A soft voice came from somewhere behind Emi, Amy and Orla, making them jump. Looking behind them, a pretty, black-haired lady in a blue houndstooth dress and black boots entered the common room.

"Let me introduce you" Theo smiled at the surprised expressions on their faces, "this is Doctor Crose, Head of St Oswald House." Dr Crose came closer and shook hands with the three new students.

"Hello and welcome" she smiled at them warmly, shaking their hands in turn. "I am Dr Sue Crose, Doctor of Edible Arts and it is lovely to have you here in our school. I hope you'll enjoy your time here - I am very glad you are in the House of St Oswald - it's actually the best house, but don't say I said that!" she whispered as the six children smiled back at her. She seemed rather pleasant with soft, gentle features and sparkling blue eyes; instantly all six children felt comfortable with her. Returning her attention to Theo, she gave her instructions.

"Theo - take our new house members to their dormitories and when you come back I will give out your timetables." Theo nodded and gathered the three together.

"Girls - your dormitories are just over there" he pointed to a door to the right of the fireplace. "I can't go in because it's the girls dormitory. But just go through the door and you'll soon find it. Mrs Hilderstone tells me she has put names on your beds so you'll know which ones are yours. Boys, you come with me and I'll take you to the boy's dormitory."

Amy, Emi and Orla looked at each other, shrugged their shoulders and left the common room, clearly happy that they had each other to explore with. Vaughan, David and Nicholas followed Theo through an identical doorway to the left of the fireplace, into a brick corridor. Theo opened the door at the end of the corridor and stepped into the boys dormitory, holding the door open for the three new boys behind him.

* * *

It was hard not to notice the beds first. There were five, white triple-bunk beds on either side of the walls with a tall white ladder running from the floor to the top bunk and between them, from the tall ceiling which was painted blue like the sky, complete with clouds and birds, hung two crystal chandeliers. As Vaughan walked in, he noticed that all the beds were made; the royal blue duvets were tucked in neatly and the crisp white pillows were all fluffed up so that not even a crease was showing. Everything he had come across in this school so far appeared spick and span - no-one had a hair out of place and there wasn't a speck of dust to be seen anywhere. He commented on this to Theo.

"Everything's so tidy and perfect here" he said, turning around to face Theo "my room at home's nothing like this! Where's everyone's stuff?"

"Ah - that's because you don't have Dr Bakewell and Mrs Hilderstone at home, do you?" replied Theo. "Dr Bakewell's a very proud man you know - proud of his achievements, his students and most of all, of his school. He is particular about a few things, but most of all, time-keeping and neatness. He can't stand mess - so, he employed Mrs Hilderstone to be Housekeeper and it's her job to make sure everything is ship-shape."

"So does Mrs Hilderstone make up everyone's beds and tidy up after them, then?" asked Vaughan, feeling suddenly guilty and offended on behalf of his mother, who always kept their house clean and tidy.

Theo laughed "oh, no - she makes sure we do it - and do it properly!" he explained. "No, we all make our own beds and tidy our own belongings away. You see those cupboards along the far wall and the chests of drawers by each bed? Each student has one of those for their things. The person in the top bunk has a cupboard and the two others each have a chest of drawers. But to be fair, as it's our first day back after the summer holiday, she will have made up these beds for us."

"How do you decide where you sleep?" Nicholas asked looking around, wondering which bed he thought he would like "can I choose my own?"

"Nope, sorry" Theo replied "there's an order. First and second years bottom bunks only. Third and fourth years have the middle bunks and the top bunks are for fifth year and lower sixth form. Upper sixth formers have their own quarters upstairs."

"How..." Vaughan began, but Theo already knew what he was about to say and answered his question before it had even been spoken.

"There's a name card on your bed and your luggage is in front of your drawers. Go on - have a look."

The boys searched the room for their bunks. Vaughan walked first up the left side of the room but none of the beds had his name anywhere. As he crossed the room and walked back down the right side, he noticed his luggage, neatly stacked in front of a tall chest of drawers to the left of the fourth bed from the back. It was only then he noticed a small envelope-sized piece of white card propped up against the pillow of the bottom bunk, with his name beautifully written in swirly blue handwriting:

Vaughan Baker
Second-Year Student

"Unpack your things and I'll meet you back in the common room in ten minutes" Theo told the boys, before leaving them alone in their new dormitory. Vaughan had never shared a room with anyone before and wondered how it would feel, whether he'd be able to sleep with all the strange noises and people sleeping in the same room as he. He wondered if he snored and if so, whether he would keep the others awake. Or would they snore and keep him awake? As these thoughts crept into Vaughan's mind he began to transfer his belongings from his suitcase to he chest of drawers, feeling very small in this huge room and hoping he would settle in soon.

* * *

With his clothes re-packed in his drawers, Vaughan and the boys returned to the common room where Theo and Doctor Crose were waiting. Seconds later Amy, Emi and Orla also appeared in the common room, having unpacked their belongings too. Seating everyone on the sofas around the fireside coffee table, Doctor

Crose produced six envelopes from her dress pocket, each sealed with a thin blue ribbon and distributed the envelopes to the children.

"These are your timetables for the year" she told them as she handed them out. "And these" she produced another six envelopes from her other pocket "are maps of Honeycomb Hall. Just in case you find yourselves lost" she added with a small smile. "Now, I have to go - I'm a very busy lady! Theo - take them to their first lesson and then you can go to yours. You have your own timetable already?" Theo nodded and raised his own envelope in response. "Great, well that's all sorted then" the teacher said, smoothing down her dress "and I'll and see you in my classes soon. Ciao" and with that, Sue Crose departed the common room leaving all four of them to study their timetables.

Vaughan looked at his timetable, the classes written down were very unusual, some of which he had never heard of before. There was Sugarcraft, Artisan Baking, Edible Arts, Natural Foods, History of Baking, Chocolatiering, Handwriting and many more.

"Handwriting?" asked David, "Why do we have a handwriting lesson?"

"It's so that when you move onto icing in the third year, you'll already have the basics of good handwriting. Think about it - if you can't write neatly using a pen, how do you expect to write neatly in icing using a piping bag?" replied Theo.

"Theo, there aren't any classroom numbers on here" said Vaughan, reading his timetable, "how will we know where to go?"

"All the rooms have plaques on the doors" answered Theo "hadn't you noticed?" Sheepishly Vaughan shook his head - he hadn't noticed anything he was too nervous and in awe of it all to have paid attention to anything small like that. "Well, all the rooms are identified on the door plaques but there's also a pattern. All the dormitories are in the towers, all the sixth form quarters are in the house towers above the dormitories; the 'Teacher's Quarters' are strictly for teachers only, the Healing Remedies class is right underneath the Hospital Quarters…"

"Hospital quarters?" interrupted Orla, "I didn't know you had a hospital in here?"

"Oh, it's not a proper hospital" Theo explained " although it is run by the school Doctor, Dr Muller-Weiss. He's a Doctor of Medicine. No, it's more a large room with a few beds where you'll be sent if you come down with anything, or feel sick. Because most of our lessons involve food, we can't have anyone ill or feeling sick in a class, it's too risky, so if you're ill you get sent to the Hospital Quarters until you feel better."

This answer seems to satisfy Orla and she nodded her understanding and allowed Theo to continue.

"Right then, your first lesson is…Sugarcraft. Oh, that'll be with Dr Crose then. No wonder she had to rush off!" he said, peering over Vaughan's shoulder to peek at his timetable. "I'll take you all down to the Sugarcraft Kitchen first, which is Dr Crose's classroom, for Vaughan, Emi and Orla's lesson, see them in and then David, Nicholas and Amy, we'll carry on to…" Quickly taking hold of David's timetable, he read where the first-years were meant to be. "…Professor Peach's kitchen. First years have Natural Foods. So I'll take you all to your classrooms then I'll have to go to my own class. Ready?"

The children nodded as Theo led them out of the common room and back onto the landing. Standing in front of the suit of armour, otherwise known as 'Ozzy', Theo took hold of the halberd which Ozzy clutched in his right hand. As Theo pulled it towards him, Ozzy's arms outstretched as he continued to keep hold of his moving weapon; his previously bent arm was now straight and the previously upright halberd was now leaning forwards. As the halberd locked in it's new position Theo let go, then they heard a rumble behind them. Turning around to see what was causing the noise Vaughan gasped; the huge coat of arms opposite Ozzy trembled slightly, then pushed itself out of the wall and slid to the left, revealing a dark hole in its wake. Theo looked at the six, bewildered children who were staring at the dark, gaping hole and back to Theo's familiar face, waiting for an explanation.

"That's how we get down" Theo informed them, pointing into the hole. "I'll go first - pop your feet in first, hold the top then let go. I'll see you at the bottom. Ozzy won't keep the passageway open for long though, so if he closes it, just pull his halberd and he'll open it again." Letting go of the top, off he disappeared, into the dark hole and out of sight, just like that. David jumped in immediately after Theo, followed by Nicholas and then Amy, before the coat of arms slid back into place, sealing the gap. With the three first-years now gone, Emi obeyed Theo's instructions, pulled the halberd and Ozzy re-opened the gap for the second-year children.

"You go next" Emi suggested to Vaughan. Vaughan nodded, thinking that as the only remaining boy, he should really show them there was nothing to be scared of, even though he was a bit unsure himself. Slowly he sat on the edge of the hole and swung in his feet, steadied himself, took a deep breath, let go and plunged into the darkness.

* * *

Whoosh - it was brilliant! "Wow", he thought, as he slid further down, "how cool is this school?" The scary dark hole turned out to be nothing more than a twisty, wooden tube - a slide! As he flew down the tube, bumping into the sides he couldn't take the smile off his face! When the slide finally spat him out, Vaughan stood up and recognised that he was now in one of the corridors Mrs Hilderstone had led them through, on their way to the Sun Room. That must be why they didn't pass anyone coming down the spiral staircase earlier, he realised. Because the staircase took you up - but the tube brought you down! The strange giant mouse-holes he'd seen earlier he now understood were the exits from the slides!

"Enjoy that?" asked Theo, grinning at him.

"Yeah!" answered Vaughan grinning just as much, before jumping out of the way as a flustered Emi appeared, almost knocking him over as she was flung out of the tube, quickly followed by Orla. Once they had composed themselves, the six children followed Theo along the corridor, across the hallway, up the staircase to the second-floor, along the landing and turned right onto the second-floor corridor. Eventually Theo stopped outside a door bearing a golden plaque engraved 'Sugarcraft & Edible Arts'.

"Vaughan, Emi and Orla - this is your class. Second-years have Sugarcraft now. Go on in and get yourselves sorted. Amy, David and Nicholas, you come with me. First-years have got Natural Foods with Professor Peach this morning!"

Chapter 14

Sugar Mice

Caroline and Verity walked along the second-floor corridor for their first lesson of the year. They were glad to be back at school - it was a place where they could experiment and let their imagination run free, creating sweets and learning tips and they never, ever got bored at school. There was just so much to learn and so much fun to be had.

As they wandered past the classroom doors, they wondered what they would be making. It was Sugarcraft with Dr Crose - one of Verity's favourite teachers.

Caroline and Verity opened the door addressed 'Sugarcraft and Edible Arts' and along with all their classmates, seated themselves at the pastel-coloured kitchen benches which filled the classroom. Each pupil had a bench to themselves, giving them plenty of space to work. Noticing that this class was made up entirely of St Oswald children, Verity breathed a sigh of relief.

"Oh good, it's just our House in this class" she called across to Caroline, who was seated at the bench on her right, in the same row. "No chance of big-headed Avery showing off, for a change." Caroline nodded in agreement. Although each child belonged to a named house and competitions between houses were encouraged, Dr Bakewell was very keen not to separate the Houses completely, therefore classes were made up of children from all Houses. This also meant that Verity and Caroline often had to put up with Avery Sorrel of St Wistan's, boasting and showing off whenever they were in mixed classes.

Feeling happier that this was a 'St Oswald Only' lesson, they quickly settled into their routine, retrieved their white hats and put on their white aprons, ready for Dr Crose's lesson to start. As they pulled their aprons over their heads and tied them at the waist, they spotted the three new scholarship pupils watching the class and copying them, quickly putting on their aprons and caps.

"Well class, welcome back to Honeycomb! I hope you all had a good holiday?" Dr Crose began, to a chorus of "yes, miss" in answer. "Fantastic! So you're all refreshed and ready to go then, are you?"

"Yes, miss!" the whole class shouted back, smiling at their bubbly teacher.

"Wonderful! Well, first of all I see we have been lucky to have three winners of the scholarship competition in our House. Congratulations, you three, you did extremely well. As Head of St Oswald, I bid you welcome to our House and also, to my class." Vaughan, Emi and Orla smiled shyly back. Dr Crose was a very cheerful, likeable teacher with an incredibly infectious smile!

"Now onto today's lesson. I thought we'd do something practical today; roll our sleeves up and get stuck in straight away. Rather than boring old written work - how does that sound?"

"Great, miss!"

"Oh, yeah!"

"Yesssssssss!"

Various enthusiastic responses echoed around the kitchen as the pupils focused entirely on their teacher. "Okay, then. I'm going to bring around some moulds and while I'm doing that I want you all to wash your hands and come back to your seats. Scoot."

Within seconds the children had vacated their workstations, frantically queuing and washing their hands at the six big white sinks under the kitchen windows, Vaughan included.

When he returned to his worktop, alongside Orla, he found Dr Crose had given him three small moulds and three white lollipop sticks. He peered across the aisle to Orla's worktop and saw she had the same kit given to her. As soon as everyone had returned from washing their hands, she explained.

"It's your first lesson of the year, so as a treat, this morning you can make sweets. Well, one kind of sweet as you'll all be following the same recipe, but you can make them into whatever shape, colour and flavour you want. Who likes Sugar Mice?" Everyone in the class put up their hand and looked at each other with increasing excitement written across their wide-eyed faces.

"Oh I am glad" Dr Crose said, pretending to be very relieved - as if there was ever a danger of a student of confectionery not liking sugar - "because that's what you'll be doing this morning. Of course, whether you choose to make a sugar mouse - or a sugar flower, a sugar person, a sugar cat or a simple mint - will be entirely up to you. Just choose a mould - or you can shape your sweet entirely by hand if you wish."

Children dived in immediately, inspecting their moulds, wondering which one to choose. Vaughan decided to use the mouse mould - as did Verity and Caroline - while Emi chose the rose mould and Orla opted for the cat-shaped mould.

The kitchen-classroom then turned into a hive of activity, with children and teacher alike buzzing around the classroom like bees. Dr Crose encouraged her pupils to share ingredients, swap flavours, to wander between the workbenches to both help and show an interest in their classmates - she believed it developed greater creativity and helped the new children make friends. She unlocked the wall cupboards, from where she produced all sorts of weird and wonderful ingredients and utensils for the children to use; glass bowls, pipettes, whisks, weighing scales; little bottles of colouring - red, blue, pink, green and yellow; icing sugar, bottles of a sticky clear liquid called glycerine, another bottle of something called glucose, white sugar, brown sugar, eggs - it was amazing!

Still grateful that their first lesson of the year was an 'Ozzy's Only' lesson, with the Head of St Oswald teaching, Verity and

Caroline watched the three scholarship winners curiously. Although the three winners had been housed together, it appeared that the two scholarship girls, Emi and Orla, had become friends already and Caroline noticed that although the new girls spoke to Vaughan, it was clear he was pretty much alone at the moment.

As the class began mixing their recipes, gooey egg whites splashing over the worktops as children whisked away furiously and others concentrated on weighing sugar, Caroline and Verity thought Vaughan looked rather lonely, being the only scholarship boy in St Oswald's. Being the more outgoing of the two, Caroline strolled over to him and spoke.

"Hi! I'm Caroline, this is Verity. Welcome to Honeycomb and to St Oswald's. Would you like to work with us? What's your name...?"

"Vaughan" Vaughan replied distracted, as he stared at the scales he was weighing his icing sugar in, waiting for the exact moment they balanced and stopped bobbing up and down. "Er...yes, okay then...thank you."

So they began helping each other and off they went, the girls helping Vaughan identify the ingredients he needed and he helping them measure them correctly. As they worked together Caroline struck up a conversation.

"So then, you won one of the scholarship places, obviously" she continued, as she cracked an egg and began tipping the yolk from one half of the eggshell to the other and back again, allowing the white to drip through the gap in the middle into the large glass bowl below, "that's a real achievement. There were about a hundred entries, you know!" She seemed genuinely impressed and Vaughan relaxed a little, feeling proud.

"Erm, thanks" he replied, copying Caroline's technique of separating the egg, trying hard to stop the yolk escaping the shell and falling into his bowl with the egg white, "there were quite a few, I suppose."

"Suppose?!" Caroline repeated as she stared at him and nearly dropped her egg in surprise, "There were! We were there, weren't we, V?"

"Yes, we were there, at the fete" Verity joined in, squirting a tiny droplet of red colouring out of a pipette and into her bowl of sugar. "Honestly, we're both really impressed that you won a place. Which one was your cake?"

"Oh, I made the Chocolate Chessboard" replied Vaughan. "I wasn't sure what to do and I sat down with my Dad to play chess because I was worrying about it and when I saw the chessboard I saw the cake in my head. So I made it." Caroline stared at him, open-mouthed. "You just...made it?" she repeated, sounding stunned.

"As soon as your mixture becomes an even colour and is smooth with no lumps left, it's ready to be poured into your moulds." Dr Crose's instructions interrupted their conversation. "Be careful when you pour - I don't really want to clean up a lot of sugary worktops after class. As soon as your mould is full you need to insert your stick if your using one. You have only a short time before it starts to set, but don't rush, pour steadily. Once your moulds are full we'll put in the fridge to cool while we record the lesson in your books. By the end of class they will be ready to eat. Just in time for break!" Caroline rolled her eyes as if this was most obvious thing Dr Crose had just said and wasn't worth interrupting their conversation for. "So, what did you say? That you just thought of a cake in your head and then made it real?"

"Yeah....why?" Vaughan asked, suddenly suspicious.

"Well, it's just that there aren't many people that can do that" she explained. "Even I can't do that yet and this is my second year. You must have a real gift, you know. For an idea to pop into your head like that and for you to be able to make it real. Wow!" Verity appeared in between them and nudged Caroline with her elbow, causing her to almost spill her mixture as she poured the gooey pink sugary liquid into her mouse mould.

"Of course he's got a gift" she said, rolling her eyes at Vaughan, "that's why he's here!" After a second of realising what the girls had said, all three of them laughed. "Anyway, come on" said Verity as she lifted her mould, "we've got some mice to make!"

Chapter 15

Rhubarb and Custard

Dr Crose's class was fun, made even better by the fact that Vaughan had made two friends already. He had wondered how long it would take him to make friends and had expected it to be at least a few days, so he was pleasantly surprised and relieved. He hated being alone and having no real friends - he'd had enough of being lonely at Honey Wood Comprehensive and desperately wanted this school to be different. Fortunately, Dr Bakewell's School was so far proving to be different in every way imaginable.

After washing their spoons and moulds, hanging up their aprons and quietly writing down in their school books what they had made in class, the heavy school bell began to dong, echoing loudly through the quiet classroom, making Vaughan jump and causing his pen to slip across the paper, leaving a crude, blue line in its wake.

"Drat" he muttered, looking at the untidy scrawl in his new book. "What was that?"

"Break" whispered Verity, closing her book and stuffing it into her bag. Following her lead, Vaughan did the same and saw other pupils gathering up their pens and books too.

"Well done class" Dr Crose applauded her pupils, "a very good start to the year. And a special well done to Emi, Vaughan and Orla. It's not easy being new in class and a year behind, but you three have done exceedingly well. Let's give them a clap." Flushing with embarrassment as the class reluctantly clapped, Vaughan slung his bag over his shoulder and popped his sugar mouse in a paper bag which he tucked away safely in his blazer pocket. He wished people would stop drawing attention to the fact that they were new. Relieved when the clapping died away after only a few seconds, Dr Crose dismissed them all and they were free to go.

"We have two breaks a day" Caroline said as they walked out of the kitchen, "one in the morning and one in the afternoon, which is actually called Afternoon Tea. Snacks and drinks are put out in the Refectory - fruit, toast and teacakes at morning break, cakes and pastries for afternoon tea - and you just help yourself. You can take what you like but you're not allowed to take any food or drinks out of the hall - Bakewell goes ballistic if he catches you. Says it encourages mice."

"He seems a bit...uptight...Dr Bakewell." Vaughan said tentatively. "I imagined him being more like a sweet shop owner, you know? Sort of... jolly and always chuckling, I suppose. Is he always...well, like he is?"

"Yes, he is" answered Verity, "but he's a genius, isn't he? They're always a bit crabby, aren't they?"

"I dunno, how many geniuses do you know then?" asked Caroline. "Besides moi of course!?" Vaughan tilted his head to the side slightly and looked quizzically at Verity, not sure whether Caroline was making fun of herself or not. His unspoken question was answered when Verity rolled her eyes at her friend, smiled and declared

"Well obviously you Caroline, but you're not quite a real genius yet" - Caroline frowned - "you're not crabby enough!" teased Verity. The pair of them roared with laughter and Vaughan couldn't help but join in. The more time he spent with them the more relaxed he became; Caroline and Verity seemed to be nice, normal girls who didn't mind having a giggle at themselves. They weren't silly and giggly like the girls at Honey Wood Comprehensive.

They were very different though, the two of them. Caroline was confident and outgoing, easy to make friends with. She stood about the same height as Vaughan though a little bit overweight;

her bobbed thick brown hair hung straight and curled neatly under her jaw. Her round face always seemed to be smiling or laughing, Vaughan noticed, her chubby cheeks rosy like apples, she was fun to be with.

Verity however was completely opposite. She was slim - almost skinny - a little taller than Caroline and her face was quite pale. She had straight blonde hair which she'd tied up in a loose pony tail and a fringe which was in the messy stages of growing out and kept flopping about over her eyes. Verity was a quiet, serious girl, not as bubbly as Caroline and wore black rectangular glasses which made her look very studious. Which of course, she was. Noticing that she often looked down at her hands unless talking to Caroline, Vaughan correctly suspected Verity was rather shy around new people. He wasn't sure what it was but something about Verity intrigued him and he hoped that the two girls would accept him as their friend.

* * *

Given that Vaughan's nerves at breakfast had stolen his appetite, making friends with Verity and Caroline had since quashed those nerves, allowing his appetite to return and causing his stomach to growl embarrassingly loudly as it did so. The three of them made their way back into the Refectory for their snacks, where they each chose a piece of fruit from the Food Table and poured some fruit juice from the Fruit Juice Fountain. They sat down at their house table with their juice and fruit and pulled out of their blazer pockets, the paper bags containing the sugar mice. They took their mice out of the paper bags and had just started to nibble them (Vaughan had bitten off the head of his) when something large, furry and unrecognisable came out of nowhere, leapt onto their table and careered across it, rucking up the tablecloth and knocking drinks over everyone as it skidded past. Children jumped up quickly trying to avoid getting soaked by the spilled drinks; there was yelling, shouting and complaining - it was utter chaos! Knocking over food, sweets, cups and drinks before the invader finally fell off the end of the table and disappeared out of sight, Vaughan suddenly realised he'd lost his sugar mouse.

"Oh look - my trousers are soaked and I've lost my mouse! I'm going to have to get some fresh trousers." Vaughan complained, getting to his feet, "What was that?"

"I've lost mine too" Verity moaned, "we should have warned you, sorry Vaughan."

"Warned me?" asked Vaughan, curious. "What about - what was that thing?"

"Those things are the terrors of the school" Caroline explained as the three of them left the Refectory and made their way towards St Oswald's common room. "Rhubarb and Custard."

"Rhubarb and Custard?" repeated Vaughan. "What do you mean? What are they?" As they meandered through the corridors, the girls told Vaughan all about Rhubarb and Custard.

"They're Professor Drumgoole's cats" Verity explained. "The tabby one is Rhubarb and ginger one is Custard. They're lovely cats actually - sometimes you might find them curled up on someone's bed - but they do like sugar mice - I forgot to warn you about them."

"So they're the school cats, then?"

"Yes, I suppose. They belong to Professor Drumgoole but yes, they're always in the school. They've been here for years, apparently. Before we started, anyway."

"The story goes that a few years ago, Dr Bakewell had a problem with mice nibbling food in the pantry" Caroline elaborated, always eager to tell a good story, "so Dr Bakewell set up mousetraps to catch them. Well, one day a St Wistan boy had been sent to the kitchens to serve detention and was dragging a sack of potatoes out of the pantry to take to the cook. But as he tried to lift the sack to carry it, he stumbled under the weight of it and lost his balance, falling backwards into the shelves, toppling them over and sending everything stored on them crashing down around him. Flour, sugar, nuts, icing sugar, sprinkles, treacle - the whole lot. Lids flew off tins, bags burst, jars smashed - you name it, it all fell down, ingredients spilt everywhere and caused a right mess. Anyway, as the boy tried to jump out of the way of the falling tins and bags, he trod on a sprung mousetrap which snapped shut across his foot and broke his toe. He went to the hospital quarters for a week and was on crutches for over a month."

"Understandably, his parents were furious with Dr Bakewell" Verity continued the saga, "and he was told off by the Culinary Council and told he couldn't use mousetraps in the school because they were too dangerous. And he should have reported the mice to the Council as soon as he found them, so he got a double-telling off. Well, he couldn't let the mice run around the school eating all the food, so he was stuck. In the end, Professor Drumgoole turned up one morning with two cats - his solution to the mice problem. He thought they would chase the mice and scare them away."

"Of course, Dr Bakewell wasn't too keen at first" Caroline added, "he was worried that they might actually catch the mice - which would have been even worse. So Professor Drumgoole buttered him up and told him he could name them. Hence their names - Rhubarb and Custard."

Vaughan looked at her waiting for the explanation - clearly he didn't know much about Dr Bakewell.

"The Doctors favourite sweet - " Caroline explained "Rhubarb and Custard!"

"So did they ever catch the mice?" asked Vaughan, interested.

"Oh no" said Verity, "we've never seen any mice at all. Maybe the cats' scent scared them away, but no, nothing's ever happened since Rhubarb and Custard came."

"That's why they like the Sugar Mice" added Caroline as they finally reached the common room, "they're the only type of mice they'll get around here now! Now you get yourself dried and we'll meet you down in the hallway."

Chapter 16

The Patisserie Plan

By morning break, Daisy Quenell, the elder of the unique Quenell twins found herself desperately missing her sister. As she had never been in a class with her twin Poppy - due to the way their birthdays put them in different school years - she didn't think she would notice her absence but she did, especially as most of her class (apart from Georgia Flavell) was already so much more skilled than she. Although the twins were now both thirteen, Poppy, being born on the first of September and only turning thirteen today, had been placed in the second-year and was the oldest in her year, whilst Daisy, being born on the thirty-first of August and turning thirteen a day earlier, had been put in the year above and was the youngest in the third-year. Of the St Wistan scholarship students, only Daisy and Georgia would both turn fourteen by the end of the school year and as such had both been put in the third-year, which meant they had got two years of catching up to do. The rest of their class had been studying at Honeycomb from the age of eleven and therefore had a two-year head-start on the scholarship girls. Naturally, Daisy and Georgia paired up and a friendship soon blossomed, each being grateful to have someone alongside them in class whom they could confide in and help each other as they worried about catching up with the rest of their year.

Earlier that morning in their first lesson of the day, St Wistan's third-years had been in the Pastry Kitchen with Madame Rougerie, a short, square, stout woman with red frizzy hair (which she tried in vain to tuck under her white cap) and an even redder face. She was French, dramatic and more than a little scary; both

Daisy and Georgia had been desperately hoping that the pastry base they made in her lesson met with her approval. As they discovered, she was not a woman to disguise her opinions or sugar-coat bad news.

Fortunately, the pastry cases they had made went very well indeed and Madame Rougerie had told the children to leave them to cool during morning break and they could collect them on their way to Chef Goodbun's class. Clearly this meant they were to be used in his class, but for what they had no idea. So with some curiosity the girls had left them in the Pastry Kitchen under the watchful eye of Madame Rougerie while they made their way to the Refectory for their snacks.

* * *

As they took a while to choose their drinks and snacks, Georgia and Daisy realised there wasn't much room left on either of the St Wistan tables. Poppy was still hovering by the snack table, deciding what to choose so she hadn't saved a seat for her sister, she hadn't even made it to the table yet. In fact, the only spaces Georgia and Daisy could find were directly opposite the annoying posh boy from their year, Percy Snodland and another boy they later discovered to be Avery Sorrel. The two boys were deep in conversation and so after giving each other the 'do-we-have-to' and 'there's-nowhere-else-to-sit' looks, the girls squeezed onto the table, hoping the boys wouldn't pay any attention to them. Fortunately just as they took their seats there was a commotion behind them, at the St Oswald table. Turning around to see what on earth all was going on, they noticed something unidentifiable yet fluffy skidding across the table top, dragging plates and cups with it, before untangling itself and becoming two cats, who promptly dropped off the end of the table just as one of the St Oswald children leapt up in the air complaining about having wet trousers! Of course, this also distracted Percy who rolled his eyes with disdain as he stared at the St Oswaldians, allowing Georgia and Daisy to sneak into their seats unnoticed. They had only been in one lesson with Percy Snodland but it became crystal clear during that lesson how he thought he was better than the new students; he had a very high opinion of himself and a very low opinion of the competition winners. Keeping their heads down and voices hushed, they quietly ate their toast and drank their fruit juice hoping not to draw attention to themselves, thankful for the commotion behind them!

But this gave the girls an advantage. Because they were talking quietly, almost whispering to each other now that the fuss had died down, they were able to clearly hear what Percy Snodland was discussing with his friend - a boy who apparently shared similar views to Percy and whom, it transpired, was in the same year as Daisy's twin sister, Poppy.

"How many of them are in your year, Avery?"

"There's two second-years in St Wistan. One boy, I think he's called Oliver and a girl - Poppy, her name is." Daisy's ears pricked up and she hoped it wasn't noticeable.

"That's only from this House though. What about the whole year - from all Houses?"

"Oh, there's quite a few. Let me see....there's a tall girl with ginger hair, a boy with mousy brown hair...a Japanese girl - she's very quiet - and..erm... oh yeah, the Japanese girl's friend. Orna or Orca, something like that anyway. The one with glasses. Why?"

"Because Avery, we both know it's not fair that these 'pupils' (he almost spat the word out in contempt) have been allowed to come here. This was our school for the elite, not just anyone who happened to bake a cake. Bakewell didn't listen to you before when you told him it was a ridiculous idea so we need to do something to prove it was a stupid idea and send these imposters back home again."

Georgia and Daisy were listening intently to every word. Though they had finished their toast and juice, they kept the drinking straws in their lips, pretending to be drinking. Neither boy appeared to have noticed them but the last thing they wanted was to be seen eavesdropping. Especially when what they were hearing sounded more and more like a sabotage plan being unravelled. They kept their heads bent low and their ears open as Percy continued.

"Look, all we need to do is make him realise that this school needs to stay a school for real confectioners. He needs to know that if ordinary kids come here he'll lose respect, the school will lose respect and that we will lose out when we come to leave. At the moment if we leave now we can have our pick of where we work, because everyone's knows you've got to be the best to come to this school. So think of what will happen once words gets out anyone can come here. So, now you see. And you, Avery, can help me. You and I think alike. You and I can help the school."

* * *

"What's your next lesson" Percy asked Avery. Avery pulled out his timetable for second-years and consulted it.

"Patisserie with Madame Rougerie. Oh great - it's a 'Mixed-House' class too". Georgia and Daisy smiled to themselves, they'd just come from their first Patisserie lesson and they could just imagine Madame Rougerie putting Avery in his place! Mixed House meant there would probably be even more scholarship students in his next class, how Avery would hate that!

"Hmmm...Mixed House, eh?" thought Percy. Then his spiteful idea came to him. "Pastry... Okay Avery, here's what we'll do. Once you start rubbing the ingredients together I want you to put a little bit of water in the bowl of one of the scholarship kids. Not too much only a little bit."

"Is that it? Doesn't seem particularly skilful. How will that do anything?"

"You'll see" said Percy cryptically.

"Alright" Avery agreed "water it is then".

The gong was struck to signal the end of break. The boys left the table first and as they walked away, Daisy and Georgia stared at each other, unable to believe what they had overhead.

"Oh my God, we have to do something!" said Daisy.

"Yes, but what?" asked Georgia. Both girls thought for a moment as the refectory slowly emptied.

"I'll tell my sister. She's in his year so they're bound to be in the next class together. She can watch him to see if he does anything." Daisy said, looking across at Poppy who was still hovering by the snack table.

"But what if he does?" asked Georgia, concerned.

"Then we'll have evidence to tell a Prefect. Or a teacher. Or Dr Bakewell.

As Georgia and Daisy got up to leave the refectory, they called Poppy over. Daisy whispered something to Poppy, who looked shocked, nodded and the three of them left the room with their heads together.

* * *

After running out of the Refectory to the boy's dormitory and quickly changing into a pair of dry trousers, Vaughan appeared out of the St Oswald mousehole in the grand hallway, where Caroline and Verity were waiting for him. Vaughan took his timetable out of his pocket to see where their next class was. Tracing the lines with his finger, he found it.

"So, next lesson is 'MH Patisserie' - what's that?" asked Vaughan.

"Patisserie is French for Pastry" explained Caroline and "MH means its Mixed-House."

"What's that then?" asked Vaughan

"It means that second-years from every house are in the lesson together." Verity explained.

"With...Madam Rug...Madam Roo...erm...." began Vaughan, reading the name of the Patisserie teacher.

"Madame Rougerie. She's a Pastry Chef but she's also Head of Student Kitchens" finished Verity who was also inspecting her timetable. "She'll be in her kitchen - that's only just down this corridor. Come on, we don't want to be late." Stuffing their timetables back into their pockets, the three of them trotted along the downstairs picture-lined corridor until they reached a door marked 'Pastry Kitchen'.

"Pastry Kitchen? What's the difference between a Pastry Kitchen and a normal kitchen" enquired Vaughan.

"There are four student kitchens" Caroline explained. "one for each type of baking. There's one for Artisan Baking - that's Chef Goodbun's; one for Chocolatieering - that's Professor Drumgoole's kitchen; one for Patisserie - which is Madam Rougerie's kitchen - this one - and the fourth one is the one we were in this morning, Dr Crose's Kitchen, for Edible Arts and Sugarcraft.

"What's the point of that?" asked Vaughan, surprised. "We do all our baking and cooking in the same kitchen at home."

"Because there are a lot more people using these kitchens" explained Verity, "one wouldn't be enough for all the classes, would it?" Realising Verity had made a good point, when he considered it, he shrugged his shoulders as Caroline also enlightened him. "And anyway, each kitchen has different ingredients and utensils. We use so much stuff it couldn't possibly all be kept in one place. Chocolatiering needs a warm room - Patisserie needs a cold room. You can't mix them, you wouldn't want hot melted chocolate dripping all over cold pastry, would you?"

"Or hot pastry melting set chocolate" added Verity.
For the first time since he'd made friends with the girls, Vaughan suddenly felt embarrassed and foolish. He didn't know any of that but once they'd told him it made sense. They knew so much more than he did already; he'd thought that if he could bake a cake good enough to win the competition that would be the hard work over,

but now it seems that the hard work was only just starting. As they made their way to Madame Rougerie's kitchen, he began to wonder if he really was worthy of studying under the greatest baker of all time, after all.

Chapter 17

The Rage of Madame Rougerie

After morning break, whilst the second-years were in Patisserie with Madame Rougerie, the St Wistan's third-years had Artisan Baking with Chef Goodbun. Apparently they were going to learn how to make a lemonade pie. Both Daisy and Georgia instantly liked Chef Goodbun. They guessed he was in his forties; he had a pleasant face and wore a crisp white tunic, a tall white chefs hat and red trousers. A slender, tall man of Jamaican descent, he smiled a lot and took his time explaining what they were doing, why they were doing it and how they were going to do it. He was quite the opposite of Madame Rougerie, who huffed and puffed a lot and charged around the kitchen like a bull in a china shop, shouting out commands. No, Chef Goodbun was much calmer and appeared to have all the time in the world for his class.

"Lemonade Pies" he began "are an invention of my own, and I for one, am quite partial to a slice!" he said with a broad smile. "Now normally, you would bake a pie all in one lesson. Both Madame Rougerie and I are Pastry Chefs; as a rule, she tends to do the sweet pastries and I the savouries. However, as we have some new scholarship students with us, whilst they are learning the basics for the next few months we shall split it between our two classes until they are at the same level as you. It will also give you a chance to perfect your own skills, of course."

Some of the class seemed to take offence to this - Percy in particular - as he rolled his eyes and audibly harrumphed. Chef Goodbun noticed and stared at him immediately but did not speak. No, Chef Goodbun was not one to give people like Percy Snodland any attention or dignify his interruptions. He merely ignored him and carried on as if he wasn't there.

Georgia and Daisy however thought it was very understanding of them to divide the class into two halves - Madame Rougerie for the base and Chef Goodbun for the filling. Little did they know, Madame Rougerie had been given no say in the matter!

They spent the second lesson whipping lemon curd into lemonade, adding lemon rind (or zest, as Chef Goodbun called it) and watching it double in size the more they whipped it. They added a special bubble-gas then poured the mixture into their pastry cases and marvelled at how the bubbles in the lemonade moved in the mixture and spent a few seconds watching them rise and pop as the yellow lemonade filling filled the pastry case.

Next they whisked up some cream, squirted some lemon juice and finally folded a little more lemon zest into the cream. With a big spoon, they dolloped the cream onto the mixture and grated some rind over the top to finish it off. It looked amazing. Georgia and Daisy were surprised at how good their pies were - Percy looked dismayed at how good their pies were. The sooner he got these intruders out of the school, the better, he thought - especially if they started becoming as good as he was.

* * *

Whilst the third-years were merrily creating their Lemonade Pies with Chef Goodbun, the second-year children took up their places at the kitchen benches in Madame Rougerie's Pastry Kitchen. In this kitchen, just like Chef Goodbun's kitchen, each student had a workstation of their own; each one contained an oven, a cupboard and two shelves below the worktop, a sunken washbasin within the worktop. There were twelve of these workstations in the Pastry Kitchen, in three rows of four; Avery Sorrel took the centre station in the front row, Caroline and Verity chose benches next to each other in the second row, with Vaughan, Florence Fitzgerald and Poppy Quenell behind them in the third row. The fourth row contained students from St Swithun's second-years that Vaughan had not yet been introduced to. That was, until Madame Rougerie insisted the class stand up one by one, to say their name and their House. As soon as all twelve children had introduced themselves to the teacher (which according to Avery was 'as waste of time' as Madame Rougerie knew all the children except the scholarship children - and Avery clearly didn't think it important for the new children to learn the names of their classmates), they began their Patisserie lesson.

"What is ze most important ingredient for making good pastry?" Madam Rougerie bellowed at her class as she strolled up and down her kitchen, gripping her rolling pin firmly in her right hand as she slapped it menacingly in the cupped palm of her left hand. Several students cautiously offered their suggestions as she passed their worktops: "flour miss?"... "quality butter, miss"... "water, miss?"

"Noh, Noh, NOH!" shouted Madam Rougerie, banging her rolling pin down on her desk, making the children jump. "Zey are just ingredients. I want to know what eez ze most important ingredient." Looking around her class, she carefully picked a student to answer.

"Verity - can you remind ze class please what zey must not forget. What is essential for creating good pastry?"

"Cold hands, miss?" answered Verity. Vaughan looked at the back of her head, wondering what on earth made her say that! Had she gone mad? You don't put hands in pastry, you put in things like flour, butter or lard!

"Very good Verity, yes." Vaughan took a double-take at his teacher. Did she just say 'yes'?

"Remember everyone - your 'ands need to be as cold as possible if your pastry eez to be ze best. Warm 'ands and good pastry do not mix. New students, you will notice washbasins fitted into your benches."

Looking around at all the other workstations, Vaughan saw indeed that each one contained a small white sink and silver tap. "Zese basins run freezing cold water only. Zey are your 'and-washing sinks. Ze 'ot water sinks for washing up are underneath ze windows." She gestured to the wall on Vaughan's left and he noticed that there were indeed six large sinks and draining boards right underneath the windows. "Now, everyone put on your tunics, grab your utensils, return to your workstations and wash your 'ands. You 'ave two minutes - chop, chop." As she gave the order to 'chop-chop' Madam Rougerie raised and clapped her hands twice, at which point the whole class scurried off, pulling on white tunics and rummaging in the cupboards and shelves under the workstations searching for glass bowls and rolling pins, before finally scrubbing their hands in the freezing cold water, ready to begin their first pastry lesson.

* * *

It soon became obvious to Vaughan that Madam Rougerie was Head of Student Kitchens, the way she patrolled her kitchen, peering over everyone's shoulders into their bowls and commenting on how well (or not) they were doing. It was surprising she knew where to look, as students were milling about all over the place, wandering between the Ingredients' Cupboards along the walls and the workstations upon which they were each working. Suddenly, Madam Rougerie stopped at Florence Fitzgerald's bench and glared at her. "What are you doing, child?" she yelled at Florence, "you are only supposed to be rubbing ze ingredients into breadcrumbs. I 'aven't told anyone to add any water yet but you're already kneading your dough. What is ze meaning of this?" Flushed and panicking, poor Florence stammered to explain. "But miss, I haven't added any water. I've just been rubbing the butter and flour together, honest."

"Child, butter and flour does not a dough make. Dough is made only when water is added. How much 'ave you added? I realise it eez your first day but I must know what 'as gone into your mixture."

"Only flour, butter and salt miss." Florence insisted. Madam Rougerie shook her head, she wasn't impressed at all. "And when did you last wash your hands?"

"Just after I put my tunic on" Florence replied.

"Good grief, girl - that was over fifteen minutes ago!" exclaimed Madam Rougerie. "Do you mean to tell me you've not washed your hands once since you've been rubbing your ingredients together?"

"Er...no, miss" Florence admitted, hanging her head. "I thought we had to wash them before we started and after we'd finished. I didn't think we had to keep washing them."

"Urgh...Florence. Zat explains your mixture sticking together zen. I'm sorry to 'ave to tell you but your mixture eez worthless and will 'ave to be thrown away. If you've not washed your 'ands and not added any water to your bowl, ze only explanation is sweat." The whole class fell silent, listening to the commotion going on at Florence's bench. Most looked very uncomfortable on Florence's behalf, glad it wasn't them on the receiving end of Madame Rougerie but one child didn't look uncomfortable or bothered at all. In fact, spotted only by eagle-eyed Poppy, one child watched the whole thing unravel with an oddly satisfied look on his face. And that child was Avery Sorrel.

"Sweat?" Vaughan and Florence repeated together.

"Yes, sweat. Because you didn't keep washing your 'ands to keep zem cold and clean, your sweat has gone into your mixture making it sticky, which means it must be thrown away. It cannot be used."

"URGH!!!" Vaughan, Florence and a couple of other pupils close-by squirmed in disgust and a boy at the workstation next to Florence put his hand to his mouth as if he was about to be sick.

"Now, now, zere's no need for any drama" Madam Rougerie informed the class, seeing Florence's flushed face drain pale with embarrassment.

"Florence, put your mixture in ze bin, wash your things in ze white sinks over by the windows and you'll 'ave to observe ze rest of ze lesson with me."

The class (with the exception of Florence) soon progressed onto kneading the dough they had just made; after ten minutes Vaughan's arms and hands were aching but he wasn't sweaty. He'd made sure to wash his hands every few minutes, just in case. He really didn't want to be embarrassed like poor Florence had been. But something about that whole drama didn't seem right to him but he couldn't work out what it was. With poor Florence's red face and sweaty pastry in his mind, he crossed over to the sink to wash his used jugs and scales. Madame Rougerie had also reminded them it was good practice to wash-up utensils as they were used, to keep their workstations tidy. Apparently, so she'd said, that was very important if you ever work in a professional kitchen and so it was a good habit to get into.

Returning from washing-up at the sink, Vaughan noticed Avery Sorrel staring at Florence with an odd, satisfied smirk on his face. Suddenly Vaughan realised what it was that was niggling him. He remembered seeing Sorrel walking past Florence's bench when she was at the sink doing her washing-up. But Sorrel's bench was right at the front of class, there was no need for him to be walking through the third row, no need to him to be anywhere near his or Florence's workstations, unless...... He thought for a moment and seeing how upset Florence looked, traipsing behind Madame Rougerie instead of kneading her dough, he decided to risk it - it wasn't Florence's fault at all and it was up to him to right this wrong.

* * *

Not wanting to make a big show, Vaughan approached Madame Rougerie who was now standing by Poppy's workbench and tried to get her attention.

"Excuse me Miss" he ventured, "Madame?" Madame Rougerie looked at Vaughan and continued to stride her way through the kitchen, Vaughan tottering after her as she prodded at the dough on each of the workstations she passed, turning to glare at Florence every so often, as if to make the poor girl feel even worse than she already did. "Yes?"

"Madame, I don't think Florence did anything wrong." Vaughan said nervously as they approached St Swithun boy's workbench at the back of the kitchen. Madame Rougerie stopped, pulled back her broad square shoulders, straightened her neck and sniffed deeply through her nose.

"I beg your pardon?"

"Madame, I'm sorry, but I don't think Florence did anything wrong with her mixture." Glaring at Vaughan, Madame Rougerie clearly did not like to be questioned - not least by a pupil, it seemed.

"Did you not see, ze mixture?" she hissed at him, through her teeth, "it was all clammy and sticky and...urgh..." she rolled an invisible ball of sticky dough between her fingers as she spoke, as if it were really there in her hands, her face twisted in disgust at the very thought of it.

"Yes miss - er - Madame" Vaughan corrected himself, "I know that but I don't think it was Florence's fault. I think someone else ruined her mixture on purpose."

"You mean sabotage?" she asked, her eyes widening, one eyebrow arching. Florence's head peered around the squat, broad frame of Madame Rougerie to hear what Vaughan was saying.

"Yes miss, sorry, Madame" Vaughan confirmed. "It's just that when Florence wasn't at her workbench I saw someone else there and I can't see any other reason for them to be there. I think this person sabotaged her."

"And who exactly might this saboteur be?" she asked, still suspicious of Vaughan's information.

"Avery Sorrell, Madame" Vaughan whispered.

* * *

Madame Rougerie strode over to Avery's bench and inspected his dough. After prodding and poking and giving a few satisfied mmm's, to both Vaughan and Florence's surprise, Madame Rougerie left him to it and said nothing to him. Vaughan stared at Sorrel who simply smirked back at him. Florence, still traipsing behind Madame Rougerie looked back over her shoulder at Vaughan; she gave a forced, small smile to thank him for trying and shrugged her shoulders, helplessly.

As the class finished and they were tidying their things away, Sorrel shoulder-barged into Vaughan, causing him to nearly drop his bowls.

"You may think you're something special" he said nastily, "but you're not. You're just a sympathy kid. Don't try and get me into trouble again - it won't work. I don't know who you think you are but you'd better watch your step." Then he piled his own dirty bowls into Vaughan's already full arms and marched off, haughtily. Verity and Caroline hurried over to help Vaughan before he dropped and broke everything.

"What was all that about?" asked Caroline. They'd seen the earlier set-to with Madame Rougerie but their workstations were too far away to really hear anything.

"I think Sorrel sabotaged Florence's mixture earlier. I saw him at her bench when she was washing her things and she swore she hadn't poured in any water but when Madame Rougerie came round, instead of breadcrumbs she'd got a sticky dough. Madame Rougerie made her throw it in the bin saying it was sweaty and Florence was really upset."

"Well you can only get dough by adding liquid" Caroline thought aloud "and sweat would do that, but poor Florence. How embarrassing."

Overhearing Caroline as she passed, Poppy joined in. "I need to tell you something" she whispered. "My sister is in the third year and at break she overheard Avery and another boy plotting to put water in someone's pastry mix. They're trying to get rid of all of us with scholarships by ruining our baking. I bet it was him that put water in Florence's bowl. I saw him looking all smug when Madame was going on about sweat in the bowl."

"It sounds like something Sorrel would do though" Verity said bitterly, "he's ever so spiteful and doesn't care about anyone else's feelings. He did look pleased when Florence was getting told off, I saw him too and thought he was just being smug. Now I reckon it's because he knew he'd got Florence into trouble. What did Madame say?"

"Nothing - that's what I found strange." Vaughan admitted. "She was more interested in inspecting his dough and because that was okay she just left it and told me to go back to my bench!"

"Typical" said Verity "he never gets told off by any of the teachers. Think's he's something special but he's not. We have to tell Madame it was his fault."

As Poppy and the rest of the class filed out of the kitchen for lunch, Poppy eager to find her sister and tell her about the sabotage, Verity and Caroline approached the buxom teacher just as she was fighting a losing battle with her thick, wiry red hair which was successfully escaping her white hat.

"Madame, just so you know, I believe Vaughan was right earlier" Verity bravely began, spurred on by Poppy's discovery. Vaughan couldn't help but admire her courage - he found Madame Rougerie a little scary, if truth be known. Looking up from her desk, Madame Rougerie looked at the three of them without speaking.

"I saw Sorrel at Florence's workstation too but I didn't think anything of it until I saw Florence walking behind you and Vaughan told me about her dough. Madame, we all know that Sorrel doesn't like having scholarships here and I think he ruined Florence's dough to try to prove a point."

"What are you going to do about it?" Caroline asked, as their teacher looked at each one of them before taking out a notebook from her desk drawer and writing on three pages. She spoke firmly and clearly as she ripped them off one by one and handed one each to Vaughan, Verity and Caroline.

"I'm going to give you all detention. Report back here during Afternoon Tea for your detention slips."

"But miss!" protested Vaughan, as Verity and Caroline both hissed 'Madame!' in his ears. "Madame! You must believe us...Florence..."

"Whezer I believe you or not is not ze question" she replied, clearly not impressed by them sticking up for Florence, "I am your teacher and you are my students. I will not have you question me in my class again. Understand? Good. Now go to lunch and read your slips to see where you will be serving your detentions."

Nodding silently, the three of them turned their backs on their teacher and left the classroom, steaming with anger at the unfairness of it all. Detention on the first day indeed - what on earth would their parents think when Dr Bakewell wrote home to tell them?

Chapter 18

The Smorgasbords

L unch was a new experience for Vaughan. At home he and his family had eaten most of their dinners on their laps - the only time they sat around the dinner table was for Sunday dinner or special occasions, like Christmas or when they had visitors. At Honey Wood Comprehensive they had a long counter, at the start of which they picked up a plastic tray which was divided into three sections - the biggest section was for the main meal, the smaller section was for pudding and the smallest section was just big enough for a drink. There, he walked the length of the counter, sliding his tray along and stopping in front of big, plump dinner ladies in blue overalls who slopped spoonfuls of food onto his tray as he passed them by, so that by the time he reached the end of the counter his tray was full and his dinner ready to eat. Here, at Honeycomb Hall, it was entirely different. Everything, it seemed, was eaten at your house table. Breakfast, snacks, lunches and (Vaughan correctly presumed) dinner.

Compared to breakfast which had amazed Vaughan, lunch was much less complicated. A selection of sandwiches were stacked on two decorative, oval-shaped silver platters, placed in the centre of each table. As they sat down, Vaughan noticed that all six tables had been laid exactly the same - two platters of sandwiches in the middle, one bowl of fruit at each end of each table and between the sandwiches and fruit bowls, were two large plates of small jellies. It was a simple lunch but the colours of the fruit and jellies make it look absolutely delicious! In the fruit bowls were rosy red apples, green apples, yellow bananas, fuzzy peaches, grapes, oranges, slices of yellow pineapple, green and red watermelon slices. The jellies also had fruits inside and were equally colourful - red, orange, purple, yellow, green and pink. Upon closer inspection Vaughan thought he saw raspberries in the red jellies, tiny orange segments in the orange jellies, grapes in the green jellies, blackcurrants in the purple jellies and pineapple cubes in the yellow jellies. Vaughan felt his mouth watering just looking at it all, he couldn't wait to tuck in!

Just as the school bell pealed one loud chime, Mr Soames appeared and ascended the steps at the far side of the Refectory, to the gong. He took hold of the large, gold baton from the base of the gong in both hands, twisted his back with his arms outstretched and hurled himself around, striking the gong right in the centre with the baton. The gong echoed through the Refectory, signalling that it was now time to eat. Dr Bakewell rose to his feet and confirmed this.

"Lunch is served" he announced "You will find a delicious array of smorgasbords on each table - please make sure you eat the savouries first before you start on the jellies. Tuck in" then he and Professor Drumgoole left the Refectory, leaving the remaining teachers to supervise lunch.

"What's a smorgasbord?" Vaughan asked Caroline, his nose wrinkled. He'd never heard of such a word before, "has he made that up"

"Dunno if he made it up" shrugged Caroline, "but he means the tray of sandwiches and sausage rolls."

"Why doesn't he just say that then?" asked Vaughan again, helping himself to a ham sandwich, "at least we'd know what he meant."

"Well I can't believe we've got detention on the first day" Caroline moaned, taking a cheese sandwich and chomping into a crisp, shiny red apple. "I mean, it's our first day for goodness' sake!"

"I've never had a detention before" Vaughan admitted, "what do you have to do?"

"We've never had one either" admitted Verity "but I think the teacher that gives out the detention decides what you do and when you do it. I suppose we'll find out soon."

"But it's not fair!" protested Vaughan. "We didn't do anything wrong, we're only sticking up for Florence, so Madame Rougerie didn't blame her for something that she didn't do."

"We had to say something" Verity reassured him. "Everything we do, in all our lessons is marked. At the end of the year we have an exam and the exam results are added to our marks throughout the year. You have to pass each year to stay here, so if Madame Rougerie marked Florence down for her mixture even though it wasn't her fault, we had to say. It's just not fair she didn't believe us."

"But it was Avery Sorrel's fault - he did it on purpose. He must have known it would give Florence bad marks. And upset her on her first day. Why would he do something horrible like that?"

"Haven't you realised what Avery Sorrel's like yet?" Caroline asked Vaughan, surprised, as she put down her apple core and grabbed a ham sandwich. "He's a snob - and a spiteful one at that. He knows exactly what he did. I think he did to get Florence in trouble and make sure she gets bad marks. Then it'll look like he was right all along."

"Right all along? What d'you mean?" asked Vaughan, confused.

Leaning forward, Caroline lowered her voice and whispered, so that no-one could overhear. "Sorrel objected to the scholarships. He stood up and told Dr Bakewell he shouldn't allow ordinary children to come here and that he was making a mistake."

"NO!" Vaughan shouted aloud in surprise, then looked around quickly as several children turned and stared at him. "Sorry!" he whispered to Caroline and Verity, sinking lower in his seat as one by one the other children stopped staring at him and turned back to their own conversations. "Avery told Dr Bakewell that he shouldn't do something?"

"He did" Caroline confirmed "so I think he ruined Florence's pastry mix to try and prove to Dr Bakewell that he was right and ordinary children can't bake here."

"But that's sabotage!" Vaughan exclaimed, outraged.

"Wouldn't be the first time" Verity commented bitterly, before pushing her plate away, standing up and walking briskly out of the refectory.

Vaughan watched as she strode out of the hall, surprised by her sudden outburst. Indeed, it was truly shocking that Sorrel could be so nasty and spiteful and unbelievable that he had the cheek to argue with his Headmaster - but Verity was quiet and shy. She didn't say anything about anyone - not even Avery Sorrel - but she seemed truly upset by this morning. Maybe it was because she'd been given her first detention, Vaughan wondered, feeling guilty. It was his fault - he'd gotten them into trouble, after all. Maybe he'd better speak to Verity and tell her he was sorry, he thought.

As he rose to his feet to follow her, Caroline grabbed his arm and shook her head. "Leave her for a bit" she advised him "she'll be okay. Don't worry." But Vaughan was worried. Verity was clearly upset and he hoped she wasn't about to fall out with him. He didn't want to upset or lose his new-found friends - especially when he hadn't meant to do anything wrong.

Sensing that Vaughan was concerned, Caroline tried to reassure him. "It's not you she's upset with. It's Sorrel. She hates him being in our classes - he really upsets her."

"Why? I can see he's not a nice person - does he pick on her?"

"No, it's nothing like that. Look, I don't think she'd like me to say too much - she gets embarrassed - but trust me, she's not upset with you. Okay?"

"Okay" Vaughan replied, feeling slightly less worried but now very curious. Verity didn't seem like the type of girl who got upset easily or disliked people so much. He finished the rest of his lunch with Caroline in silence, privately wondering what on earth Avery Sorrel had done to hurt Verity so much.

* * *

Dr Bakewell took a cup of tea from Professor Drumgoole as they returned from the refectory and once again sat in the Headmaster's Office, discussing the events of the morning. Dr Bakewell picked up the round, jammy biscuit off the saucer and tucked into it as he asked the Professor - who was also enjoying a biscuit with his tea - how things were going. "So Derek, what are your first impressions?"

"It's very early days, George" Professor Drumgoole began cautiously, brushing chocolate biscuit crumbs from the corners of his mouth, "but so far, all seems to be going well."

"Really?" Dr Bakewell peered over the top of his round, tortoise-shell glasses at the Professor, as he placed his teacup back in it's saucer. As it chinked back into place, he raised his head to look at his colleague properly.

"I hear Clementine has already issued three detentions - one of them to a scholarship winner - on their first day, for heaven's sake."

It didn't take long for word to pass round the school. Although the children didn't know it, there was nothing that happened at Honeycomb Hall that didn't reach the ears of the all-hearing, all-seeing Dr Bakewell.

"Ah. Yes, that is true" confirmed Professor Drumgoole. "Three St Oswald students were given detention; the new student Vaughan Baker, along with Caroline Coleman and Verity Rose."

"Verity Rose?" exclaimed Dr Bakewell in surprise. He knew Verity well and she was an excellent pupil. "Go on."

"Apparently there was an incident in her class involving another scholarship student...Florence Fitzgerald, I believe it was. Anyway, as I understand it, Verity, Caroline and Vaughan tried to explain to Clementine that she'd made a mistake and, well, you know Clemmy - she wasn't too pleased with that and gave all three detention."

"Hmmm....she's probably just asserting her authority. Letting them know she's boss" Dr Bakewell pondered out loud, as he paced his office, thinking.

"Avery Sorrel was also involved" Professor Drumgoole stated bluntly. Dr Bakewell stopped in his tracks and turned to face his friend. "Sorrel? How? What had he done?"

Professor Drumgoole noticed the way Dr Bakewell asked what Sorrel 'had done' - rather than ask how he was involved, which could have meant involved in any way. Dr Bakewell knew very well that Sorrel must have been the trouble-maker behind it all, not one of the innocent ones. Although all the children in the school were important to Dr Bakewell, he did have a particular dislike of Avery Sorrel, though he would never admit it to anyone else or let it show. In return, Avery Sorrel refused to give Dr Bakewell the respect he deserved; it was fair to say they had a mutual dislike of each other. Nevertheless, Dr Bakewell had to be told what had happened and so Professor Drumgoole relayed the entire story to the Headmaster, as it had been told to him.

"...and so Sorrel snuck up to Florence's bowl in her absence and poured in a little water, turning her breadcrumb mix into dough. Vaughan witnessed this and at the end of the lesson he approached Clementine to tell her what he'd seen." Professor Drumgoole concluded.

"And Verity? Caroline? How did they get caught up in this?"

"They were supporting Vaughan. I imagine they'd told him about the marking system. It was very brave of him to have approached Clementine, in my view."

"And the poor boy suffers a detention for his honesty and bravery in looking out for his fellow classmates." pitied Dr Bakewell. "And Avery?"

"Got away scot-free, I'm afraid" said Professor Drumgoole. Dr Bakewell shook his head, tutting. "Typical" he muttered. "Well, I can't undo the detention, but keep your eyes and ears open for me, Derek. And keep a close eye on Sorrel. This is his second year now - he might start to get cocky. Especially with the scholarship children."

Professor Drumgoole nodded thoughtfully. "Are you sure you can't undo the detention? It seems awfully unfair."

"Yes, it is unfair. But nevertheless, Clementine was the teacher of the lesson and she has the right to give detentions where she deems it a suitable punishment. No, if I overrule her we'll have children thinking they can question teachers, children thinking detentions can be overturned if they complain and respect within the school would soon fall. No, the detention will remain but I'll speak to Clementine and make sure it's an easy one. Send her in, will you, when you next see her."

Recognising this as an instruction to leave the office, Professor Drumgoole acknowledged his orders with a polite nod of his head before leaving George Bakewell deep in thought, sat behind his beloved oak desk.

Chapter 19

The Forest of Forgetfulness

A fter lunch the second-years made their way back to the Sugarcraft Kitchen for Edible Arts, an interesting lesson which, Verity told Vaughan, wasn't a lesson open to first-years, so he was very lucky to have joined the school as a second-year. Vaughan was glad because it meant that in this class at least he didn't have a year of catching-up to do; in this class at least they were all learning the same things, at the same time, together.

As this was also a mixed-house class, the scholarship children from St Wistan and St Swithun hadn't yet met Dr Crose, so she introduced herself then asked each of the children to tell her their name and House. Once the introductions were over Dr Crose excited her pupils by declaring that for this lesson they would go exploring in the school grounds.

"But Doctor Crose" Oliver Eddington raised his hand as he spoke, "haven't the other second-years in class already explored everywhere? Is it just us scholarship children going exploring or the whole class?"

"Well, Mr...Eddington, isn't it?" Dr Crose asked, as Oliver eagerly nodded his head, impressed that she knew his name already, "we shall all go exploring together, for the following reasons. Number one - this class only begins in the second-year at school and I have no doubt that students who enrolled last year will have walked past a lot of edible art many times without noticing. As you progress, you will imitate a lot of flowers and plant life you see here in my Sugarcraft lessons. It is my job to introduce you to the delights we have here in our very own gardens and Professor Peach, when you meet him, will explain to you all about the properties of

Natural Foods. Edible Arts and Natural Foods are closely entwined so I suggest you pay close attention to our classes. Number two - however creative and imaginative I may be, I have yet to find a way of being in two places at once!" She smiled warmly at her class as they chuckled in reply.

Once the mirth died down, she spoke again but her tone became different; she now sounded quite serious and the smile on her face faded as she continued.

"I must insist that once we leave the classroom and venture across the gardens that we all stay close together. We shall be walking close by the Forest of Forgetfulness, so for your own safety no-one is to wander off or stray from the rest of the class."

Vaughan looked apprehensively at his classmates wondering why Dr Crose had become so serious when she mentioned the forest. He'd played in forests before, he quite enjoyed running through the trees, listening to the sound of the wind and birdsong as he'd rustled through the leaves and twigs. Forests weren't scary places, he thought, at least not in daylight. What a strange thing to warn them about.

"Ready?" Dr Crose's voice jolted him back from his daydreaming with a start. "Pick up your notebooks and pencils and follow me." The class obediently gathered their belongings and, lining up behind their teacher, duly followed Dr Crose out of the school and into the gardens, chattering amongst themselves excitedly.

* * *

"The Forest of Forgetfulness?" Vaughan whispered to Verity as they stepped along the wooden boards carefully positioned through the vegetable patch, taking care not to lose their balance and fall off into the cabbages surrounding their feet, "what's that?"

"It's a huge forest behind the school farmhouse that's so big it goes far beyond the school boundaries. No-one has ever gone in one side and come out the other, so it's never been mapped - no-one can say for certain how big it really is." she whispered in return.

   "Apparently, it's so full of trees that all look the same, it's easy to lose your sense of direction" added Caroline, rushing to keep up with the two of them, "and once you've lost your way you can't remember how to get out. The further in you go the more lost you become, hence its nickname, the 'Forest of Forgetfulness'. You forget which path you've taken and can't retrace your steps." Vaughan was listening to this tale so intently he didn't notice a very large, low-hanging pumpkin, whose vine had climbed the wooden pergola which framed the vegetable patches, allowing the pumpkins to grow all over the wooden frame. He bumped squarely into it, causing it to swing wildly. Stepping back in surprise as the pumpkin swayed to and fro like an enormous orange conker, a giggling Caroline put out her hands and gently steadied the rocking fruit as Vaughan rubbed his forehead, tutting.

   "Of course, there is another rumour about how it earned its name" Verity said. "There are others who have said that it is so beautiful inside that it fills your whole mind and all your senses so much so that you forget about everything outside the forest. Nothing outside matters - any worries, problems - the magic and beauty of the forest makes them all disappear; totally forgotten." Vaughan preferred this rumour and wanted to believe that Verity's tale was the real reason behind its nickname, but sensibly he decided that in truth it was probably a mix of the two. He made a very important note in his mind never to enter the forest alone.

* * *

During class, Dr Crose pointed out several plants which according to Verity and Caroline, she had been spot on earlier - even though they'd walked this way many times over the last year, they hadn't paid any attention to the plants before. They had been tasked to draw each plant in their books as Dr Crose gave examples of what they could be used for.

'Lupins - providers of the mystical Moondew. Gives a sparkly, dewy like texture' Vaughan wrote in his book as they proceeded past the tall fountains of multi-coloured lupins and their masses of starry leaves.

They had stopped four times to make notes about certain plants before Vaughan looked up and saw a farmhouse a few minutes walk away. Behind the farmhouse stood trees so tall they looked as though they almost touched the sky. They stretched along the horizon as far as Vaughan could see. He reasoned that it must be the Forest of Forgetfulness, but what a strange little house in front. As they continued towards the house, he wondered if some sort of Gate Keeper lived there, guarding the forest and helping those that had become lost inside. Raising her hand to halt the procession, Dr Crose enlightened them.

"Children, this house belongs to a very important friend of our school. In this house lives Farmer Lambrick. He looks after the animals that provide our school with many of our foods, grows our vegetables and has often rescued those poor souls lost in the forest. Come." She beckoned them towards the white-washed walls and sparsely thatched roof of the higgeldy-piggeldy house and as the class gathered around on the little gravel path which led to the old wooden front door and waited eagerly to meet the school farmer, the door swung open and onto the cobbled path he stepped.

* * *

The battered wooden door creaked open on its rusty hinges and onto the path stepped a man at least in his sixties, clutching a brown chicken in his hands which was thrashing about wildly, clucking and squawking. Farmer Lambrick looked at the children as walked past them without saying a word, the chicken continuing to flap its wings while squawking loudly as he walked to the end of the house then turned left, behind the house and out of sight. There was a soft 'thump', a click of a bolt then he reappeared - minus the chicken.

"Mornin'" he called cheerily to the assembled class. "Oi imagine Dr Crose 'as already introduced me, but just in case, moy name is Farmer Lambrick." He gave a big, toothy grin to the children which they politely returned, though in silence and very shyly.

"My, yer're a quiet lot, ain't yer?" he said, craning his head forwards and tilting it as he looked at them. "What's she done...told yer some 'orror stories about me? Cause if she 'as...they're all true!" He said, before laughing heartily and winking. His face was tanned and weather-beaten, with deep-set lines and wrinkles around his eyes and forehead, yet somehow there was something very reassuring and warm about him. He spoke with a very broad West-Country accent and Vaughan thought he was exactly how a Farmer should look and sound.

"Now, now, Lambrick" Dr Crose interrupted, "we have some new students in our class - well, in our school in fact, today. Let's not scare them straight away, shall we?"
Turning to face her class, she explained. "Don't take too much notice of Farmer Lambrick here. He enjoys his little jokes and loves to make up stories. Don't you Lambrick?" she called over her shoulder.

"Oh, Oi'm just sayin', that's all....Poor old Farmer never gets visitors and when he does he's told off fer bein' friendly....poor Farmer..." Farmer Lambrick said soulfully as he shook his head sadly and put his hands in his pockets, scuffing the ground with his shoe, pretending to be upset.

"He likes to play-act, too" Dr Crose informed her pupils, as she rolled her eyes. "He enjoys having visitors."

"And whoy not!" Lambrick jumped back to life, and put his hands on Dr Crose's shoulders. "Yer see children, yer 'ave ter enjoy life! Yer take what yer've been given - and yer makes somethin' good out of it. Isn't that roight, Dr Crose? That's what yer'll teach 'em to do, isn't it? Take somethin' ordinary, sprinkle a little bit o' Bakewell magic over it and create somethin' beautiful and new."

"Oh, yes, Farmer Lambrick - that's very true. Thank you." Vaughan and the rest of the class were watching this little performance with interest. Farmer Lambrick had managed to transform himself from being a weird, lonely, old Farmer into a jolly, likeable man in less than five minutes. Maybe this was all an act, Vaughan wondered.

"As you know, Oi'm the school Farmer" Farmer Lambrick continued. "Moy job 'ere is to provide you youngsters with all the food yer need to keep you healthy and strong and the extras for yer ingredients for yer lessons. Fancy a tour?" A tour? Vaughan thought - of a tiny little house? He must be joking again.

"We'd be delighted, thank you Lambrick" Dr Crose accepted. "Children, please follow Farmer Lambrick and remember to stay close together." As the class shuffled behind Farmer Lambrick, they walked to the end of the house where he and his noisy chicken had disappeared earlier. Turning the corner to walk to the back of the house, once again Vaughan was taken by surprise.

Behind the house was a huge area of land which was completely hidden from view when you approached the house, with several smaller grey, stone buildings. He realised too that the forest wasn't right behind the house as it first looked, it was a good five minutes walk away at least. They walked through a home-made wooden gate which had been made of thick, sturdy tree branches tied together, into a fenced off area which was currently alive with chickens running around, pecking and clucking at their feet as they walked through. There must have been about fifty chickens, Vaughan thought, all different colours and sizes. Treading carefully through the chicken coop, they exited through another similar home-made gate at the far end, next to which stood a huge wooden chicken house.

"Quickly through the gate!" Farmer Lambrick shouted as he held it open, swiftly shooing away any chickens that dared to make an escape attempt whilst the gate was open. As the final person, Dr Crose stepped through, Farmer Lambrick swung the gate shut with a 'click', right in the beak of an adventurous white chicken trying to make a dash for freedom.

"Anyone 'ave eggs fer breakfast this mornin'?" he asked. Caroline, Orla and two other children put their hands in the air. "Hope yer thanked 'em as yer walked through, then" he said mysteriously. "All eggs 'ere come from moy chickens. Best eggs in the world, they are. Fresh air - plenty of exercise and good ol' chats with Lambrick here produce the foinest eggs in the world." he stated proudly.

"Lambrick!" Dr Crose's voice cut through his daydreaming.

"Hmm...? Oh, oh yes!" he muttered, "now then where was Oi? Oh yes. The veg. All the veg yer see 'ere is grown just for you. Dr Bakewell - great man - wants to make sure that his students eat only the most natural food possible. He says 'fruit and vegetables produce healthy children. Healthy children have healthy minds. Healthy minds produce imagination, experimentation and creation. Everything a good baker needs to have.' And who am Oi to disagree? Great man, Dr Bakewell. Expects a lot, moind you, but gives a lot."

"Lambrick!" Dr Crose interrupted his drifting off the point again.

"Sorry" he said to Dr Crose, as he pulled a pretend sad-face at the children, making them smile. "Well, moy point is that yer should know where yer food comes from and how it grows. Almost everythin' you eat comes from moy land."

"And the flowers that you can find on Farmer Lambrick's land are also edible" Dr Crose informed them. "I want you to inspect the vegetables you see growing here and draw in your books their pictures; Farmer Lambrick will help you learn which flower is from which vegetable. You have ten minutes before end of lesson."

The class scurried in all different directions in the enormous vegetable patch, which Farmer Lambrick had divided up into several areas. Caroline and Verity noticed that right at the far side of the vegetable patch, next to the forest were some beautiful big yellow flowers. The three of them walked to the edge just as Lambrick saw them heading towards the forest.

"Hey, you three" he called, as he jumped up and quickly ran to catch them up. "Where're you going?"

"Just over there to those big yellow flowers Sir" Vaughan answered.

"Well you be careful" Lambrick said, "that goes roight up to the Forest. Just make sure you don't go beyond those yellow flowers. I'll be watching you."
'Blimey' Vaughan thought, 'it's only a forest.' "We won't Sir" he promised.

Chapter 20

Afternoon Tea

Vaughan kept his promise and the whole class walked safely back to the school just in time for afternoon tea. Returning to the Refectory, he noticed the food table had changed yet again. The Refectory was fast becoming his favourite room of the school - every time he entered it, it looked different. Now, each of the house tables was covered with a white table cloth, there were plates and tea cups laid out for the pupils and the food table had changed beyond recognition.

This afternoon, it was laden with cakes. Vaughan, Caroline and Verity took a plate from their table and went to choose their snacks. Vaughan was surprisingly hungry again and reasoned it must have been the walk to Farmer Lambrick's and the cool, fresh air that made him hungry; seeing all the colourful cakes and choices before his eyes now made him feel ravenous!

He took a while before choosing, there was so much available. He looked at the plump iced buns, the huge chocolate muffins, the danish pastries. Then he noticed the lemon drizzle slices, the jam scones and the shortbread slices. Verity walked to the far end of the table, towards the gong and took a cherry bakewell cake; Vaughan followed and found yet more confectionery! Victoria sponge cake, angel cake, fruit cake and finally almond slices. Feeling greedy but unable to choose just one, Vaughan took an almond slice and a jam scone. Returning to the table he wasn't in the least surprised to find Caroline eagerly tucking into a large chocolate muffin! They sat down together and wolfed down their cakes and gulped their tea, conscious not to be late for reporting to Madame Rougerie - they did not want to upset her any more!

Dr Bakewell was as good as his word. Clementine Rougerie vacated his office during Afternoon Tea looking rather flushed and not at all happy. Caroline, Vaughan and Verity reported to her office as soon as they'd finished afternoon tea, as she had instructed, to receive their punishments slips.

With trepidation they approached the door to the Pastry Kitchen. Still feeling that he was to blame for this sorry mess, Vaughan walked on ahead of the girls and knocked the door three times.

"Enter" a gruff voice beckoned from behind the closed door. Vaughan turned the doorknob and the three ventured nervously inside.

Madame Rougerie was seated at the teachers desk, facing them as they set foot in her precious kitchen. "Sit" she gestured to the three workstations in the first row. Silently, Vaughan, Caroline and Verity inched themselves up onto the wooden stools and nervously awaited their detentions.

"I 'av 'ere, your detentions' she sniffed, waving three envelopes in her right hand, glowering at the cowering children. Surely she can't still be angry, Vaughan thought as she tossed the envelopes dismissively onto each work bench.

"As you will see, you 'av been given detention for zis evening. Make sure you are at ze Time-Keepers Clock at six o'clock zis evening, ready to serve your detentions. Zat will be all" she spoke swiftly and firmly, "you may go."

She looked so angry the three of them decided not to say anything other than a quick 'yes, miss' each, before stumbling off their rickety stools and rushing towards the door. "And don't run!" Madame Rougerie shouted after them, as they hurriedly escaped the kitchen and closed the door behind them.

"Phew" said Caroline, breathing a sigh of relief, "glad that's done. Crikey, she looked furious!"

Opening her envelope Verity looked puzzled. "Our detention isn't with her. It's with Farmer Lambrick."

"Farmer Lambrick?" Caroline repeated "you sure?"

"T's what it says here" Verity confirmed, "see for yourself." Vaughan and Caroline ripped open their envelopes and read it for themselves. Sure enough, it was there in writing and signed by Dr Bakewell:

This detention slip has been issued to:
Caroline Coleman, Verity Rose and Vaughan Baker
In punishment for:
Insolence to Madame Rougerie and questioning a teacher
They are hereby instructed to serve detention with:
Farmer Lambrick
When & Where:
September 1st - six o'clock pm - at the Time-Keepers Clock.
Signed: **Dr G Bakewell**

"You both seem a bit...surprised." Vaughan said after they'd all read their detention slips. "Why? What's up?"

"It's just that normally, the teacher that gives out the detention is the one that oversees it. You know, so the teacher knows that you've served it and that you did whatever you're supposed to do, properly. And, they record it on your school report." Caroline informed him.

"And I've never heard of pupils being given the same detention together before" Verity added.

"Maybe it's because we're all in trouble together?" Vaughan suggested, "we said the same thing, at the same time, to the same teacher, in the same class."

"Hmmm...I s'pose...." Verity pondered, "but Farmer Lambrick's not a teacher. It's very odd."

Vaughan thought about this and realised Verity was right - why would they serve a detention with a Farmer not a teacher? It all seemed very strange...

* * *

Newly re-fuelled from their Afternoon Tea of cake and tea and curious about their forthcoming detention, Vaughan, Verity and Caroline made their way to the last lesson of the day - Handwriting. Vaughan found this lesson the least enjoyable today as it reminded him of being told off at his old school, and writing lines as punishment.

The teacher, Mrs Higgins, demonstrated the techniques of copperplate writing, which she explained was vital for them to master. She explained how it would give them total hand control which was crucial not only for writing, but for making tiny decorations for sweets and cakes and of course, for when they progress to icing writing on cakes.

They spent the whole hour trying to trace copperplate writing through transparent paper and as it took so much concentration, the whole class was spent in almost complete silence. Vaughan was extremely glad when he heard the school bell toll it's heavy peal five times, signalling the end of class and beginning of free time.

Chapter 21

Detention

The children passed free time exploring Honeycomb Hall, the girls showing Vaughan the shortcuts they knew and taking him to the rooms they hadn't yet visited, like the Library the Hospital Quarters and the Ballroom. In fact, they spent so much time exploring that Vaughan suddenly worried that they might have lost track of time and be late for their detention. As he began to worry about this another thought struck him which he'd forgotten to ask earlier. "Oh, I forgot to ask you - what's the 'Time-Clock' and where is it?" he asked as they stepped from the ballroom back into the Grand Hallway. He dreaded the thought of being late for detention.

"Just there, by the staircase" Verity pointed across the grand hallway to the Grandfather Clock which stood proudly facing the ancient black front door.

"Oh, the Grandfather Clock!" Vaughan said, smiling. What a funny name to call it - all clocks tell the time, he thought to himself. "Why didn't she just say so?"

"It's not a normal clock" answered Verity, "look."
The three of them walked along the passageway and stopped in front of the clock. Vaughan peered at it's face - he remembered from before it had seemed strange but he hadn't had a chance to examine it until now.

As all clocks do, it had two hands. Only the hands of this clock weren't hands at all but wooden spoons. There was one big one which pointed straight up to where the number twelve usually is and a smaller one. The face itself was divided up into slices, so that it almost looked like a cake about to be served. Instead of twelve numbers circling the clock face there were little pictures, each in it's own slice of clock, the picture being at the widest part of the slice, the outer edge of the clock-face.

"That's weird!" he exclaimed. "Where are the numbers?"

"Right in the middle - around the small circle" Caroline pointed.

As the slices narrowed there was a number in the thinnest part of the wedge. These numbers circled around the centre of the clock face, where the spoon handles were fixed. Vaughan noticed that these numbers went from one to twenty-four, and discovered there were indeed twenty-four slices of the clock.

"But the numbers aren't really that important. It's a Time-Keeping Clock, for keeping the time, not telling the time."

"How.....?" began Vaughan but his voice petered out as he realised he didn't exactly know what to ask without sounding dumb. Fortunately Verity explained how it worked without him having to ask and feel silly.

"The twenty-four slices show the twenty-four hours of the day. The ones in blue show night-time and the ones in yellow show daytime." It was only then that Vaughan noticed the face was split almost in half, with the background colours of the slices showing various shades of blue and yellow. That made sense, he thought.

"The symbols in each slice tell you what you should be doing during that hour. Look." She pointed to a pale yellow slice with a picture of a sunrise - the number in this slice was 5. "This tells you it's five o'clock in the morning. See, the number tells you what hour of the day it is, the yellow tells you it's daytime. The next one, number six, has a bell symbol in it because that's what time the school bell tolls, to wake us up." Moving on to some other slices, she explained their meanings. "This symbol here - the black teacher's mortar board, means lesson time. That's also why there are more of them. See, the first one is in slice number 9 because the first lesson starts at nine o'clock." Vaughan noticed this and slowly all the other pictures and slices started to make sense - he was starting to understand how to read it.

"I think I get it" he said. "This one here that has the number 13 in" (which was right at the bottom where a normal clock would have a number six) "shows a dinner plate with a sandwich on, so...that means...that means it's lunchtime?"

"Yeah, you've got it!" cheered Caroline. Together they showed him all the remaining pictures and what they meant. Vaughan had already learnt that the mortar boards indicated lesson time and the sandwich at 13 meant at one o'clock in the afternoon it was lunchtime; he now learnt that the soap and toothbrush at 7 meant that seven o'clock was the time to get up, washed and dressed; the milk jug and cereal bowl in slice 8 told them breakfast began at eight o'clock; the fizzy drink in slice number 10 and cupcake in slice number 15 meant these were the times for morning break and afternoon tea.

There was also a bright shining sun for number 12 indicating midday; an open book in number 18 for homework and study time and a dinner plate in number 19 for dinner-time. According to the symbols of the clock, at eight o'clock it was time for a bath or shower and bedtime was obviously at nine o'clock, for in the slice numbered 21 was a picture of a patchwork-quilted bed. The darkest slices of the clock face were numbered 22 through to 3 and showed various stages of the moon cycle; the full moon shining brightly right at the top of the clock to indicate midnight.

All this Vaughan understood after it had been explained to him (the hardest part he found was learning the night-time hour numbers of a twenty-four hour clock), but oddly he spotted no picture in slice number 17 - five o'clock in the afternoon.

"What's happened here?" he asked pointing to number 17. "Has the picture fallen off?"

"No!" Caroline smiled and Verity chuckled, "there's no picture because that's our free-time.

"Oh" Vaughan replied. Now he could read it he understood what it meant but not it's purpose. It was pretty but not very useful, he thought.

"But what are you supposed to do with it?" he asked the girls. "How do you know what the real time is?"

"It's a Time-Keepers Clock; it's for Time-Keeping not Time-Telling. It tell's you where you should be at the stroke of every hour." Caroline told him. "Dr Bakewell hates people being late. So he had this clock made especially to show you the hour of the day and what you should be doing."

"Only the small spoon moves" Verity added "the big spoon always points straight up and never moves. When the bell in the clock tower strikes, the small spoon then jumps straight into the next slice."

"So if we're here - in the hallway - when the small spoon moves into the 6 o'clock slice, where the open book is...."

"Then it means we're late. Well, we would be if we were supposed to be somewhere else at six o'clock. But as we've been told to be here in the hallway, we'll be right on time."

"That's not very helpful though, is it?" mumbled Vaughan under his breath "what's he point of telling you you're already late?" Verity shrugged her shoulders in answer.

At that point the small wooden spoon did indeed slide into the six o'clock slice of time just as the bell in the clock tower pealed six times. Whilst it was tolling, Farmer Lambrick appeared from the corridor behind them.

"Oi take it you three are waitin' fer me then" he asked, making Vaughan jump.

"Yes, sir" he answered "we were told to be here at six o'clock for detention."

"Mm, Oi was told. Well then, let's get to it. Come with me."

He ushered the three of them together and led them back down the picture-lined corridor, past the kitchens and the pantry and out of the back door.

"Where are we going?" asked Verity, surprised because she's always presumed detentions were served in the classrooms. But they were heading outdoors into the cool air.

"Ter the kitchen. Honeycomb's kitchen, not the student ones. Tradesman's entrance, of course" he smiled, "best place to get it."

"Get what?" asked Vaughan, intrigued, as they exited the school and walked a long a path towards some trees.

"The raw ingredients" said Farmer Lambrick, "of moy magic compost."

"COMPOST?!" squealed Verity and Caroline together, "but that's made from..."

"Yep" the farmer agreed and stopped in front of an almost hidden arched doorway. Grinning at them he rapped the door with his fist, "rotting food!" he said. The three children gave way to pulling faces at each other, with the additional 'urgh' and 'eeuw' mixed in for good measure.

The door opened before them to reveal a headless man standing in front of them. Headless only because the big sack he was carrying in his arms blocked his face from view; all the children could see were black and white checked trousers and the bottom half of a stained, white tunic-top. The children's exclamations of disgust slowly quietened down, then suddenly..... "Verity?"

The anonymous headless man who had placed the sack on the floor (revealing a head firmly fixed to his neck as he did so) spoke as he straightened his back and stood up. He was anonymous no more.

"Dad!" squeaked verity.

"Dad?" thought Vaughan, "that's Verity's Dad?"

"Well - what are you doing here? Why aren't you in the study or library? It's six o'clock."

"It's alroight Tony" Farmer Lambrick broke the awkward silence "they're just helpin' me. They don't have much 'omework apparently and they're using their toime to give an old Farmer an 'and with his compost collection." he explained cheerfully. Verity was quite taken aback by this - it wasn't entirely false - they had been given no homework today and if they weren't serving detention then this would be extra free-time, but she felt both uncomfortable yet relieved that the detention hadn't been mentioned. Until...

"Oh, I see." replied Verity's Dad. "I heard a whisper that they'd been given detention."

"Ah. Yes, that is true" admitted Farmer Lambrick as Mr Rose looked questioningly at his embarrassed daughter, "although, according to Dr Bakewell, it wasn't deserved and will not be recorded on their permanent school report." At this, all three children felt hugely relieved. Leaning forward, Lambrick whispered into Mr Rose's ear.

"Our friend Avery Sorrel caused some mischief in Madame Rougerie's class this morning - sabotaged one of the new students. These three tried to explain to Clementine what had 'appened but she didn't take koindly to it. Issued all three of 'em detention." He stepped back and continued speaking at the normal volume. "So, he asked me to take their detentions as he knew Oi could use the extra hands."

Staring at the floor, nervously kicking the dust with her feet, Verity raised her eyes to meet her father's.

"Well, I was surprised to hear Verity had been given detention" admitted Mr Rose, "but explains it very well. You stay here a moment and I'll get the rest of the sacks. And Verity - it's alright, sweetheart. I'm not cross or disappointed in you, I'm proud of you for sticking up for your classmate." He returned to the kitchen and brought out another sack of food waste before wishing them all a pleasant evening and closing the door.

The sacks were heavy. Farmer Lambrick suggested that they carry a sack between two people as they had a long way to go. So off they set, Farmer Lambrick and Verity carrying one sack with Vaughan and Caroline sharing the weight of the other and together the four of them staggered across the fields under an ever dusky sky, to the farmhouse just visible on the horizon.

* * *

When they reached the farmhouse, they dropped their heavy sacks and Farmer Lambrick invited them in for a cup of tea to thank them for their help.

Standing in the hallway, Lambrick spoke, breathlessly. "You thirsty, you three? It's 'ard work carrying those sacks - do yer want a cup o' tea before we carry on?"

Surprised, they all said 'yes, please' and Farmer Lambrick disappeared into the kitchen, telling them to make themselves at home. They looked at each other without saying a word, shrugging their shoulders and stepped through the first open door they saw - which happened to be the living room. Stepping inside they looked around the homely living-room and it's mismatched furniture as they heard the kettle bubble and boil in the next room. Moment later, Farmer Lambrick appeared with a tray of four steaming mismatched mugs of hot tea, and gestured them to sit down.

"Thank you" said Verity as she took the first mug and settled herself into a cosy pink armchair, "but aren't we supposed to be working hard as a punishment, considering this is our detention?" she asked as she sipped her tea and found it a little too hot at the moment.

"Ordinarily, yes" agreed Farmer Lambrick, "but word travels around this school. From what Oi hear, you lot have got this detention because you were tryin' to help someone else." All three muttered and nodded their agreement. "So Oi don't believe yer should be punished at all. Oi think yer should all be applauded, meself. So come on, drink up an' be proud of yerselves. Dr Bakewell is" he added, mysteriously.

Chapter 22

Dormitory Revelations

The children were both surprised and relieved that their detention was so easy. They had no idea what to expect but hauling compost to the farmhouse and chatting with a Farmer over a cup of tea was not something any of them expected. Returning to the school at seven o'clock for dinner, they were glad it was over with and with a weight off their shoulders, happily tucked into dinner.

Again the Refectory had been transformed for the final meal of the day. Plates and cutlery were laid out for each student on each house table as it had been for Afternoon Tea, but this evening there were trays, bowls and casserole dishes of food on each house table and the long snack table was full of pudding. Dr Bakewell welcomed the students to dinner as Mr Soames sounded the gong, the signal that they could tuck in.

Vaughan helped himself to sausages, mashed potatoes, peas and gravy; Verity spooned cauliflower cheese from a casserole dish onto her plate and Caroline piled her plate high with roast beef, carrots, peas, roast potatoes and Yorkshire pudding. The smells wafted around the large room and soon the noise of chatter was drowned out by the scraping of knives against empty plates. Finishing their meals, Vaughan, Verity and Caroline took their dirty plates to the snack table where they piled them up and helped themselves to spotted dick and custard for pudding. Yep, Vaughan thought, these were the best school dinners he could ever have imagined!

The first night at Honeycomb Hall felt strange to Vaughan. He had his own room at home - in fact, he'd never spent a night away from home before - unless you count the night at the B&B when they'd been making their way to the school, but even then his family had been with him. No, this was his first night away from home, away from his family and he felt a little homesick and strangely lonely, despite sharing a dormitory with just over thirty other Oswaldian boys.

Obeying the Time-Keepers Clock, he showered, brushed his teeth and climbed into bed for nine o'clock. He lay there in silence as the rest of the boys in the dormitory gabbled on to each other, discussing their day, their lessons, what they were looking forward to learning in the forthcoming year and how good it was to be back together again. Clearly being in bed for nine o'clock did not necessarily mean going to sleep at nine o'clock, Vaughan realised. He lay in bed listening to the chatter around him and recalled the events of the day. It had been a big day for him - starting this wonderful new school, making friends with Caroline and Verity, very regrettably receiving a detention, and meeting Farmer Lambrick. He yawned - it had been a very full day, his brain was even more tired than his body was. Eyes heavy with tiredness, he closed his drooping eyelids and allowed sleep to take over in a matter of minutes, when he dreamed of the Summer Fete; baking huge giant fairy cakes as big as buckets, of winning an award for his bucket-cakes and seeing Avery Sorrel squashed under the bulk of Madame Rougerie when she sat on him unknowingly during a picnic, Avery's arms and legs waving wildly in the air for someone to pull her up and rescue him!

The girls dormitory was quite similar. Everyone was in their bunks - well, on someone's bunk by nine o'clock, also chattering and giggling, clearly enjoying each other's company again.

Verity and Caroline's bunks were next to each other. Both girls sat cross-legged on Caroline's duvet, along with Emi and Orla. As Emi and Orla were the only scholarship girls in St Oswald, Caroline called them over to sit with them on their bunk.

Both Emi and Orla gladly accepted the offer and squeezed on, asking Verity and Caroline for guidance and sharing their nerves and concerns. As they talked, the four girls opened up and Caroline admitted that although they were glad to be back at school, they were very angry they were given a detention.

"You got a detention?" asked a shocked Emi.

"When?" asked Orla, "What for?"

"Remember when Madame Rougerie had a go at Florence in Patisserie, accusing her of not washing her hands when her breadcrumbs turned into dough when Florence swore she hadn't put any water in?"

"Yes?" Emi and Orla chorused.

"Well, we don't think it was Florence. You know Vaughan - the new boy from our House? Well, we've made friends and he reckons he saw Avery Sorrel in Florence's spot when she was washing up at the sink. Putting two and two together, we think he had something to do with it. So we told Madame Rougerie" explained Caroline.

"But we can't prove it" continued Verity. "When Vaughan told us it made sense because right from day one when Dr Bakewell told us in assembly he was going to run the competition, Avery objected. We thought it was pretty brave of Vaughan to stand up for Florence like that, so we backed him up. We thought, if we agreed - if there were three of us telling her the same thing, that she might listen. But instead she gave all three of us detention." Emi and Orla stared at Verity and Caroline agog. Slowly, Orla spoke.

"You were right" she said quietly, "it was Avery Sorrel."

"How do you know?" asked Verity. Orla explained. "We've made friends with Poppy Quenell from St Wistan. Anyway, after Patisserie, she told us that this morning during break her big sister Daisy had overheard some boys talking in whispers about setting up some plan to get rid of all us scholarship kids. The last thing Daisy heard them say was that their next class was pastry making and it

- 127 -

would involve water. Then they left the table. That must have been what they were planning - they must have done it against Florence. Which means you were right."

"I knew it!" squealed Verity, both angry and delighted. Angry that Sorrel had been so conniving, so mean and downright spiteful but delighted that not only had he been caught out but that now several others knew what he was like. Now there were more of them to watch out for him. It also meant that they had been very wrongly punished.

"That could be really useful" Caroline said thoughtfully. "Avery Sorrel is in St Wistan's House too, so if Daisy knows she was right, they both might be able to keep a close eye on him."

"Ooh, like spies, you mean?" asked Emi excitedly.

"Kind of, yeah!" agreed Caroline. "We can only see him when we're in mixed-house classes but as Poppy's in St Wistan with Avery, she'll be in all his classes. And on his table in the refectory."

"Well, I'll ask Poppy and she can ask Daisy - I don't know Daisy very well. I don't know if Poppy would want to, she's quite shy - but she might, now we know for sure that Avery tried to get Florence into trouble." said Orla honestly. "Why Daisy too?"

"Because we think that the other boy Avery Sorrel was talking to was Percy Snodland." Verity continued, knowing what Caroline was thinking. "He's almost as bad as Avery but he's a year older - he's in the third year. Which means..."

"Poppy can listen out for what Avery's up to and Daisy can listen out for Percy! It's perfect! We can have a spy in each year! No-one would think it strange that two kids in different years spend a lot of time together if they were twins." Caroline finished Verity's sentence for her. It was a habit that sometimes irked Verity but on this occasion she didn't notice. She was far too pleased that at long last, snotty, spiteful Avery Sorrel might just get his comeuppance.

Chapter 23

The Farmer's Market

Putting on his Grandad cap and green wax coat, the weathered old Farmer checked his pockets for his wallet, found it and satisfied he placed it carefully back in his coat pocket and buttoned it up to keep it safe. He pulled on his old, green wellington boots and as the grandmother clock in his hallway chimed seven o'clock, he walked out of the farmhouse into the foggy half-light of the Autumn morning, pulling the rickety door shut behind him.

Over the fields he plodded, squelching through the muddy terrain and rain-soaked grass, glad he was wearing his wellingtons. After a few minutes he arrived at the rear of the school and knocked on the arched door in front of him. It was answered almost immediately.

"Alright Tony?" he said.

The man who answered the door smiled at him and replied. "I'm alright mate, you? You ready then?" he asked as the Farmer nodded in reply.

"Ar, all set. Been looking forward ter this, first market of the year's always the best, in't it?"

"You're not wrong there" replied Tony. "Got everything then?"

"Ar" Farmer Lambrick confirmed again, as Tony pulled on an old raincoat and Farmer Lambrick took some keys from his other pocket.

Together they walked across the side of the school towards a cluster of trees, behind which sat two vehicles; a quaint little old Citroen dolly car with a rounded roof and bonnet, coloured pale lemony-cream and maroon; next to it a battered old Land Rover with huge muddy tyres. The two vehicles had been cleverly hidden behind the trees so that if you looked at the school from the front, all you could see were the trees. The smaller cream car was hidden behind the green Land Rover, which itself was camouflaged perfectly behind the evergreens.

The two men approached the Land Rover and jumped in the front, Tony occupying the passenger seat and Farmer Lambrick settling into the driver's seat.

"Market Day - here we come!" announced Farmer Lambrick as he started the engine and slowly trundled the noisy vehicle out from it's camouflaged hiding place and down the school driveway, through the wrought-iron gates and onto the lane beyond where it rumbled and growled it's way to market.

* * *

Going to the Farmer's Market was a treat for both Tony and Farmer Lambrick. Being a Farmer in his youth, Farmer Lambrick loved to catch up with people and have a chat; he enjoyed seeing what the Farmers were rearing and getting tips off the stall holders about 'the best way to do this' or 'a better way to try that' and so on. Tony enjoyed the Farmers Market because he was the School Chef. A great chef a few years ago who ran his own restaurant, he enjoyed going to the market with Farmer Lambrick because he could listen to how the food had been grown, how the animals had been kept and if they'd been well looked after. It was very important to him, to give the students proper food.

Of course, Farmer Lambrick grew most of the school's fruits and vegetables himself. But he didn't really keep any animals - not for meat anyway. He might have been a Farmer but he had always hated that side of farming and decided that he was going to become vegetarian. How the other Farmer's had laughed when they found out! But Farmer Lambrick hadn't cared - until one day he lost his job. Refusing to move from the farmhouse to the slaughterhouse, he was told he had to find another job and found himself lucky enough to have been hired by Dr Bakewell. It was at the school he befriended the School's Chef, Tony Rose, who respected Farmer Lambrick's beliefs and so they came to the Farmer's Market together, once a month, to buy meat for the school. Dr Bakewell had suggested the idea originally and they both thought it was brilliant. Who better than a Farmer and a Chef, to choose the best food for his pupils? And so here they were, for the first Farmer's Market of the school year.

The stalls were plentiful with all sorts of produce. Meat pies, pork pies, fresh rabbits, vegetables, fruit, eggs (duck, hen, goose and ostrich), an amazing selection of jams and cheeses and so many people bustling about with their baskets it was hard not to lose each other. Eyeing up one of the meat stalls, Tony was asking questions about the chickens being sold, when something on the stall behind caught Farmer Lambrick's eye. Something on the stall moved.

"Hang on 'ere, Tone" he nudged his colleague "there's summat strange over there, Oi'm goin' to 'ave a nose." Tony nodded vaguely acknowledging him, though he was far to busy haggling over the price of the chickens to pay much attention. Farmer Lambrick pottered off curiously, feeling himself strangely drawn to the stall behind.

* * *

Surprisingly he found himself at another meat counter. But there was nothing odd about it. All the usual trays of meat, price flags and lists of meat that could be ordered. The only strange thing he noticed was a wooden cage behind the counter, against the stalls rear wall. In the cage was a plastic pig - nothing unusual about that, seeing as this was a meat stall. Nothing usual so far that was, until the plastic pig snuffled and moved.

" 'Xcuse me?" Farmer Lambrick spoke to the stall holder who had just handed a bag of mince to a customer.

"Yes?" the stall holder wiped his hands down his apron, "can I help you?"

"Did that pig just move?"

"What, him?" the stallholder jerked his head as he pointed behind him with his thumb. "Not much meat on him. Runt of the litter. Won't get much for him, that's for sure. Thought of raffling him off, can't really afford to keep him til he's bigger."

"I'll take 'im off yer 'ands if yer loike" said Farmer Lambrick immediately.

"Now hold on, I know he's not got much meat on him, but...."

"I'll have him!" another voice had overhead and joined in the conversation. Looking to his left, Farmer Lambrick saw who he had been put into competition with. "I'll have him, keep him a few months then when he's nice and fat, he'll do nicely for Christmas." With horror, Farmer Lambrick realised he was in competition with a butcher. Staring at the ruddy-faced, overweight butcher he felt responsible for the fate of this little pig; he had to save him from the butcher who wanted to turn him into Christmas Dinner. Staring back into the shiny, jet-black, innocent eyes of the caged little pig, he knew he couldn't let that happen. But what could he do? What could he do, he wondered?

* * *

He took his wallet out of his coat pocket and peered inside. There was just enough to cover the meat needed for the school with only a little left over. He picture Dr Bakewell's face in his mind then looked back at the little pig, who seemed to be pleading with him, staring back with unblinking round eyes.

"I'll give you thirty" said the portly red-faced butcher "take it or leave it."

Farmer Lambrick peered inside the wallet at the money Dr Bakewell had given to him.

"Forty" he said, making his decision as he slapped down four, ten-pound notes on the counter. The butcher stared at him and rifled around in his own pockets. "Sixty."

Gulping Farmer Lambrick made his final decision and prayed it was enough. He knew he would have some explaining to do when he got back to the school. "Oi'll give you a hundred" he declared.

The stall holder was taken aback. A hundred pounds was usually what he would sell a healthy sized pig for, not a little runt of a piglet like this one. He looked at the butcher.

"I'm done" the butcher said, "he's not worth that" and stuffing his money back into his pocket he marched away.

"Looks like he's yours then!" grinned the wide-eyed stall holder, unable to believe it. To think, earlier he was going to raffle him off for just a few pounds, too! Beaming but a little anxious, Farmer Lambrick took hold of the crate carefully and carried the piglet safely back to meet Tony.

"Almost done" said Tony without looking up, "just the sausage and pork to get then we're finished. WHAT THE...?" he exclaimed, finally looking at Farmer Lambrick and the square wooden cage he was holding.

"Loike 'im?" asked Lambrick, "Oi just bought 'im off that stall over there."

"I know I like fresh meat, but that's a bit too fresh. What have you got that for?"

"Oi'm keepin' 'im" said Farmer Lambrick proudly, "he's my new pet. Only trouble is that Oi spent half our meat money on 'im."

"Have you gone mad?" whispered a worried Tony in a low voice "what're we supposed to tell Dr Bakewell? He's going to notice we haven't got enough meat to last the month, you know. Did you think of that when you went on your animal crusade?"

"Oi know" admitted Farmer Lambrick ruefully, "Oi was hopin' to get 'im for free. Almost did too, but this big fat butcher overheard and wanted to 'ave 'im fer his Christmas dinner. Oi had to save 'im, look at 'im. Look at how cute and lovely he is" then he started cooing and making silly faces at the pig, who wriggled in his cage and snorted back.

Being an understanding man, Tony decided not to tell him off - after all, they were both caring men and Farmer Lambrick had just saved the life of this little piglet. This was a farmer who would rather lose his job than harm an animal, Tony remembered.

"Look, I'll think of something" he assured the worried Farmer "I'll make sure the meat we have got goes that little bit further. Or we'll just have to eat more veg this month, that's all."

"Cheers, Tone" smiled Farmer Lambrick, "yer a chef in a million!"

Chapter 24

Rasher

"Ha! Oh-ho! Ha!" Dr Bakewell's stilted, forced laugh made Farmer Lambrick wriggle uncomfortably. "Oh ho, very funny" he said, as an artificially wide grin peeped out from below his gingery-grey moustache and fixed itself across his face, so he looked somewhat like a Cheshire cat, as he looked from Farmer Lambrick to Tony Rose and back again.

"I think, Sir" began Tony "it would be a great idea to have a meat-free month. Or a meat-free fortnight. Be a nice change and we could tell the students it was a special 'Harvest Celebration' or something. Only food from the ground until the 'celebration' was over by which time we will have gone to the next market and can have meat again. What do you think?" Dr Bakewell's face dropped and the forced smile vanished instantly. You could almost see it slide off his face, pulling the corners of his mouth down into a firm, straight line as it did so. "You are joking, aren't you?" he asked. "Where's the meat you bought?"

"No Dr Bakewell, Sir, we're not jokin'. Oi 'ad to get him, he was just lyin' there in a crate and he looked so sad. He looked roight at me - could feel his eyes burnin' their way straigh' to moy 'eart - it was as if he was callin' me to 'im, pleadin' fer me to rescue 'im."

"Poppycock! Pigs don't converse with people. Are you seriously telling me that you spent half the school's monthly meat budget - a whole month's worth - on...on...on a pet?" Dr Bakewell's usually ruddy face grew redder and redder with every passing minute, so that it clashed oddly with his greying ginger hair. There was no disguising the fact that he was extremely angry with Farmer Lambrick.

"Oi know it seems - well, odd" protested Farmer Lambrick as Dr Bakewell rolled his eyes in disbelief, "but Oi just 'ad this feelin' Oi was meant to 'ave that pig. Oi've always wanted a pig and it just felt that Oi was meant to 'ave this one. Oi won't do anythin' like it again Sir, Oi promise" he finished humbly.

"Hmph. Damn right you won't" muttered Dr Bakewell. Then he switched his attention to Farmer Lambrick's accomplice - Verity's father, Tony Rose, the School Chef.

"You have half your monthly meat ration. What can you do?"

"Manage" Tony replied. "I can manage, Doctor."
Placated but clearly not happy, Dr Bakewell lifted his chin, stretched his neck upwards, rolled his shoulders back and inhaled deeply through his nose. "Do what you can, Tony. If you need any extra fruit or veg, help yourself to Farmer Lambrick's patches."

"By all means, certainly, anythin' you ask" grovelled Farmer Lambrick.

"I wasn't asking" snapped Dr Bakewell hotly as Farmer Lambrick hung his head and decided it would probably be best not to speak. He hadn't ever seen Dr Bakewell quite this angry before.

"Just make sure the children don't go hungry and they don't notice a difference in the quality of the food. Last thing we need are complaints from the parents."

"Yes Dr Bakewell, I will" agreed Tony, relieved. He was very fond of Farmer Lambrick and more than half expected Dr Bakewell to demand they return the pig to the market, which would have left the poor Farmer heartbroken.

"And YOU" he directed a steely glare back at Farmer Lambrick, "don't ever - EVER - do anything like this again, do you understand me. Consider yourself warned. You're not the only Farmer around here, you know." Farmer Lambrick nodded vigorously and silently as he stared ashamedly at his feet. "A pet pig, of all things. First cats now a pig. Be a zoo soon if my staff get their way" muttered Dr Bakewell to himself as he walked away from the two men, standing there like naughty schoolboys outside their Headmaster's Office.

When he was out of earshot Farmer Lambrick spoke to Tony. "Anythin' you need from my land, you can 'ave it. Do yer think yer will be able ter manage?" he asked with genuine concern and a touch of worry.

"I hope so mate, I hope so." Tony sounded less certain now than he did earlier, when he'd told Dr Bakewell he would manage. Then he'd sounded confident; now he sounded unsure. "Are you absolutely sure you've done the right thing, buying that pig? You can see how angry Dr Bakewell is."

"Oi know and if Oi was 'im watchin' me - or anyone else watchin' me - Oi'd think Oi was crazy an all - or stupid. But for some reason Oi can't explain, Oi just 'ave this feelin' in me bones that savin' that little runt of a pig is gonna be the best thing Oi've ever done. Yes mate, Oi'm absolutely, positively, definitely sure.

* * *

Farmer Lambrick couldn't wait for Vaughan, Verity and Caroline to pay him a visit. He was certain that they'd fall in love with the little piglet just as he'd done a few days earlier. When Saturday morning arrived he waited at the fence for them, almost bursting with excitement and grinned when he saw the three familiar figures trudging through the uneven damp grass of the fields towards him.

"Alroight, you three?" he welcomed them enthusiastically grinning from ear to ear, unable to hide his excitement any longer.

"Alright Lambrick!" smiled Vaughan back, "You look happy today!"

"Ar, that Oi am Vaughan, that Oi am."

"Why?" giggled Caroline, laughing as Farmer Lambrick began hopping from one foot to the other, "what's happening today? Ooh, have you got some new biscuits? Chocolate ones?"

Verity rolled her eyes and smiled. Trust Caroline to think of biscuits!

"No, it's not biscuits!" Farmer Lambrick replied, "But come on in and yer can 'ave yer tea and biscuits then Oi'll tell yer." Removing their wellies at the front door, all three children followed Farmer Lambrick into the tumbledown farmhouse, eager to know what had got the old Farmer so excited that he was behaving like a schoolboy!

As the children sat down in the cosy living-room they heard the sound of boiling water coming from the kitchen, followed by the unmistakeable high-pitched whistle of the kettle; moments later Farmer Lambrick appeared in the doorway with his round tray, carrying four steaming cups of tea and a plate of biscuits.

"Ooh, they are chocolate!" squealed Caroline as she dived in and helped herself.
Shaking her head slightly with amusement at Caroline's obsession with chocolate, Verity urged Farmer Lambrick to continue with his story.

"Never mind the biscuits! Why are you so excited then, Farmer? Is it your birthday or something?"

"Oh no, nothin' loike that. Although it feels loike all moy birthdays come at once! Anyway, yer remember gettin' into trouble with Madame Rougerie fer doin' what yer felt was roight? An' gettin' a detention fer yer efforts?" All three children nodded glumly; it was still a sore point for all three of them. "Well, the same thing 'appened to me just this week."

"You?" spluttered Caroline, half-way through chomping her biscuit and spraying crumbs everywhere. "Sorry. You? Got a detention?" she finished, wiping her mouth clean.

"Nah, not a detention. Oi got into trouble. With Dr Bakewell."

All three of them looked amazed. What on earth could Farmer Lambrick have done to get into trouble with the Headmaster and why would he now be really happy about it?

"That doesn't make sense." said Verity, confused. "How can you get into trouble with Dr Bakewell?"

"And why would that make you so happy?" added Vaughan.

"Oi think it'd be best if Oi showed yer, Oi aint so good wi' words. Come wi' me."

The four of them put down their scalding-hot cups of tea and the children followed Farmer Lambrick firstly to the front door to collect their wellies, then back through the farmhouse to the back door. All four of them pulled on their wellies before stepping outside through the back door and noticing a new addition - a square muddy pigsty. In the middle of the sty was a pink piglet, no bigger than a jack russell dog, oinking and sniffing the ground.

"Oh wow!" said Caroline loudly, "it's a piglet!"

"This is the little fellow that got me into trouble recently. He was about to be sold to a butcher and Oi rescued him. Course, Dr Bakewell wasn't too happy with me, 'cause Oi spent most of the school meat budget on 'im, but yer know, look at 'im! Had to 'ave him, didn't Oi? Oi've always wanted a pig yer know."

"What's his name?" asked Verity, trying to coax the pig towards her.

"Well, Oi wanted somethin' that suited 'im. He's a boy and Oi rescued 'im from a butcher, saved 'im from bein' someone's Christmas dinner, so Oi've given 'im the first name that came ter me."

"Which is...?" pushed Vaughan, smiling at the happy grunting piglet rolling in the mud.

Farmer Lambrick smiled with pride. "Rasher!" he laughed.

Chapter 25

Windfalls

The days passed quickly as the children learned new skills and Farmer Lambrick devoted himself to his new pig and almost before they noticed, October arrived, bringing its traditional bright colours and cool breezes. Autumn had now truly claimed the land; the fruit trees in the orchard were full of fruit ripe for picking, the leaves on the trees were becoming fewer and the last determined few that held fast to the branches were beautiful shades of orange, red and yellow. Caroline and Verity put on their duffel coats before walking out into the gardens for their first lesson of the day. Although the sun was out and shining brightly, there was a light breeze and a cool chill to the air; as they wandered through the gardens to the orchard, they passed the gardener, Cuthbert Flowerdew, raking the leaves that had recently fallen and waved cheerily; they walked from the open gardens through the twiggy rose arch until they came to the orchard itself.

The orchard was Verity's most favourite place in the school grounds. It was divided into mini-orchards; pear, apple, cherry, plum and damson trees grew here, with student-made, trodden down pathways of mud criss-crossing the orchards and separating the fruit. Verity loved the orchard the most because she said it didn't matter what time of year it was, it was always beautiful. With so many trees, in the spring it smelled like freshly washed clothes and the masses of blossom were always floating around in the wind, falling on and decorating anyone who passed by. In the summer, it was full of green leaves and birds, whose bird-songs were so hypnotic you could listen to them as the birds flitted from tree to tree, for hours. In Autumn, the leaves fell to the ground creating a carpet of red and brown hues and the fruit was ripe for picking (not to mention the occasional apple they scrumped if they were really hungry). In the winter, after all the leaves had gone, the branches of the trees stood out starkly against the white sky; but it was when the trees were covered with snow and icicles and the ground became a thick blanket of snow that Verity found it the most enchanting. She loved to walk in fresh, thick snow and feel the cold, soft flakes fall gently onto her face as she danced around. Last January, during her first Winter at Honeycomb Hall, she sneaked out at night-time to dance in the snow under the stars and the inky black sky although she caught a nasty cold and had to stay in the Hospital Quarters for a week to recover.

In the pathway, Verity and Caroline met up with Vaughan and their teacher, Professor Peach. This was Vaughan's first outdoor lesson and he wasn't sure what to expect. Understandable, as Professor Peach was indeed an unusual teacher. He was about sixty and rather plump around the tummy; he had thick, uncontrollable grey hair which, when he put on his glasses, made him look a little like Einstein. Today he was wearing his peach suit-jacket, white and orange check shirt, brown corduroy trousers and an orange-and-yellow bow tie.

"Do you reckon he's wearing that so that if the new students forget his name his suit will remind them?" Caroline whispered, as they giggled quietly. They laughed about him sometimes but deep down they both liked him very much; he was a gentle man who, for as long as Verity and Caroline had known him, had never shouted at a pupil for any reason - everyone did as he asked, when he asked; he was one of those teachers that everyone liked.

Caroline and Verity watched for a while, as Professor Peach produced four wicker baskets, gave instructions on harvesting 'windfalls' and explained how they could be used in baking.

"Any apples already fallen on the ground are called 'windfalls'. The name is such because it is the wind that has caused the apple to fall off the branch. They may be bruised, show signs of coddling moth or been half-eaten by a squirrel or bird. However, do not presume that this means they are not suitable for baking. Quite the contrary. You will find these very useful for recipes that require small quantities of apple; for example for stewing or chopping. You of course now know the difference between cooking apples and eating apples - we shall today collect windfall cooking apples only." Professor Peach continued to explain how to spot good windfalls and bad windfalls. As soon as he had finished his instructions, he gave the class free rein to roam amongst the apple trees and collect a basketful of windfalls each. "Sort yourselves into four groups of equal-ish size, collect a basket and return to me in half an hour with them full. Off you go!"

As the class divided themselves up into groups of two or three, Caroline, Verity and Vaughan grabbed a basket and headed off into the apple orchard.

"Do you really use apples off the ground in baking?" Vaughan asked Verity. It seemed strange to him, he thought if they'd fallen off they must be rotten inside.

"Oh yes, quite a lot" she told him. "As long as they've got no worm holes or been half eaten by a squirrel! Apples are apples, there's no difference in the taste."

"Unless you pick one that's got a worm in it" said Caroline.

"Ewwwww!" Vaughan and Verity said together.

They spent the next half an hour collecting apples and putting them in the basket and messing about, filling each others coat pockets and hoods with apples, trying to see who could hold the most before tipping them into the basket.

"Hey, I've got a joke for you two, speaking of apples" said Vaughan, picking up a whole apple and biting into it, enjoying his first lesson outdoors. "What's worse than finding an apple with a worm in it?"

"Dunno" said Caroline, shrugging her shoulders.

"What?" asked Verity, emptying her hood of more apples.

"Finding an apple with half a worm in it!" he laughed pretending to have found one in his apple and imitating being sick.

"Oh shut up, Vaughan" sighed Caroline, chuckling, "that's disgusting!" and she tossed a small apple out of their basket at Vaughan, playfully.

"Come on you two" said Verity seriously "stop messing about - we've got some foraging to do!"

Chapter 26

A Bath Tub of Grub

Since Farmer Lambrick had brought Rasher back to his farm, the little pig seemed to grow daily. Farmer Lambrick had created a small, make-shift pigsty for Rasher, in between the cabbage patch and the potato patch, using the two stone walls of the two existing vegetable patches for its sides. It was very quick to do - he simply constructed a waist-high wooden fence just in front of the forest and securing it between the existing stone walls, thus created a small square pigsty.

Vaughan, Caroline and Verity used their free-time to visit him and Farmer Lambrick, who was glad of their company and interest in Rasher. He had someone - three someones to be exact - who loved Rasher as much as he did. Dr Bakewell was still annoyed with him despite Tony having done a fantastic job disguising the lack of meat in the school dinners.

This had given an added benefit to Farmer Lambrick that he hadn't considered before - as the school children had eaten more vegetables and fruit, all the left-overs could be used to feed Rasher. So while everyone's dinners had been healthy and varied, Rasher had had an abundance of food during his first month with the Farmer and both pig and students were absolutely glowing thanks to it.

One Saturday morning, Vaughan, Verity and Caroline made their way to the farmhouse for what had now become their weekly weekend treat: a mug of hot scalding tea and toasted tea-cakes, a chat with Farmer Lambrick, squirting water in Rashers pigsty to make the ground freshly muddy, watching Rasher roll around wallowing in the new mud then rinsing him clean with the hosepipe, before filling up Rashers food trough with the left-overs Verity's Dad routinely gave them.

Farmer Lambrick stayed in the farmhouse to wash up and let the children play with Rasher outside. They finished giving Rasher his mud bath and walked to the front of the farmhouse where they picked up the buckets of scraps they had earlier left by the farmhouse door. Carrying the heavy buckets they returned to the sty, lifted the latch, opened the gate and trod through the wet, squelchy, ankle-deep mud to the food trough. Using both hands they raised the heavy buckets and tilted them downwards, pouring their contents into an old bath-tub which Farmer Lambrick had cleverly decided to use as a pig trough. If there was a way to re-use anything, Farmer Lambrick would usually find it! He didn't believe in buying anything new, as he often said, he liked 'things wi' character and a bit of 'istory to 'em' - which went a long way to explaining why the all furniture and crockery in his house was mismatched and looked rather the worse for wear.

Just as they had poured out the dregs from the bucket, Rasher trotted over and immediately began noisily chomping his breakfast; as he did so they felt a strange tickle across the back of their knees. Each thinking it must be Rasher - before realising Rasher was beside them, head buried up to his ears in the leftovers - all three swiftly spun around and saw the great blur of fur which had brushed their legs; out of nowhere Rhubarb and Custard raced across the pigsty and leapt onto the higgledy-piggledy stone wall which separated the pigsty from the cabbage patch and sat there above the recently re-filled 'bath-tub-of-grub' (as Caroline affectionately called it), staring down at its contents. Rasher looked up from his food trough and seeing the two cats peering down at him, let out a loud 'oink' of surprise. Rhubarb jumped down into the mud and sauntered brazenly around the sty and over to the bath tub.

Following Rhubarb's lead, Custard also jumped off the wall and into the muddy sty. Realising his precious leftovers were in danger, Rasher trotted away from the bath-tub towards the fence and turned, facing the cats and the side of the bath-tub. Lowering his head, he snorted and charged like a bull at the two cheeky cats, who were greedily munching their way through the pigswill looking for remnants of chicken and fish.

The cats, of course, leapt elegantly into the air and landed gracefully on the wall above the trough, just in time to see a very upset Rasher charge head-first into the side of the trough, knocking it over and spilling its contents all over the muddy ground. Immediately Rhubarb and Custard pounced back down, sniffing out tasty chunks of tuna, cheese and whatever else they could find, leaping here and there as Rasher tried desperately to scare them away.

Finally, after a while of being chased around in circles, Rhubarb and Custard were at the far end of the pigsty, in front of the wooden fence that Farmer Lambrick had built. Concentrating with all his might, Rasher lowered his head once more, stamped his trotters and thundered across the sty as fast as his short stumpy legs would allow, doing a very good impersonation of a small, pink, raging bull.

He almost got his targets too, literally just missing Custard by a whisker, as Custard squealed in horror. Fleeing to the right and landing on the wall separating the pigsty from the potato-patch, Custard avoided his angry snout; behind him Rhubarb pounced to the left to the safety of the cabbage-patch wall, successfully dodging the angry pig's trotters as they thudded into the soft ground, splattering mud everywhere. But Rasher was going so fast he couldn't stop that quickly. He wasn't as agile and quick-footed as the cats. He managed to stop running but the mud was soft, having been freshly soaked that morning. He skidded through the mud, across the sty and crashed head first into the little wooden fence loving built by Farmer Lambrick, which instantly shattered into pieces. Splinters flew through the air and Rasher, Rhubarb and

Custard all squealed as the splinters showered down upon them like stinging raindrops, a cacophony of noise that penetrated through the walls of the farmhouse to the tuned ears of Farmer Lambrick, who had finished washing up and had just sat down at the kitchen table to drink his tea.

Hearing the commotion, Farmer Lambrick jumped out of his chair, spilling his tea over the table and ran to the kitchen window, which overlooked the vegetable patches and pigsty. "RASHER!" he yelled through the window, "NO!"
Seeing the chaos outside - the school cats in the pigsty covered in mud, pigswill strewn all over the ground, a jagged, gaping hole in what used to be a wooden fence with Rasher and the three children panicking, he dashed out of the house as fast as he could.

* * *

Farmer Lambrick was a few seconds too late. Already spooked by the smashing of the fence, the rainstorm of splinters and the ear-splitting noise of Rhubarb and Custard screaming in fright, Rasher paced frantically around the sty, imitating a miniature rodeo bull. Leaping over the stone wall with an agility that surprised the children, Farmer Lambrick raced to calm Rasher down. But that was the last straw for Rasher. On top of everything else scaring him, the sight of Farmer Lambrick jumping into his sty and running at him, was too much. He looked in front of him as Rhubarb and Custard sprinted out of the sty and scrambled up a tree on the edge of the forest. He looked behind him and saw Farmer Lambrick bearing down upon him quickly, he looked back in front at the cats and saw the hole in the fence - his door to freedom. He was still panicked, he had little time to think; so he did what his instinct told him to do - he ran.

Straight through the gaping hole, jumping over the shallow ditch that bordered the forest, he ran after Rhubarb and Custard who were perched safely on a branch of a forest tree, backs arched, hissing at him. He ran away from Farmer Lambrick who was shouting, calling his name. He ran away from the three children who were running after Farmer Lambrick, calling him. He was angry, he was scared but most of all, he was hungry.

* * *

Hot on the trail of the feline food thieves, Rasher thundered on through he Forest of Forgetfulness as Rhubarb and Custard leapt from branch to branch, trying to avoid the raging beast below them, as all three animals ventured deeper into the forest and disappeared from sight.

Realising they had stepped foot inside the forest, Farmer Lambrick stopped abruptly and outstretched his arms just in time, as Vaughan, Verity and Caroline ploughed straight into them, almost toppling into the ditch.

"No" he said "yer'll get lost. You three stay 'ere 'case he comes back an' if he does yer can block 'im in the sty. Oi'll go." Farmer Lambrick dashed back to the farmhouse and reappeared with a hand-drawn map and a thick rope with which he intended to lasso the naughty pig. He ventured into the forest alone, leaving Vaughan, Verity and Caroline behind, feeling very put out. Just because they were children they didn't see why they should be left out - after all, they could probably run faster than Farmer Lambrick any day.

After a short while and the children had just about stopped sulking, they heard rustling and Farmer Lambrick reappeared with Rasher securely held by the thick rope which was wrapped around his neck like an impromptu dog collar and lead. Relieved to see them both back, the children rushed to greet him and fuss Rasher.

"You naughty little pig" said Verity, rubbing Rasher's back, "you scared us running off like that."

"Don't do that again or it'll be the stew pot for you" teased Caroline.

"Thanks fer waitin', you three. But he'll be alroight now. Yer'd better get yerselves off before the teachers start lookin' for yer and find Rasher." Slightly surprised at being dismissed so, the children reluctantly returned to the school.

"What's the matter with him today?" asked Caroline, "He seems a bit grumpy."

"No idea" shrugged Vaughan, "probably just shocked Rasher ran off. Anyway, let's go back and see what's for lunch - I'm starving!"

Chapter 27

Bonfire Night

As Autumn settled in across the land and the weather grew gradually colder, the children practised making Autumnal-themed foods and sweets; Dr Bakewell was a keen believer of teaching according to the season and felt the children worked better that way.

It certainly seemed true to Vaughan; he had heard children talk about 'Orange October' and wondered what it meant. Now he realised - almost everything they ate or worked with was one shade of orange, red or brown. Of course, the St Swithuns' said this was their month because orange and brown were their House colours, but everyone knew this was rubbish - St Swithun's feast day was the fifteenth of July!

Vaughan, Verity and Caroline had great fun during October, preparing for Hallowe'en and baking with the food harvested from Cuthbert's prized gardens and Farmer Lambrick's vegetable patches. They made pumpkin cheesecake, butternut squash samosas, meringue toadstools, 'rotting' apples, eyeball jelly, pumpkin pie, orange muffins, carrot cake, bat biscuits, zombie zinger sweets and iced mummies to name but a few. They were kept warm by Mr Rose's hearty meals; beef stews, vegetable soups, chicken casseroles, lamb hotpots, sausage and mash, pork casseroles, pasta bakes and hot fresh bread rolls were the order of the month, boosted by stodgy puddings such as sticky toffee pudding, chocolate fudge cake, treacle sponges and bakewell tart - all with lashings of cream custard and consequently the children looked forward to their warming dinners every night.

Once Hallowe'en had passed, they wondered what they would do next, for Christmas seemed such a long way away. Over the next few days, the children watched Farmer Lambrick collecting wood and storing it up outside his farmhouse, curious as to what he was doing. But they had forgotten Bonfire Night was only five days away. Dr Bakewell may have been old-fashioned but he did encourage such celebrations - especially when it gave rise to creating new confectionery suitable for such traditions.

During morning break on the first of November, the children were very excited to see a large bowl labelled 'Popping Candy' on the snack table. Caroline was just about to grab a handful when Mr Soames took hold of her arm and stopped her. "Sorry Caroline, that's not for snacks."

"But it's on the table" protested Caroline, "it must be. Oh go on, can I have some? Please?"

"I just put it down for a second to tie my shoe" the butler explained, "I have to take it to Professor Drumgoole. Sorry" and picking the bowl back up he strode out of the Refectory and the door swung shut behind him. Sulking, Caroline scuffed her way back to Verity and Vaughan, telling them how mean Mr Soames was not to let her have any.

"But we've got chocolatiering next anyway" said Vaughan as the three of them made their way back to the snack table. "Maybe it's for use in class."

"We've never used it before in class. We've never had it before" she continued, sulkily as she picked up a bowl of apricots.

"That doesn't mean we're never going to use it, though. Maybe Vaughan's right?" suggested Verity sensibly, pouring herself a glass of fruit juice. They made their way back to the table to finish their snacks before the bell rang again, signalling it was time to make their way to the next lesson.

In Professor Drumgoole's class Caroline was surprised, excited and annoyed to see the very same bowl of popping candy right in the middle of the long table. She was surprised and excited because she really wanted to try some but realising Vaughan and Verity had both been right earlier, she was annoyed about that and annoyed with herself for being so sulky. However, the lure of the popping candy soon sweetened her mood and got rid of her annoyance!

Also on the table were bowls of white, milk and dark chocolate, bowls of mini marshmallows, slabs of nougat, sausages of marzipan, digestive biscuits and ginger nut biscuits. Professor Drumgoole explained that they were to create their very own 'Bonfire Night Delicacy' in class using any or all of the ingredients on the table. More excited than ever before, the children washed their hands, put on their aprons and hats and began experimenting.

Laughter and fun filled the classroom. Verity crushed up some biscuits, mixed in the popping candy and coated it all with milk chocolate to stick it together, making what she called 'Biscuit Bonfires'. Vaughan coated marshmallows in white chocolate, rolled them in the popping candy and then re-coated them again - this time in dark chocolate - to make 'Marshmallow Volcanos' and Caroline used everything - she stirred marshmallows, biscuits, popping candy, nougat, marzipan, all fused together with melted chocolate and rolled into large balls, creating 'Exploding Gobstoppers'. Then came the time for the test - eating them.

The rest of the class had been equally imaginative with their creations and their names: Emi created 'Guy Fawkes Fizzlesticks', Orla made 'Skyrockets' and there was also Choco-lite, Catherine Wheels and Traffic Lights to name but a few. Professor Drumgoole was very impressed with the class and allowed them to try three sweets only, as the rest would be saved for Bonfire Night itself. As they taste tested their creations, they were even better than they had hoped. The chocolate melted deliciously in their mouths exposing the popping candy, which then started to fizz and explode on their tongues, like little fireworks bursting into life in their mouths and crackling in their ears. Then, when the explosions fizzled out, they were left to crunch the biscuit or chew the marshmallows. They had so much fun, the lesson seemed to go by incredibly quickly and they were all disappointed when Professor Drumgoole told them it was time to clean up and write down their recipes.

* * *

Bonfire Night itself came around very quickly. On Saturday the fifth of November, Vaughan, Verity and Caroline were visiting Farmer Lambrick as usual and were surprised to see him lugging old branches and twigs and broken furniture across the fields. Hurrying across the damp, leaf-strewn fields, they called out to him.

"Lambrick!" Vaughan called first, his breath a visible fog in the cold November air. "What are you doing?" Farmer Lambrick looked up, rather red-faced and a little out of breath.

"Oh, mornin' you three" he replied, straightening his back and puffing heavily. "'fraid Oi 'aven't got much time ter stop this mornin', got ter get the bonfire built up ready fer tonoight."

"Why have you left it til last minute?" asked Caroline, concerned. "You could have built this days ago, bit by bit. Would have been easier for you."

"Arr, Oi could 'ave" agreed Farmer Lambrick, "but what do yer think a bonfire full o' leaves an' twigs looks loike to a little animal - say, loike a hedgehog?"

"Erm...probably like a den" suggested Verity.

"I bet it looks warm and cosy - like a little home!" added Caroline, excitedly.

"Or a safe place to hide or sleep?" offered Vaughan, shrugging.

"Exactly! At this toime o' year all sorts o' little critters are lookin' fer somewhere to 'ibernate. And a lovely big pile o' wood and leaves would look very appealin' indeed. Last thing we want is some poor animal ter crawl in 'ere at noight, settle down and go into 'ibernation. No, yer should only build a bonfire on the day it's goin' ter be lit, otherwoise you'll end up wi' roasted hedgehogs or mice and all sorts, and we can't 'ave that." The children considered this and decided he had a good point. But the poor farmer looked exhausted lugging all that wood about.

"Course not!" exclaimed Verity, "that'd be horrific. But you do look tired - how about we help you build it?" she looked at Caroline and Vaughan who nodded their agreement. "Yeah, course we'll help" they agreed. So the four of them spent the next half an hour raking up the fallen dry leaves and dragging broken bits of furniture, fallen tree branches, rotten birdhouses - as much wood as they could find - across the muddy grass into a growing pile in the field, inside the circle which Farmer Lambrick had marked out with pebbles. Working so hard, they soon found themselves getting so hot they had to take off their winter coats and hats they were getting so sweaty! The pile of wood soon grew taller than the children and they finished by throwing wooden sticks as high as they could, to reach the top. When they had finished and all the wood had been used, they stepped back to admire their handiwork; the children craned their necks up to view the tall, triangular bonfire which stood before them, almost ten feet tall.

"Crackin' job, thanks you three" said Farmer Lambrick gratefully, "Oi was startin' to get a bit achy doin' all that on moy own. Yer've saved me quoite a bit of toime - ready fer that cup o' tea now?" The children grinned and nodded - their hands and noses were starting to grow cold again now they'd finished all that hard, physical work - and were quickly putting their coats back on.

"Ooh yes please" answered Caroline, as she wrapped her scarf around her neck and slung the tassle end over her shoulder, "got any chocolate biscuits today?"

* * *

As evening drew closer and the nights got darker, the children wrapped up warmly to go out and celebrate bonfire night. This night was the only time of year they didn't eat dinner in the

Refectory - instead, they ate outside, so Vaughan had been told. He was quite curious to see how this would be done, where would the chairs be? Would they have to sit on the damp and muddy ground? He was very intrigued which only added to his excitement.

The pupils gathered in the grand hallway and waited for the wooden spoon on the Time-Keepers Clock to slide into the seven o'clock wedge - dinner time. As soon as it signalled seven o'clock and the school bell finished pealing, they raced through the corridors and out into the frosty night air, stumbling over the wet, uneven grass of the fields as they rushed towards Farmer Lambrick's. As they approached, the smells of hot food wafting through the air tickled Vaughan's nostrils and made him feel incredibly hungry. As they neared the bonfire, he realised the tables that had been used for the Summer Fete were being put to use again, but this time they had been laden with steaming hot food. He looked and Caroline and Verity who grinned back at him.

"Isn't this great?" beamed Verity, "just take what you want when you want." He looked at the tables before him, wondering what to eat. There were platters of sausages, chicken legs, bread buns, jacket potatoes, baked sweet potatoes and spare ribs. There were cauldrons of chilli, grey peas, boston beans, pumpkin soup, baked beans and trays of toffee apples - it was both simple yet full of choice at the same time. And best of all, the chocolate bonfire nibbles they'd made earlier were also on the table, along with others he presumed must have been made by the other classes and a tray of cupcakes with long stick stuck in each cake. He grabbed a paper plate and piled on some sausages, spare ribs and bread. Caroline helped herself to a sweet potato and some spare ribs, while Verity chose a bowl of boston baked beans. When all three of them had taken some food they hovered around the bonfire waiting for Farmer Lambrick to light it. When almost all the children were there, Farmer Lambrick appeared, grinning, and started the countdown.

"You ready, kids?"

"READY!" they chorused, then joined in the countdown.

"Ten....nine....eight....seven....six....five.....four.....three....two.. ...one....Hooray!" Farmer Lambrick lit the bonfire and everyone cheered as they watched the firewood glow first red then orange, before coming to life with crackles and sparks. Finally the fire took hold, providing a welcome warmth to the cold children as they chatted and tucked into their hot buffet. They 'oohed' as they watched the flames lick the branches and the sparks jump higher, the flames leaping and dancing into the sky, crackling loudly as the wood split in the heat. Once the fire became a huge pyramid of orange, living heat, Farmer Lambrick made his way to the food tables. Calling for attention he made one more announcement.

"And now, toime fer dessert!" he called, as he lit a match and one by one lit the tall sticks which were protruding from the cupcakes. The sticks instantly sprang to life, sparks flying from them in all directions, making their way down the stick to the icing. "Sparklers" Verity whispered to Vaughan, as they watched, mesmerised. Once the sparklers had gone out, the children were allowed to take the cakes.

At half past seven Professor Drumgoole appeared through the smoke, carrying a large crate. He stopped just before the bonfire and the crowd of chattering children, in an empty part of the field. He took out several fireworks and placed them in rows, digging them into the ground. Once he had stuck all the fireworks firmly into the field, Vaughan and the girls watched as he got out a long length of tape and wrapped it around all the fireworks, going from one to the other until they were all attached to this thread. Once he finished, he made his way to the bonfire and made an announcement.

"Children, are you all enjoying the bonfire so far?"

"Yes sir!" loud and enthusiastic replies echoed around, with smiles alight as the flames reflected in the eyes of the children.

"So are you all ready for the fireworks now then?" Gasps and 'oh yeah', 'fireworks!' confirmed the children were indeed looking forward to the display. "Okay, you all stay here and get ready then. Here we go!"

Professor Drumgoole returned to the fireworks and lit the fuse of the first one - a rocket. As the flame crept towards the rocket, Vaughan saw the light also trickle along the thread that ran through each firework and realised the Professor had made a fuse to light them all, one after the other. Having lit the first rocket Professor Drumgoole returned to the children and stood with them, faces skywards as they 'ooh-ed' and 'ahh-ed' as the fuse reached the firework and the rocket climbed higher and higher, whistling loudly, before bursting into a bright red explosion of sparkles which floated gently back down to the ground, just as the second rocket whizzed its way noisily up into the air.

As Vaughan and the girls watched the fireworks, Verity thought she heard a strange noise. Nudging Caroline, she asked if she'd heard it too.

"It'll be the fireworks" Caroline said dismissively.

"It's not that kind of noise." Verity insisted, "Where's Farmer Lambrick?" Looking quickly around them, the girls realised Farmer Lambrick was nowhere to be seen. This was odd, as they knew he was looking forward to the bonfire.

"Have you seen Farmer Lambrick?" Caroline asked Vaughan irritably, annoyed at being distracted from the fireworks. She loved bonfire night and thought Verity was being a bit of a worry-wart.

"What? No" said Vaughan half-heartedly, as he watched a cocktail of multi-coloured fireworks screaming and fanning across the sky. Caroline turned back to Verity.

"We don't know where he is" she shrugged, unconcerned. "Probably indoors - he was quite tired after building the bonfire, remember." Not content, Verity persisted. "I'm going to find him. I heard something. He might have fallen down and no-one's going to know with all the noise."

Reluctantly, Caroline agreed. "Okay, okay - we'd best let Vaughan know where we're going." Caroline nudged Vaughan and cupping her hand between her mouth and his ear, to shield her voice against the cacophony of noise surrounding them, she told him Verity was worried because Farmer Lambrick was nowhere to be seen and in between the explosions of fireworks, she'd said she'd heard strange noises coming from the direction of the farmhouse.

"I'm coming too" said Vaughan immediately and the three of them abandoned the fireworks display to go and check on Farmer Lambrick.

* * *

The nearer they got, the louder and more frequent the noises became. They heard bumping, things being knocked over and finally they heard Farmer Lambrick's voice shouting over the noise. "No! Calm down! It's okay, it's alroight! Sshhhhh....Sshhhhh! Come 'ere! No!" Worried, the children ran around to the back of Farmer Lambrick's house and realised with horror what was happening.

Rasher was running wildly about in the pigsty - Farmer Lambrick was in the middle of the sty having fallen down and was having great difficulty getting up. Every time he managed to get to his knees, he would either slip over again in the quagmire of the sty or be quickly knocked off balance as Rasher kicked and butted furiously like a rodeo bull. "He's gone mad!" wailed Caroline, agog.

"It's the foireworks" spluttered Farmer Lambrick, "RASHER - CALM DOWN....they've sent 'im haywire. They're scarin' 'im. RASHER!" Scared, the children could see Rasher was in great distress, running in circles, but they were also worried about Farmer Lambrick. Rashers trotters could cause him serious harm and he either kept slipping or Rasher kept bumping into him every time he tried to get to his feet. "CRAWL TO THE WALL" Vaughan shouted, as the Farmer, who was coated from head to toe in mud, dodged the stampeding, snorting pig. Lambrick just about managed to crawl - still slipping - on all fours, out of the path of the deranged Rasher, to where the children were stood on the other side of the stone wall. Vaughan and Verity leaned over the sty wall to grab Farmer Lambrick's arms; he raised his hands and between them, the children pulling with all their strength and the farmer managing to regain his balance, he finally got to his feet.

"Look at you!" said Verity, "you're filthy!"

"Never mind him - look at Rasher!" shouted Caroline "He's going to try and charge the fence down!" The four of them watched as Rasher charged headlong down the sty towards the fence. "RASHER!" yelled Farmer Lambrick, "NO! He's going to knock himself out, I've strengthened the fence - he can't...." But he was stopped mid-sentence by Rasher. Rasher had no intention of trying to smash through the fence - he'd done that once before and watched as Farmer Lambrick repaired it with thicker branches. No, pigs are intelligent animals, Rasher was no fool. He wouldn't smash through the fence, he'd....

"LOOK AT THAT!" squealed Verity, "HE'S JUMPED THE FENCE!" for Rasher had indeed leapt with all his might and cleanly jumped the uneven tree-trunk fence, his curly pink tail bobbing frantically as he charged into the safety of the Forest of Forgetfulness and disappeared into the eerie darkness.

"It's moy fault!" Farmer Lambrick sobbed helplessly, "Oi fergot animals get scared boy foireworks! Oi've lost 'im and it's all moy fault!"

"No, it isn't" said Verity sternly, surprising both Caroline and Vaughan. "You saved that pig's life, my Dad told me. You rescued him once, you can rescue him again. Now, do you or do you not know your way around the forest?"

"Roughly, yes. More than anyone else, at least" nodded Farmer Lambrick. "Right then" said Verity. "You'll need torches, do you have any?"

Buoyed by Verity's calm attitude, Farmer Lambrick soon calmed down and returned to his senses. "Oi do" he confirmed, standing up tall and looking as though he was about to do something extremely important. "And Oi'm okay now, thank you Verity. Sorry about that - think Oi was just shocked. Oi know what Oi'll do."

"And what's that?" asked Caroline "How are you going to get him back?"

"Oi'm goin' to walk into the forest, foind moy pig and bring 'im 'ome."

Chapter 28

Mission: Rescue Rasher

"What? You can't!" said Vaughan, "the forest's too big. You'll get lost too."

Farmer Lambrick smiled his slow, lop-sided smile at Vaughan. "Nah, Oi know what Oi'm doin'" he said. "Come on - Oi'll show yer." Removing the muddy, leaf-encrusted wellies at the door, he led the children into the farmhouse and into the living-room they usually sat in, when they had their weekend visits. He lifted the lid of the old antique trunk that Vaughan pretended was a pirate treasure chest, its rusty hinges creaking as they flexed open. Inside was an unusual assortment of ropes, metal clips, luminous tape, harnesses and torches.

"This 'ere's moy emergency trunk. Now then, let's see..." he muttered as he rummaged around and rifled through its contents. Vaughan, Verity and Caroline looked quizzically at one another and shrugged, not understanding what Farmer Lambrick was doing.

" 'Ere she is" he finally said, lifting a large coil of thin red rope. It looked brand new compared to the other dull, rough looking ropes. It was almost shiny. Placing the red rope on the floor at Caroline's feet he delved back into the emergency trunk and pulled out a black harness. As he stepped into the harness and pulled it up around his middle, he explained.

"Oi'll tie meself off to moy fence" he began "and as Oi walk through the forest Oi'll circle a tree every few metres to keep the rope noice and toight and straight. Then, when Oi want to come back Oi turn around and follows the rope back again." His explanation made sense but seeing Farmer Lambrick all geared up in ropes and a harness made them feel quite anxious.

"But alone you can only go down one path at a time" Vaughan piped up. "If you can do it using ropes, we can all do it using ropes. There's enough there for us to have a rope each, then between us we can go down four paths at a time and have a better chance of finding Rasher."

Verity's eyes widened in surprise and she tried to discreetly shake her head at Vaughan, hoping Farmer Lambrick wouldn't notice.

"Thank you fer yer offer Vaughan, but no. Yer need t' know what yer doin' in there. It's much too risky fer three young children ter venture in, let alone on their own and in different doirections. Think about it - what would yer do if a rope got snagged on somethin' sharp and snapped? Then we'd have you to find as well as Rasher. No, yer best off stayin' 'ere."

"Has a rope ever snapped?" Vaughan was not to be put off easily.

"Well....no."

"Look, we're wasting time. You choose the ropes, you fasten them to us and we'll only walk in a straight line. As soon as we reach the end of the rope, we'll turn around and come back."

"And what do yer intend to do if yer actually foind Rasher?" asked Farmer Lambrick. 'Ah' thought Vaughan. He hadn't got that far in his plan of action.

"Whistles!" shouted Caroline eagerly as Verity turned to her friend in amazement. "If you have whistles, we'll each take one. Whoever sees Rasher blows three times loudly on their whistle! It's what policemen in olden days used to do, to attract attention!"

"Ye're roight there, gal" agreed Farmer Lambrick. "Alroight then, let's get yer harnessed up but yer must promise ter keep yer ropes toight, yer torches on and walk straight ahead only. It's bad enough losin' a pig - if Oi lost a child Oi might lose moy 'ead too" he sighed, with a sad smile. They nodded their agreement as Farmer Lambrick threw a harness and torch to each of them; Vaughan grabbed his and smiled gratefully at Caroline, who was now rather excited by the idea of this rescue mission, as she clutched her harness and grinned back.

As Farmer Lambrick clipped ropes to their waists, Vaughan looked up and smiled at Verity. Unlike Caroline, Verity didn't smile back. In fact, she looked pale and rather uncomfortable with the quest Vaughan had volunteered them for. She hadn't bargained on venturing into the forest themselves - especially at night.

"Now - only go straight, moind" Farmer Lambrick reminded them. "Keep lookin' over yer shoulder ter make sure yer rope's in a straight loine and every so often walk all the way 'round a strong tree, to keep the rope toight. Roight, well then, that us all set." he confirmed as he tugged at everyone's harnesses one last time to check they were secure.

Walking out to the sty and standing between the fence and the edge of the forest, Farmer Lambrick stood each child against a tree and placing his hands on their shoulders, he positioned them exactly in the direction they were to walk. Vaughan stood to the left, then Farmer Lambrick, then Verity on Farmer Lambrick's right and Caroline on Verity's right; in that formation they fanned out through the forest and began to walk.

"Don't forget to circle yer ropes around the trees."
It was the last thing Vaughan remembered hearing as he ventured further into the eerie beauty of the Forest of Forgetfulness, the trunks of the trees soon hiding any view of the farmhouse behind him. As darkness encompassed him and silence descended, the wall of trees and canopy of branches blocking out the sound of the bonfire celebrations just a few minutes walk away, he suddenly felt completely alone. And rather frightened.

Chapter 29

Find of the Century

It was Verity that found him. Head down, snout grubbing through the damp leaves and soft ground, snuffling and snorting as he flicked his head up every now and then. She froze for a moment, suddenly fearing that the whistle might scare him away - or worse, he might charge at her. But Farmer Lambrick had said that that was what they should do, so, she took a deep breath, put the whistle to her lips and -

'PSWHEEP, PSWHEEP, PSWHEEP' She blew three times and a piercing, shrill sound echoed throughout the trees, scaring the birds who squawked and flapped their wings as they swiftly took flight, branches rustling and leaves falling as they escaped the ear-splitting whistle. Hundreds of birds rose into the air all at once, their small dark forms invisible against the inky black sky, but the noise of the flapping of hundreds of wings and the flow of air they generated blew gently against the leaves on the trees, creating a spooky, scary atmosphere around Verity. She wanted to turn around and run away, out of the forest, out of the darkness, back to the safety of the farmhouse, to the light and warmth of the bonfire, to her friends. But she didn't. She didn't move anywhere. She stood frozen to the spot, staring at Rasher. Rasher didn't move anywhere either. He just carried on ferreting around the tree roots, flicking up balls of mud with his muddy snout and chomping them down, oblivious to Verity and the shrill piercing of her whistle.

"Hold on!" Farmer Lambrick's voice spoke from somewhere in the distance. Aware that if Rasher did run before Farmer Lambrick arrived they might lose him for good, Verity leant forwards, arm outstretched, but she didn't have enough rope left; as she strained to reach the pig, the rope around her middle dug uncomfortably into her stomach making it difficult to breathe, so she had to stop reaching and stood up straight. 'What to do, what to do?' she thought as she looked around, racking her brains for ideas.

"Rasher" she called softly, "oh Raaa-sherrrr". Rasher raised his head, tilted it to the left and looked straight at Verity. She couldn't believe it! "Ra-sher" she called again, putting out her hand again, hoping he would come to her, but he lowered his head and plodded on to another tree close by, where he pawed the ground with his trotter and again began furrowing the roots with his snout.

Farmer Lambrick could be heard making his way through the forest but he still wasn't in sight yet. 'What am I going to do?' Verity thought as she flopped down on the ground.

"OW!" she exclaimed, jumping up and rubbing her bottom - she'd sat down on a stone. Swiping her foot back and forth through the leaves on the forest floor to kick it away, she shone the torch on the ground but noticed that where she'd just cleared away the leaves, there were no stones or rocks where she'd sat down. Just a flat, muddy, forest floor. What had she sat on, she wondered? Putting her hands on her bottom she felt it again. Whatever it was, was in her coat pocket - the harness she was wearing had rucked up her coat around her back and top of her legs. She fiddled with her coat pockets and lifted out the offending object - it was an apple! She looked at it wondering where on earth it could have come from - then she remembered. Windfall harvesting in Professor Peach's lesson. Vaughan or Caroline must have put it in her pocket when they were messing about. What luck she hadn't noticed and taken it out before!

Holding it in her outstretched hand, again she softly called Rasher's name. Again, Rasher raised his head and looked at Verity - and spotted the delicious looking apple sitting there temptingly in the palm of her hand - yellowy-green, large and juicy looking. He sniffed the air and turned a little, facing Verity. He trotted nearer and stretching out her arm as far as she possibly could, balancing the soft apple in her fingertips, Verity held her breath as Rasher took a cautious bite, froth building at the corners of his mouth as the sharp tang of the fruit excited his taste buds, apple juice dribbling down his face as he tucked in. Then -

WHAM! Farmer Lambrick appeared through the trees and pounced on Rasher who squealed in shock; Verity jumped back in surprise and the half-eaten apple dropped to the floor. Swiftly coiling a small rope around Rasher's neck to create a makeshift collar, Farmer Lambrick took control of the situation and Verity began to breathe again.

"Well done Verity" he congratulated her "excellent idea ter coax him with an apple. Best get 'im 'ome now - look at the state of 'im" he said tenderly, looking at the mud which was almost completely covering Rasher's face.

"I'm surprised he wanted it, given all the mud he's eaten" said Verity, shining her torch at the base of the tree where Rasher had been busy foraging. "Look at all that mess and piles of mud he dug up. He ate most of it too, the greedy pig, that's only the bits that he left."

Puzzled, Farmer Lambrick went and looked at the ground where Verity was pointing. Rasher ate almost anything but it was always food - he'd never known him eat mud or earth before. Farmer Lambrick lifted up the balls of mud that Verity's torch was shining on, twizzled them around in his fingers and looked closely at them before sniffing them. Verity thought this was most odd and feeling embarrassed looked around at anything but Farmer Lambrick.

"This isn't mud" he suddenly said, with a strange expression on his face. "Roight...erm...do you 'ave an 'andkerchief?" he asked Verity quickly, as he felt his pockets to see if he had any himself.

"Er...no..." Verity replied, wondering why he wanted a handkerchief when he didn't have a cold or a runny nose.

"Vaughan! Caroline!" he yelled into the forest "can you 'ear me?"

"Yeah! ouch"

"Yes, Farmer"

Two voices shouted back.

"Do either of you 'ave an 'andkerchief?"

"No"

"Yep, I do!" Vaughan had one.

"Stay there, Oi'm coming to get yer. Yer'll never believe this!"

Completely bewildered, Verity took hold of Rasher's rope-lead as Farmer Lambrick handed it to her.

"Keep 'old of him, Verity" he said firmly "he's a little treasure!" Then he disappeared back through the trees, the way he had come through earlier.

About ten minutes later he reappeared with Caroline and Vaughan alongside him. The three friends stood together with Rasher and watched Farmer Lambrick wrap three lumps of mud in Vaughan's handkerchief, with the greatest of care. Looking from one to another, all three of them shrugged, indicating that not one of them knew why he was doing this and privately thought he had lost the plot.

Popping the handkerchief safely in the pocket of his waistcoat, Farmer Lambrick took hold of Rasher and together the four of them traced Verity's rope back out of the forest and after tying Rasher's rope safely to a post in his sty, they went back into the farmhouse.

"Farmer, I think we'd better be getting back now" Verity said, aware that time was getting on and the bonfire was almost at an end.

"ooh yes, Oi'll come with yer. Don't suppose yer know where Dr Bakewell will be 'bout now, do yer?" asked Farmer Lambrick.

"Dr Bakewell?" asked Caroline. She looked up at the grandmother clock hanging on the wall - it was a quarter to nine. By nine o'clock they would be expected to be in bed. Oh heck, she thought, we're going to be late - we'll be in trouble again!

"I suppose he'll be in his office, we're supposed to be in bed by nine so I don't really know."

"Roight then, we'll have ter hurry. Come on" he ushered them out of the house and they scurried across the fields as quickly as they could, hoping to catch Dr Bakewell before the clock struck nine.

Chapter 30

Dr Bakewell's Treasure

They just made it in time. The small spoon on the Timekeepers Clock hadn't yet swung into Bedtime Hour.

"Roight then" Farmer Lambrick said quickly, head and eyes darting about all over the grand hallway, "which way?"

"Which way?" repeated Vaughan, "Which way - what? Dr Bakewell's office?"

"Yes of course 'is office" he replied hurriedly, "where is it?"

"Oh - I, er, I don't know" Vaughan told him.

"Oi don't expect you to know Vaughan - girls, which way?"

"But we don't know either" said Caroline, slightly offended, "we've never been there. Pupils don't, usually, unless your in big trouble. Haven't you been before?"

"No - Farmer's don't, usually" snapped Farmer Lambrick, clearly a little frustrated. Tensions were starting to run high although the children still had no idea why. Then a thought struck Vaughan.

"Find Hilda" he blurted out. Caroline and Verity stared at him with confusion and mouthed 'who?'

"Hilda - Mrs Hilderstone"

"Oh!"

"She'll know. Or Professor Drumgoole. Come on!" urged Vaughan, now caught up in the urgency of the moment.

They quickly scoured the area but Professor Drumgoole was nowhere to be found. Then, with just minutes to spare, Mrs Hilderstone appeared from the picture-lined corridor, dusting the floor with her long black skirt as she glided into view.

"Mrs Hilderstone, Mrs Hilderstone!" the children chorused breathlessly as they rushed to her. "Can you tell us where Dr Bakewell's office is please? We need to see him urgently."

"Goodness me, slow down!" said Mrs Hilderstone wispily. "I'm afraid you'll get lost trying to find it all by yourselves. If it's urgent, I'll take you myself" she offered kindly. Smiling, she held up her ginormous keyring showing off all her keys. "I know a shortcut!" she added cheekily, with a twinkle in her eye.

Swiftly the four of them followed her down the picture-lined corridor until they came to the Sun Room. Raising her bunch of keys which clanged noisily, she rummaged through each one before selecting the one with a sun shaped handle. Turning the key in the lock she opened the door to the dark, unoccupied Sun Room. It looked very spooky at night time; the large sun-shaped mirror over the fireplace reflected the moonlight and the moonlit shadows of the plants against the walls managed to completely change the formerly bright, sunny, cheerful room into a very gloomy, ghostly room. The children were very glad Mrs Hilderstone was there to lead them through the eerie room, their eyes fixed firmly to their Housekeeper so as not to let the shadows play tricks on their minds.

"This is the shortcut to the Teacher's Wing" Mrs Hilderstone explained, "and this - " she stopped outside an ordinary looking wooden door "is Dr Bakewell's office. Good luck." She smiled at them as she rapped the door three times with her wizened knuckles, before turning around and gliding away, like a ghost into the eerie darkness, blending into the shadows and disappearing from sight.

"Come in" boomed a formidable voice from behind the door. Farmer Lambrick stood in front of the door, ordered the children to follow behind him, took a deep breath, twisted the brass door knob and opened the door.

* * *

Dr Bakewell's office was like no other office Vaughan had ever seen before - he very much doubted any other Headmaster's Office would look or smell like this one.

If he had been asked to describe it in only one word, he would have been hard pressed to choose between 'gold' or 'shiny'. As they entered the most hallowed of offices the first thing they saw was a large, wooden trophy cabinet, full of trophies of gold, silver and bronze and wooden shields, both large and small. Each shelf was brimming with awards, there was hardy any room left for any more to fit.

The floors were as all the others - polished, shiny, wooden floorboards. The walls were a delicious caramel and cream colour; caramel on the bottom half and cream on the top with thin wooden rail separating the two. At first glance it reminded Vaughan of a toffee sundae and he strangely wondered if the wall would taste of toffee or caramel, if he licked it. Framed certificates decorated the walls, an indication to visitors of Dr Bakewell's skill and experience.

As they stepped over the threshold into the office itself and closed the door behind them, they felt their bodies tingle; it was as if something magical happened just stepping foot inside Dr Bakewell's personal office. Children hardly ever entered this room. As their eyes scanned the office, marvelling at all they could see, they noticed an old, thin, wooden table pushed against the wall on the left, earlier hidden from view by the open door. This long table was laden with culinary gadgets and Vaughan found it incredibly hard not to wander over and mess with them they were so tempting, sitting there all shiny and clean - Dr Bakewell's own personal tools - desperate to be used, to be touched, to pass on a glimpse of the magic and wonder of Dr Bakewell's confectionery.

There was an old-fashioned weighing scale, with a large gold dish and black lead weights; an array of wooden spoons of all different sizes; honey stirrers which Vaughan recognised from when his Dad had brought some home from work; copper icing syringes;

squares of shiny gold paper; an enormous red leather-bound book which was currently closed but almost called out to be opened and read, to bare its soul to the eyes of its reader and pour it's contents into the reader's hearts and minds, giving itself immortality.

Above this chemistry table of cookware were two rows of long, thin shelves which ran the whole length of the table, one above the other. These narrow shelves contained cream square jars which upon closer inspection by Vaughan (which took the form of him craning his neck towards them and squinting), contained herbs and spices. The top shelf appeared to contain the herbs (Vaughan managed to read the labels of the Parsley, Sage and Lavender jars) while the bottom shelf contained the spices. Vaughan discreetly took a couple of steps towards the table and began to read the spice jars: Saffron - Nutmeg - Cinnamon - Cardamon - then -

"Yes?"

A deep, throaty voice cut through his inquisitive snooping and brought him back with a jolt. He suddenly remembered that he was standing in Dr Bakewell's office - the Dr Bakewell's office! Quickly swivelling around, he saw Dr Bakewell, sitting behind an old oak desk with a curious expression on his face. Farmer Lambrick, standing right in front of the desk, quickly removed his flat cap and twizzled it around nervously in his hands as he spoke.

"Dr Bakewell, sir" he began, with a slight nod to the Headmaster, "we've found - the children and Oi - or rather, Rasher an' Oi..." Dr Bakewell stared at him as the stammering Farmer couldn't get his words out quick enough. "Look" he decided to show the Headmaster their find instead.

Placing his shabby grandad-cap on the corner of Dr Bakewell's desk - causing the sour Headmaster to huff and roll his eyes in displeasure - Farmer Lambrick reached into his waistcoat pocket and gently took hold of the ball of mud he'd so carefully carried all the way from the forest and held it out in the palm of his hand.

"What is this?" asked Dr Bakewell, clearly unimpressed and bewildered by the Farmer's nervous excitement.

"Oi can't say fer sure, Doc" (again, Dr Bakewell took another sharp intake of breath and fidgeted uncomfortably in his chair at being referred to as 'Doc') "but Oi think this moight be one o' them natural truffles" and he ever-so-gently unwrapped the folds of the handkerchief to reveal the little ball of soft brown mud that sat within.

Clearly this meant something to Dr Bakewell - at the mention of the word 'truffle' his head lifted up and he leant forward to get a better look.

He took off his round tortoise-shell glasses swapping them for a pair of gold-rimmed, half-moon spectacles which he balanced expertly on the end of his bulbous nose. He reached out his hand and with the lightest of touches, took hold of the mud-ball himself.

Standing safely behind Farmer Lambrick, Vaughan, Verity and Caroline looked silently from Dr Bakewell to each other, each of them asking the same, unspoken question through their eyes - what on earth was going on? Peering around the Farmer, they watched with great curiosity as Dr Bakewell first rolled the ball in his fingers, then lifted it to the light glaring down from the small chandelier, sniffed it, tapped it and finally put it to his ear and shook it.

"Just a moment" he said curtly, looking at no-one in particular as he placed the ball back onto the handkerchief on his desk. He stepped from behind the desk and opened a door in the wall by the trophy cabinet, which Vaughan hadn't noticed before, he was too busy inspecting the spice jars. Opening the door, Dr Bakewell leaned into the gap and shouted.

"Derek! Come in here a moment, please" then he took back his seat behind the desk, staring at his four visitors as he rubbed his moustache thoughtfully with his fingers and waited for Professor Drumgoole.

Moments later, the Professor appeared through the door, slightly out of breath.

"Yes, George.....Doctor?" he added, as he noticed the presence of Vaughan, Verity and Caroline. Not doing the Professor the same courtesy of using his professional title in front of students, Dr Bakewell explained.

"Derek - what do you make of this?" he asked, handing the puzzled Professor the handkerchief containing the ball of mud before returning to his desk to await the Professor's opinion. Delicately holding the small package in his fingers, Professor Drumgoole inspected it closely. He too sniffed it, weighed it in his palm and also held it up to the light, as if he expected it to suddenly become see-through. He placed it in the palm of his left hand whilst his right hand rolled it back and forth, from wrist to fingertip. Then, with hands that were now quite dirty, he put the ball underneath his nose - so close that it almost touched his nostrils - closed his eyes and sniffed as he ever-so-gently squeezed the mud between his fingertips and quietly gasped. Vaughan and the girls couldn't take their eyes off him, he was fascinating. They hadn't a clue what he was doing but it looked intense and they were mesmerised. Professor Drumgoole then opened his eyes, raised his head to look Dr Bakewell in the eye as a huge smile spread across his sharp-featured face.

Chapter 31

School Saviours

"I do believe we have ourselves..." Professor Drumgoole began, carefully chipping off pieces of hardened mud from the ball with his fingernails until a small, brown sphere remained in his palm, sitting amongst the debris, "...a one hundred percent genuine, natural chocolate truffle!"

"Good gommins!" exclaimed Dr Bakewell, who, having watched Professor Drumgoole release the truffle from its protective mud shell, was now standing on his feet and leaning forward over his desk, his stocky tweed arms slightly bent at the elbow, his hands rolled into a ball. In fact, the knuckles of his hands resting on his desk were the only thing keeping him upright and preventing him from belly-flopping onto the desk in shock. He stretched out the palm of his right hand, into which Professor Drumgoole placed the truffle and he too stared open-mouthed at this cherry-sized, powdery brown orb.

"Where did you get this?" Professor Drumgoole enquired of the children as Dr Bakewell flopped back into padded leather his chair, twirling and smelling his new-found treasure.

"In the Forest, sir" replied Farmer Lambrick. "Yer see, Rasher - moy pig - ran off and we went searching fer 'im. It was Verity 'ere that eventually found 'im." Verity stepped forwards to describe what she had seen. The fact that neither Dr Bakewell or Professor Drumgoole had made any comment at the mention of them searching the Forest of Forgetfulness told Verity that not only were they not in trouble (for which she was extremely relieved) but that this truffle was obviously so important that it didn't matter how or where it had been found.

"Well, we were all roped off to a tree at the edge of the forest, by the farm, so we could find our way back and not get lost" she started, feeling obliged to make sure Farmer Lambrick didn't get into trouble himself for letting them wander into forbidden territory. "I had almost reached the end of my rope when I heard something grunting and snorting. I stretched a bit further, shone my torch around and found Rasher prodding the ground with his trotters. Every so often he stuck his head in the ground and swung his head left to right and back again, like he was shaking the leaves about with his snout. Then after a few swishes he'd nudge his head forward and out rolled the clumps of mud. Then he'd eat them."

"How many times did you see the pig do this, Verity?" asked Dr Bakewell, gently placing the truffle safely back into the handkerchief.

"About three times then Farmer Lambrick managed to catch him."

"Do you think you could remember which path you took into the forest - or where the tree was?"

"I wouldn't be able to remember the way Sir, no" answered Verity honestly as Dr Bakewell's face fell, full of disappointment. "It all looks the same and it was dark. But my rope was one of Farmer Lambrick's new ones and I remember some of the dye rubbing off on the bark when I circled the trees, like Farmer told us to. I can show you where I started and we might be able to trace it - you know, follow the trees with red circles around them! Are we really not in trouble, then?" Conscientious as ever, she had to be certain.

"Oh my dear child, not at all!" assured Professor Drumgoole. "You have just done the school - and Dr Bakewell - an incredible favour. You may well have just saved this school from being closed down and saved all our futures with it!"

"Save the school from - being closed down? What do you mean, Sir?" asked a stunned Caroline, speaking on behalf of all three bewildered children.

"You'd better sit down" said Professor Drumgoole heavily, as he led them to a settee next to the wooden bookcase. "This may come as somewhat of a shock."

* * *

"Honeycomb Hall - or more precisely, our school - was in danger of being closed down." Gasps of surprise, 'what?' and 'no!' immediately escaped the mouths of Vaughan, Verity and Caroline. Raising his right hand to show there was more yet to say, Professor Drumgoole calmly quietened them. "We needed more children. More children to teach and more fees to maintain the school. The less children we have the less money we have to take care of all the repairs that need to be done." A lightbulb switched on in the minds of Verity and Caroline, right at that very moment. "Oh!" they whispered in unison together, "the concrete icing!" and stifled a chuckle.

"Yes" confirmed the Professor, overhearing their whisper "that was a solution Dr Bakewell made for one tiny problem. But there are more repairs yet to be done, more bills to be paid and most of all, more children to teach. What's the good of being a teacher if you have no-one to teach?"

"However" Dr Bakewell decided to join in the explanation, "I still have my standards. This school is the best in the world and the only school of its kind in England, so we had to ensure that our students are the cream of the crop. The 'best of British' so to speak. Not the richest - no, that doesn't matter at all - the most talented. That's what's important. The most creative, inspiring; with a lot of potential for us to nurture. Children with promise, that we can mould into great confectioners; children who want to learn because they have a natural gift, regardless of what their parents do or how much money they have. The best bakers of the future, that's the kind of pupil I want in my school."

"And so the idea of the fete and the competition was born" concluded Professor Drumgoole, answering the question that all three children had been pondering ever since the fete was announced - why? "We would gain more children, more people would hear of our school and want to come in the future; more children would be inspired to create their own confectionery and the money raised at the fete has been enough for us to carry out the most urgent repairs. If more children attend the school and we have fetes which excite people's interest then it would be much harder to close the school." The minds of Vaughan, Verity and Caroline were spinning fast, taking in all this information. It was an awful lot to digest in five minutes - especially for a twelve year old. It made sense, their explanation, even though it came as a huge surprise. But there was something that didn't quite fit. One thing that none of them understood. Finally Caroline voiced what all three of them were thinking.

"Sir?" she spoke directly to Professor Drumgoole, out of respect. "What did you mean when you said we had done Dr Bakewell a favour and saved the school? I don't understand." Dr Bakewell replied.

"I presume you've heard of truffles - you will have no doubt, Caroline?" Caroline nodded her head in answer. "Eaten them on special occasions, perhaps? Well, truffles are very rare items of confectionery. So rare in fact, that for years bakers and chocolatiers have been trying to copy the exact taste and texture of real, home-grown truffles. Natural truffles only grow in certain places - ancient woodland usually, but they are extremely difficult to grow - they need special soil conditions, not too dry yet not too wet. They need a certain amount of light - too dark and they rot; too light and they shrivel up. They grow underground, which not only makes them difficult to grow but incredibly difficult to find. It is usually pigs that are used to find them, as they can smell the truffle through the earth. Unfortunately, although a pig can be trained to find a truffle, the taste is too tempting for them and more often than not, once they find one they immediately eat it."

"So that's what Rasher was eating, then?!" Verity realised, "They weren't balls of mud he was eating, they were truffles!"

"Hmm...yes, I expect he was" replied Dr Bakewell seriously, as he raised his eyes and looked directly at Farmer Lambrick, who sensibly avoided his eyes and fidgeted nervously with his cap, realising that if these truffles were so rare, his pig had found them, indeed, but the rest of his find was quite possible gurgling away in his pig's stomach! Farmer Lambrick was quite glad when Vaughan diverted the Headmaster's attention from where the remaining truffles may be, with another question.

"So, the Forest of Forgetfulness - is that an ancient forest then?"

"Apparently so" answered Dr Bakewell honestly. "If it wasn't, the truffles wouldn't be able to grow. I wasn't aware of the fact but I suppose it must be."

Snatching onto this revelation, Farmer Lambrick took at chance at redeeming himself with the Doctor, who still hadn't quite forgiven him for spending half the meat budget on Rasher.

"So, if Rasher 'adn't jumped moy fence and escaped into the forest, we wouldn't 'ave known that we've been growin' truffles all this toime, would we? Maybe this was whoy Oi felt Oi was meant to save 'im. If Oi 'adn't bought Rasher, we wouldn't 'ave found the truffles, would we?"

"Apparently not" admitted Dr Bakewell reluctantly. He did not like to be proved wrong.

Chapter 32

Christmas Preparations

With Christmas approaching, the children were kept so busy they hardly had any time to visit Farmer Lambrick. The school always broke up for the Christmas holidays on the last Friday before Christmas Day, which this year fell on Friday 21st December and Professor Drumgoole thought it would be a good idea for the children and parents to spend the last evening of term together at the school before going home for Christmas, so Dr Bakewell decided to put on a Concert, much to Professor Drumgoole's amazement. Dr Bakewell managed to persuade Cherry Bakewell, who had sung at the Summer Fete, to come back and star in the concert. Everyone was very excited about this, especially since Georgia Flavell had discovered that Cherry was now a professional singer, appearing larger-than-life on billboards and posters in the big towns and cities.

The last week before Christmas was chaos. Lessons were nearly all practical because Dr Bakewell wanted to show-off his pupils' talents. They made scented orange pomanders, edible wreaths, stained-glass biscuits, gingerbread decorations, spiced marshmallows, chocolate-dipped Christmas trees, truffles, marzipan snowmen, Christmas cakes and mince pies. Everything they made would be used to decorate the school and eaten at the Christmas Concert. In fact, for the first time in his life Vaughan was getting bit fed-up of baking. His fingers were stained by all the food colouring they were using and starting to get sore. He was really looking forward to the holidays - he just hoped his Mum and Dad wouldn't want him to do all the baking at home too!

* * *

Walking arm-in-arm along the picture-lined corridor one morning after breakfast, Verity and Caroline were discussing what they were hoping to hear Cherry sing at the concert, when they heard a funny, high-pitched 'ooooooh'. As they turned the corner into the hall they spotted Mrs Hilderstone balancing unsteadily on a stepladder, standing on tip-toe, arms outstretched, trying to hang a paper-chain decoration on the chandelier above her head.

As she lifted up her left foot for balance to stretch a tiny bit further, she realised immediately it was an inch too far. She overbalanced and wobbled; the ladder rocked, she toppled forwards and the ladder began to collapse beneath her.

"Aaargh!" she screamed as she fell, unexpectedly landing on top of Caroline who had raced towards her to try to catch her and stop her falling. Under the frail weight of Mrs Hilderstone, Caroline herself slipped and tumbled backwards into Verity; both children fell to the floor with a very shaken and shocked Mrs Hilderstone on top of them.

Mrs Hilderstone's scream had attracted a lot of attention and a crowd soon gathered around them as children came running from every direction to see what was going on. Along with the children, the first adult to rush in was Mr Soames, the butler. Seeing Mrs Hilderstone on top of the children in a heap on the floor, he immediately sent the spectating children away, assuring them that she was alright and there was nothing for them to see. But inside, Mr Soames was concerned. Mrs Hilderstone was a tiny, delicate lady whose falling over days were long gone.

"Hilda!" called Vaughan, dashing down the staircase over to the crumpled heap of bodies on the hall floor, "are you alright?"

"I think I've broken my ankle" moaned Caroline as she tried slowly to sit up.

Mr Soames reached out his hand and as Mrs Hilderstone took hold he gently helped her to her feet. "What on earth were you doing?"

"Just trying to hang up the decorations for the children" she said sheepishly, "I wanted it to be all Christmassy for them, you know, especially with the Concert."

"Hilda, are you okay?" Vaughan repeated as he pulled Verity out from underneath Caroline, who was still lying on her back wincing in pain. Mr Soames looked at him, confusion written across his face.

"Hilda?" he asked "I think you've had a bump on the head. Her name's not Hilda, it's......."

"Yeah we know her real name's not Hilda" Verity jumped in, her composure regained, "it's our nickname for her. You know - Hilder-stone - we just shortened it to Hilda instead."

"Well, you should really call her Mrs Hilderstone" Mr Soames scolded them, "it shows respect. But seeing as you helped her and broke her fall, I'm sure you can be forgiven. Hilda, indeed!" he chuckled, shaking his head in amusement.

"Actually Bert, I quite like it. Yes - Hilda - these three can call me that. I could have broken something if they hadn't appeared when they did."

"Speaking of which, we ought to take you to Dr Muller-Weiss, just to make sure you haven't broken any bones."

"I'm fine, honestly. There's no need to make a fuss" Hilda protested, but Mr Soames and the three children wouldn't take no for an answer.

"I'm sure you are but it won't hurt to check" argued Mr Soames.

"Yes, I think you should" agreed Vaughan.

"Better safe than sorry" Verity added.

"I'll come too, my ankle really hurts" Caroline complained.

Looking at the children who were clearly concerned about their housekeeper, Mr Soames held out his hand again. "Come on Hilda" he said with a smile as he used her new nickname, "I'll see you to the Hospital Quarters. You too Caroline. Are you alright to walk?"

"I think so" said Caroline as she hobbled up, leaning on Vaughan for support. "Ow! Maybe not."

"You concentrate on Caroline" Mrs Hilderstone told Mr Soames as she rubbed her wrist, "I'm fine to walk. It's only my wrist that's sore, there's nothing wrong with my legs."

"Alright, if you insist" Mr Soames said with a sigh, as he draped Caroline's arm across his shoulders and placed his left arm across her back, to support her as she tried to walk.

"Meet you later" Caroline called over her shoulder, as she limped up the stairs, aided by the Butler and Mrs Hilderstone.

"Thank you very much for your concern" added Mrs Hilderstone with a nod "but don't worry. I'm fine and Caroline will be too."

Vaughan and Verity watched the three of them hobble their way up the staircase looking like they were taking part in a strange three-legged race, as they made their way to the Hospital Quarters. Suddenly they realised they were alone together without Caroline for the first time. It felt strange, they felt like they were missing something, even though she had only been gone a few moments.

"So then" said Vaughan looking around the hallway, not sure what to do next.

"So then" said Verity, looking at the strewn paper-chain and fallen stepladder "better clear up this mess."

Chapter 33

Thirty-Two Degrees

The lead up to Christmas was a very exciting time at Honeycomb Hall. The children were creating all sorts of incredible foods, guided by their incredibly talented teachers. In Sugarcraft, Dr Crose had taught them to make little winter roses which could be used for edible cake decoration on Christmas Cakes; in Artisan Baking, Chef Goodbun taught them how to make stained-glass biscuit decorations to hang on the Christmas trees and Professor Drumgoole introduced them to one of his favourite delicacies - chocolate Christmas truffles.

Truffle making with Professor Drumgoole was a hoot. But truffle making proved to be very tricky, very delicate, but above all else, very, very messy.

As the second years of St Oswald's entered the Chocolate Kitchen, they saw the wooden kitchen table covered completely in white greaseproof paper; silver bowls laid out ready for each pupil with pink and white marshmallows scattered all over the table, like confetti at a wedding. Taking their seats and trying hard not to eat the marshmallows, the class listened with keen interest as Professor Drumgoole stood at the head of the table and began the lesson.

"What you are trying to create" he explained "is a velvety-soft delicacy which - when placed on one's tongue - melts slowly and steadily, allowing the liquid filling to ooze over your tongue. The flavour should fill your mouth, tingle your gums, flow through your veins and move upwards towards your brain, so that until it has completely melted away you can think of nothing but the flavour and texture of that ball of smooth liquid, coursing through your veins and warming your body." He spoke with such smooth, velvety-soft tones that Caroline sat staring at him unblinking until she almost started dribbling and hastily wiped her mouth with the edge of her sleeve. "Now, does anyone know where truffles come from?"

Several children put their hands up and offered their suggestions in turn as the Professor pointed at them one by one to answer. Orla O'Brien was selected first.

"Switzerland?" Professor Drumgoole shook his head and pointed to Caroline.

"Belgium!" chanced Caroline. Again Professor Drumgoole shook his head and pointed elsewhere.

"Japan?" suggested Emi Kemura timidly. Professor Drumgoole shook his head once more.

"No, none of you were correct, although some good guesses. Both Switzerland and Belgium do indeed create some of the finest chocolate but no, that wasn't what I was looking for. Although it was a little unfair of me to ask, I admit. No; proper truffles - the real deal - grow naturally. They're not made by people at all but by nature; they grow underground so they're never seen."

"Really?"

"He's teasing!"

"No way"

"He's having us on!"

"It's a joke! They're chocolate!"

"Yeah, chocolate doesn't grow, it's made!"

The class were having a difficult time believing the Professor. Comments of disbelief echoed around the kitchen as student after student agreed with the one before and disagreed with their teacher.

"Oh, doesn't it?" asked Professor Drumgoole. "The cocoa bean - from which all chocolate is made, comes from the Cacao Tree which is grown in hot countries like Ghana, Ecuador, Mexico and Brazil. It's been grown and used for years by ancient cultures.

In fact, the Aztecs used to prescribe chocolate as a medicinal cure for a lot of illnesses and ailments. But I digress."

Caroline looked at Verity and whispered, "I wonder if he can persuade Dr Muller-Weiss to give us chocolate medicine when we're ill?!" and they both chuckled.

"No seriously, natural truffles are very rare and very expensive. As such they are considered to be among the most finest confectionery one can eat. For years chocolatiers have tried to imitate and perfect the natural truffle. Some have come close - very close indeed" he nodded towards Avery Sorrel who puffed out his chest and smiled smugly at his classmates at this comment "but no-one has yet managed to get it exactly right. Just so." He pinched the air with his thumb and forefinger as he said 'just so' as if to put an invisible full stop in the air. Sorrel abruptly stopped smirking at the others and shrank back down into his seat.

Professor Drumgoole handed out bowls of liquid chocolate and thin thermometers. "There are two very important rules in truffle making which must be followed. Does anyone know what they are?" Caroline raised her hand and Professor Drumgoole noticed. "Yes Caroline?"

"You need to use plain chocolate."

"Yes, indeed you do. For the first part at least." confirmed Professor Drumgoole. "Do you know why?"

"If you use milk chocolate it doesn't set properly and tastes sickly?" Caroline offered.

"Excellent, Caroline, excellent! That is true class. Plain - or dark - chocolate sets a lot quicker. I'll explain why milk chocolate gives a sickly taste shortly. Does anyone know the second rule?" No-one put their hand up to answer this, not even chocoholic Caroline, who seemed to be in her element in this class.

"No suggestions? Alright, it's a little technical but you must make sure the chocolate reaches exactly thirty-two degrees before you do anything. Those temperature gauges will show you how hot your chocolate is. Dip them in the bowls I've just given you and you'll see." The class obediently dunk their thermometers into the thick, shiny brown liquid in their bowls and watched the readings as they crept up. Vaughan's, Verity's and Caroline's read thirty-five, thirty-four and thirty-two degrees. As they watched their temperature readings Vaughan leaned to his left spoke quietly to Verity, who sat in between Vaughan and Caroline.

"How did Caroline know that you have to use dark chocolate?"

"Oh - her Dad's a chocolatier like Professor Drumgoole" Verity told him. "Plus she's a chocoholic." Spotting Caroline sneakily running her little finger around the bowl and craftily lapping up some of the chocolate, they both stifled a giggle.

Once the temperature had cooled down to the required thirty-two degrees Professor Drumgoole allowed them to begin. Handing out jugs of cream and more empty bowls he divulged further top-secret truffle making tips.

"The cream is double-cream" he said, tapping the side of his thin nose with his forefinger. "Any other cream and it just won't work. Believe me, I've tried! And this is why you must always use dark chocolate - if you use milk chocolate, when you blend in the cream there's simply too much dairy for it to work. It becomes sickly, doesn't set properly and you won't have the all-so-important oozing of liquid on the tongue. You just end up with chocolate flavoured milk. Now, the secret of good blending is to -"

"Add the chocolate to the cream" Avery Sorrel's sing-song voice interrupted, sounding bored and uninterested.

"Yes. Thank you Mr Sorrel. Although it is good manners to raise your hand when answering a question in class. Or indeed, at least wait for one to be asked." Professor Drumgoole said curtly, staring at him unimpressed. "Well, as our new teacher Mr Sorrel points out, you do need to measure out your cream first and add your chocolate to the cream. Twice as much chocolate as cream please, everyone! Mix your mixture thoroughly then fill these piping bags" (he made his way along either side of the table distributing long plastic piping bags to each student). "Pipe your truffles quickly before they set. Off you go!"

It was like a messy, noisy race. There was cream being splattered all over the table, chocolate slopping up and over the sides of the bowls as children stirred their mixture furiously. Metal spoons clanged noisily against the sides of the bowls as chocolate was whipped into the cream; splashes of chocolate flew all over the place, landing unexpectedly on the children. "Look - its raining chocolate!" Emi giggled to Orla as drops landed on her face.

After a few seconds of stirring Vaughan noticed his mixture thicken which quickly transformed into a sticky brown paste. He opened his icing bag, filled it with the gooey mixture and snipped off the point at the bottom of the bag, ready to squeeze out the chocolate and create his first-ever truffles.

* * *

It was surprisingly difficult to do. He twisted and squeezed the bag but he really had to force out the chocolate; he was sure he was pulling funny faces and going red as he used all his strength trying to pipe it out. Professor Drumgoole had made it look easy when he swirled his nozzle and immediately produced perfect twisty pyramids. Vaughan looked at Caroline's pyramids, which looked a lot more like the Professor's than his did. Looking back at his own efforts he pondered that they looked more like dog-poo than anything else. The more he tried the harder it became. Professor Drumgoole came and watched everyone in the class and told Vaughan it was because his mixture was setting too quickly. He must have let his temperature drop below thirty-two degrees but he shouldn't worry as it was a good first effort.

As Caroline's were all done she offered to help Vaughan. "I'll give you a little tip" she whispered quietly after Professor Drumgoole had moved onto the next struggling pupil, "hold it in your hand and squeeze it a bit more first. The heat from your hand will warm it up and help soften it." But she hadn't realised just how much of Vaughan's chocolate had set and as she held it she felt solid lumps of pure chocolate blocking the nozzle. She twisted and squeezed with all her might (going even redder than Vaughan had) but only a small tube of mixture plopped out, nowhere near enough to twirl into a twisty pyramid.

"It looks more like a turd than a truffle" Vaughan admitted to Caroline and they fell about laughing. Verity came to see what was going on and they all agreed that Vaughan had made some awful truffle pyramids but fantastic truffle-turds! Unfortunately Avery Sorrel overheard them and in an attempt to embarrass Vaughan, immediately told the whole class, in his gleeful, smarmy way.

"Hey, has anyone seen what Vaughan's made? Look - he's made truffle-turds! Even said so himself! Ha ha ha - can't even squeeze chocolate out of a bag properly, ha ha ha! Some confectioner you're going to be" he added spitefully as he walked past Vaughan, 'accidentally' bumping into Vaughan's shoulder on purpose.

"Thank you, Mr Sorrel" Professor Drumgoole cut him short, "it's not as easy as you might think, when you haven't had any practice. I'm sure your first truffles weren't perfect either" he said pointedly, peering at Sorrel from raised eyes. Sorrel awkwardly settled back into his seat and turned away from Professor Drumgoole, glaring at Vaughan. Ha - he clearly didn't like being put in his place, Vaughan thought to himself. He sidled up to Caroline and whispered. "Have you done this before then?" He thought this was everyone's first go a making truffles.

"No, Sorrel's father is a Chocolatier like Professor Drumgoole. He and my Dad trained together for a while when they were younger. Unfortunately Avery thinks he's something special when it comes to making chocolate and truffles 'cause his Dad is one of the best truffle makers in the country, although I'd never admit it to him. He's big-headed enough already."

Looking at his pathetic mounds of chocolate mixture, feeling disappointed, Vaughan perked up as Professor Drumgoole explained there was more to do yet. No wonder his looked nothing like any truffle he'd seen before - he hadn't finished yet! Dusting his hands with cocoa powder, Vaughan picked up each dollop of chocolate and one by one, rolled them into neat balls. Ah, he thought, now they were starting to look more like truffles!

When all his 'turds' had been magically transformed into tidy balls of chocolate with a simple roll of his hand, he felt a lot happier. Very messy, but happy. Vaughan thought he was even messier in this lesson than when he'd been practising baking at home all those months ago, covered in flour. Looking at his dishevelled pupils, Professor Drumgoole ordered them to go and wash their hands and return without delay.

Less than five minutes later he was faced with a class all sparkly-clean (apart from the cocoa-covered aprons). Now they were ready for the next stage.

Melting more chocolate - to the all-important thirty-two degrees - Professor Drumgoole told them that now was the time they could choose what kind of truffles they were going to make. Apparently the 'only limit is your imagination', so he said.

The class had a whale of a time experimenting, creating their own unique truffles. Verity hid one of hers inside a marshmallow which she then covered entirely in chocolate; Caroline dipped hers in white chocolate and then rolled it in coconut so that it looked like a snowball; Vaughan dipped his into white chocolate, then dark chocolate and repeated it several times so that when you bit into it, it was stripey inside. Emi spent ages creating 'truffle gobstoppers' - she dipped it in chocolate so many times it became the size of a golf-ball before she stopped! The rest of the lesson they were allowed to experiment with different types of chocolate, coatings and flavourings. To make them Christmas truffles, Professor Drumgoole had brought out little bottles of special festive flavourings - aniseed, spice, orange, hazelnut, cranberry and mint, to add that little extra something to the truffles. Not one tray was the same as another and Vaughan couldn't remember ever having so much fun in a lesson before.

At the end of class they proudly presented Professor Drumgoole with their trays of truffles for him to store. He explained that they would be eaten at the Christmas Banquet along with other creations from other classes. As Vaughan again washed his hands at the end of class, he could hardly wait to try them. 'Roll on Christmas!' he thought, with a smile!

Chapter 34

The Absence of Dr Bakewell

The following morning during breakfast, the three children noticed Dr Bakewell's chair remained empty. School notices were, as usual, read out by Professor Drumgoole, who merely glossed over Dr Bakewell's absence as if it was quite run-of-the-mill. Which according to Caroline, it was anything but.

"As you may have noticed, Dr Bakewell is not able to join us this morning" acknowledged Professor Drumgoole as he stood, holding the big red book of School Notices in his hands. "This is nothing for you to be concerned about, he is simply occupied elsewhere and shall return shortly." A muttering broke forth amongst the students, mainly commenting how un-curious they were as to Dr Bakewell's whereabouts. Verity however, seemed both intrigued and concerned.

"I hope he's alright" she admitted to Caroline and Vaughan, "it's not like him to miss a school gathering."

"Actually, he's never missed breakfast, lunch or dinner" Caroline whispered, more for Vaughan's benefit than Verity's - she already knew this. "Verity's right, this is really strange. Something must be going on."

"Something big" nodded Verity, biting her bottom lip in thought.

"What if he's in trouble?" asked Vaughan "what if it's something to do with Rasher? Remember how furious he was with Farmer Lambrick for buying him?"

"He has been in trouble before - remember when we told you about the mice in the pantry, ages ago?" Verity continued in hushed tones.

"Yeah but that was really serious. He had to go to the Culinary Council because a parent complained and they ordered him to their offices in London" clarified Caroline. "That's as high and serious as you can get."

"I thought that was the Council of Confectioners" Vaughan said, surprised. "Who are the Culinary Council then?

"First of all there's the Council of Confectioners" Verity explained. "They make sure all the confectionery - you know, sugar and sweets, cakes, pastries and stuff, is safe to eat. Then, above them is the National Association of Master Bakers."

"The who?"

"The National Association of Master Bakers. They're higher and more important as they rule over the Council of Confectioners but also all the baking methods, bakers and recipes as well. So they're responsible for more than just confectionery."

"Then above both of them comes the Culinary Council" added Caroline. "They oversee everyone - confectioners, bakers, chefs, cooks, farmers, butchers - basically anything to do with food. They're as high as you can get. That's why it was so serious when they called in Dr Bakewell last time. But that was a completely different situation."

"But we don't actually know where he is, do we?" Vaughan reminded the girls. "How do we know it's completely different?

"We don't - but we know a man that does, I bet" Caroline said. "Let's ask Professor Drumgoole - he knows everything."

"Then there's only one thing for it" said Vaughan "we have to ask him. If Dr Bakewell is in trouble, we have to help."

* * *

The three students hammered their fists on Professor Drumgoole's office door. As soon as morning break arrived they sacrificed their fruit snacks for knowledge. They had convinced themselves Dr Bakewell was in need of help and only they cared enough for their grumpy Headmaster to assist. Only they could rescue him.

Very quickly the door was answered, leaving Vaughan, Verity and Caroline rapping their knuckles against fresh air for a few seconds as the door to the office opened.

"What on earth's the matter?" asked a very taken-aback Professor Drumgoole.

"Professor, where's Dr Bakewell?" Vaughan spoke first.

"Is he in trouble?" Caroline quickly followed.

"We have to help him!" Verity added lastly.

"One at a time, please!" Now would you like to come in instead of standing in the doorway, behaving hysterically?" Professor Drumgoole spoke kindly although the children could tell he was also annoyed at the interruption. They also felt a little upset by his sharp words, they didn't think they were behaving 'hysterically' at all.

"Sorry" they mumbled, heads hanging as they stepped into his office, the Professor closing the door behind them. Gesturing them to stand in front of his book-strewn desk, Professor Drumgoole took his seat and allowed them to continue.

"Well, you three? What seems to be the problem?"

"Sir, we need to find out where Dr Bakewell is" said Caroline firmly.

"We're worried he could be in trouble" added Verity, hoping this would explain their so-called 'hysterics'.

"Do you?" Professor Drumgoole spoke quietly as he raised his eyebrows in surprise. A slight smile crept across his lips for a second and almost immediately vanished, but not before Vaughan had seen it. He wondered why the Professor would smile at such a serious matter. "And why might that be?"

"Come on Sir, you know Dr Bakewell never misses a school gathering. This is the first time we've ever known him not be at a meal with us. It's not right, something's up" said Caroline earnestly.

"We're worried he might be in trouble with the Council, Sir. About Rasher." Verity decided to come straight to the point. Time was ticking. "We know he's been in trouble once before - the whole mice thing - so if he's in trouble again, we want to help him. Let's face it, pigs are a lot bigger than mice so he might be in even more trouble this time."

The slight amused smile reappeared on the Professor's face as he looked at the three worried faces before him. "Ahh. Yes, that was a most - unfortunate - incident, I do agree. And you three incredibly clever children are right about two things. One - Dr Bakewell has indeed been summoned to the Council of Confectioners..." Gasps of shock and exclamations of 'no!'; 'I knew it!' and 'told you!' simultaneously escaped from the mouths of the children until Professor Drumgoole raised his hand to call for silence.

"Dr Bakewell rang the Council of Confectioners himself. He wanted to discuss something with them and as they deemed it both important and urgent, they requested he meet them in person. Hence he is currently not in school, as he is simply conducting school business at the Council of Confectionery in London."

"But last time..." began Caroline

"Last time was different. Last time he was answerable to the Culinary Council who as you should know, are far more powerful than the Council of Confectioners. As I said, this time Dr Bakewell contacted them. This time he's hoping for good news."

"And what's the second thing we're right about?" asked Caroline.

"It does concern Rasher."

"I knew it!" Verity couldn't help herself. "He is going to be allowed to keep him, isn't he? Farmer Lambrick, I mean?"

"Oh yes, you see as long as Rasher isn't kept in the school grounds as such, Farmer Lambrick can explain his presence by saying Rasher is simply his pet pig."

"But he is his pet pig! Hang on - isn't the Farmhouse on school grounds?" queried Vaughan.

"Again, yes."

"Sir, I'm getting really confused here. What does Rasher have to do with the Council of Confectioners and what difference does it make whether he lives in the school grounds or not?" asked Vaughan, who felt as though his mind had become a whirlpool of information, swirling round and round without actually getting anywhere.

"Look, seeing as it's largely due to you three, then I'll tell you. But this must be kept private. Not a word to anyone, you understand? Not even all the teachers know yet." Vaughan nodded his agreement while Verity and Caroline made a criss-cross shape over their hearts, promising they wouldn't tell. This was unbelievably thrilling - they were going to hear some news so important, so exciting and so private that they would know before the teachers! Professor Drumgoole trusted them enough to let them in on something that so far only he and the Headmaster knew! Anticipation burning within them, they pulled up three chairs, eyes shining brightly and ears blocking out any other noise, eager and ready to be let in on the big mystery.

* * *

"Alright. The truffles Rasher uprooted in the Forest of Forgetfulness are genuine rare, natural truffles. I'm certain of it. Which, as you know, mean that if we harvest and sell them, will very likely prevent the school from being closed. But we don't hold that power - we're only a school. That power, to certify them as natural truffles and enable us to harvest and sell them can only be granted by the Council of Confectioners. Dr Bakewell has taken the samples saved by Verity to the Council to await their verdict."

"How does this affect Rasher then?" asked Vaughan.

"Because the only way truffles can be found is by pig" explained the Professor. "Dr Bakewell's plan is to firstly get the Council to certify that they are genuine truffles. If they confirm this, they will then want to know how they were found. Then and only then can Dr Bakewell tell them about Rasher. It will also be another way to prove how real they are.

"But what if they say they're not real truffles?" asked a worried-looking Verity, again biting her bottom lip.

"Then there will be no need to mention Rasher. Don't you see, we win either way. Real truffles dug up by a pig, mean Farmer Lambrick gets to keep Rasher on school grounds as a working truffle-pig. If they're not one hundred percent truffles, they were simply found by a student at the edge of the forest who then brought them to me. If Rasher is discovered, he is simply Farmer Lambrick's pet, nothing else."

Suddenly it all made sense. "So Dr Bakewell really isn't in trouble then?" asked Verity, weakly.

"No Verity, he isn't. Quite the opposite. But I'm very proud of the way you three showed concern and wanted to help him. I'm very aware some of the students don't understand our Headmaster and think him grumpy, but you three can clearly see there's more to him than meets the eye. Your loyalty to Dr Bakewell is both heartwarming and impressive. But it doesn't run to you avoiding detention for being late for class. I'll be sure to inform Dr Bakewell of your loyalty and concern, but break's almost over. For goodness sake run to your lesson before you're late - you've got Madame Rougerie next!"

He smiled as the three children jumped up, scraped their chairs back and ran to the door smiling. "Thanks Sir!" they shouted over their shoulders as they opened his office door and raced down the corridor. Professor Drumgoole stood in the doorway, the small smile creeping back across his face as he watched them go, all three of them hurrying down the corridor to avoid the wrath and detentions of Clementine Rougerie!

"NO RUNNING IN THE CORRIDOR!" He heard the voice of Prefect Theo Banks in the distance, shouting at the children he'd just told to run and he chuckled. He closed his office door behind him and lost in thought went back to his desk, wondering both how Dr Bakewell was getting on and how very impressed he had been again, by Vaughan, Verity and Caroline.

Chapter 35

The Council of Confectioners

Shielding himself from the continued rainstorm which had awoken him early that morning and had yet to cease, Dr Bakewell stood under his burgundy umbrella, staring at the four-storey Georgian house which loomed up out of the ground before him. Spindly black railings stood firm at the side of the stone steps and descended from the front door down to the basement, the windows of which were barely visible above the pavement and stood level with Dr Bakewell's feet. Droplets of rain dripping rhythmically from the edge of his umbrella, Dr Bakewell inhaled deeply, thrust his chin upwards to straighten his neck - as he often did in times of contemplation or anxiety - and marched firmly up the wet, stone steps to the bright red door, the only splash of colour against an otherwise grey day. Framed top and side by bright white carved columns the door stood out contrastingly against the brick of the house and the black shuttered windows.

Above the door was a small semi-circular window and carved into the stone frame between the window and the door itself, were the initials 'C.O.C.O.A.' Although it had a brass door-knocker in the shape of a lion's head in the centre of the door, Dr Bakewell did not use this to knock. Instead he pressed a button on the square metal pad on the right of the door, which sounded a quavering voice, almost muffled by crackles, in response.

"Yes?" came the crackly, short acknowledgement of his presence.

"Ahem" Dr Bakewell cleared his throat before introducing himself. "Doctor George Bakewell of Dr Bakewell's School of Confectionery."

"Enter." The lady to whom the quavering voice belonged was clearly not one for conversation, thought Dr Bakewell, as he shook the raindrops from his umbrella before tucking it under his arm and opening the now-unlocked door.

He stepped foot inside the old house, it's real-fire warmth giving a much-needed welcome from the cold, damp, winter weather outside; the sudden change in temperature caused his tortoise-shell glasses to immediately mist up the moment he stepped into the hall, temporarily blinding him with fog. Closing the door behind him, he stood in the hallway of the old Georgian house, placed his old battered briefcase on the coloured mosaic tiles beneath his feet and allowed his glasses to slowly de-mist in the warm hallway. After almost a minute, once the mist on his lenses finally evaporated and he was able to see clearly again, he tidily stood his soaking wet umbrella tip-down in the umbrella stand, hung his black bowler hat and trench-coat on the wooden coat stand opposite and fiddled with his tie. No sooner had he adjusted it to make sure it was absolutely dead-centre, the owner of the crackly voice appeared in person.

A smartly dressed Jamaican lady, roughly the same age as Dr Bakewell, entered the hallway; she wore beige skirt suit, black blouse and pearl necklace that hung low across the dark blouse. She wore no make-up and her wiry, steel-grey hair was tied-up, clasped in a gold hair-slide at the nape of her neck. The only item which softened her harsh appearance were the matching pearl earrings which hung discreetly from her earlobes.

"Doctor Bakewell." She smiled and shook his hand, her welcoming smile bringing an unexpected warmth to her plain features. "Good morning. I hope you had a pleasant journey?"

"Good morning, Mrs Beard" he replied courteously, recognising her at once and shaking her hand. "Pleasant enough thank you, considering this awful weather."

"Yes, well, not a lot one can do about that I'm afraid. Still, it is December - what would you expect? Do take a seat."

She gestured him towards the room on the right, where she had appeared from earlier, which clearly doubled as both waiting room and Reception Area. Dr Bakewell took a seat with his back to the window, making sure he would not be distracted or become hypnotised by the soft pitter-patter of the raindrops on the window and the watery paths they made when they merged together and trickled down the glass.

Mrs Beard sat behind her cluttered desk. For a very smartly dressed woman, her desk was contrastingly messy - yet she appeared to know where everything was. For the whole ten minutes Dr Bakewell sat in the waiting-room-come-office, not once, he noticed, did she look through one pile for something only to find it in another. Noisily typing away on her old typewriter, occasionally referring to some papers, whatever she wanted always lay hidden in the pile of folders or papers she selected, she never re-searched through a second or third pile.

The old black Bakerlite rotary telephone suddenly rang, it's receiver almost rattling in it's holder as it loudly sprang to life, it's unexpected piercing shrill causing Dr Bakewell to jump. Mrs Beard didn't jump - she simply stopped typing on her typewriter for a moment, extended out her hand and calmly answered the call without even lifting her eyes from her work.

"Yes? Very well, I'll send him now. Thank you." Succinct as ever, Mrs Beard turned her attention to Dr Bakewell. "They're ready for you, Dr Bakewell. First floor, second on the right."

Dr Bakewell rose, picked up his briefcase, gave a courteous dip of the head and a mumbled 'thank you' as he passed Mrs Beard's desk on his way out. Already focused on her work, Mrs Beard did not speak in reply, nor even look up. She merely carried on reading a letter from one pile of papers and making notes in another, before returning to her typewriter.

Every step Dr Bakewell took stole a little of his breath. By the time he reached the top of the stairs he was quite out of breath and flushed. His heartbeat had quickened - he could tell by the way his heart was hammering against his ribcage, though whether it was fear, excitement or nerves he couldn't tell. He sat his briefcase down for a moment while he wiped his sweaty palms against his trousers and again adjusted his already perfectly positioned tie. Stifling a cough to clear his throat, he picked up his briefcase, knocked and opened the second door on the right as instructed and strode purposefully into the room, closing the door behind him. He wanted no eavesdroppers to this conversation, after all.

* * *

Dr Bakewell knew the three members of the Council that sat before him. On the left as he faced the panel of Councillors was Tommy Albright, an elderly fellow older than Dr Bakewell, with more lines and wrinkles around his eyes than a screwed up map - a product of years of squinting at tiny, intricate, detailed icing. He was an icing genius but his years of perfectionism had taken a toll on his eyes, leaving him so short-sighted he now relied on a magnifying glass to read. Next to Tommy, in the centre of the panel sat the Head of the Council, Confectioner Frank Chewdle. Confectioner Chewdle had a reputation for being a tough cookie, a very difficult man to please, but it was not he whom bothered Dr Bakewell the most. He liked Tommy Albright very much for he was a pleasant and fair man; he respected Frank Chewdle and admired him. No, the man that unsettled Dr Bakewell the most was the man sitting on Frank Chewdle's left hand side - chocolatier Henry Sorrel. Owner and founder of 'Sorrel's Sweets' he had a very high opinion of himself and rather a low opinion of Dr Bakewell. This was unfortunately a trait he had also passed down to his son - Avery Sorrel.

Greetings over, Confectioner Chewdle began the meeting. "Well, Dr Bakewell, you have a very interesting claim. May I ask when this discovery was made?"

"Yes, it was on bonfire night. The fifth of November" he added unnecessarily.

"Uh-huh" Confectioner Chewdle took the lid of his fountain pen and began to write in a large, leather-bound book which lay on the table in front of him, looking up only to hear Dr Bakewell's answers.

"And the discovery was made where?"

"In the Forest of Forgetfulness."

"Uh-huh." More note writing in the book.
Frank Chewdle then removed his glasses with one hand and addressed the other two councillors. "Dr Bakewell contacted me at the beginning of last month with a very interesting claim. I requested his attendance here for us to consider his claim. Dr Bakewell, for the benefit of the Council, please state the nature of your business here today." Dr Bakewell cleared his throat.

"I believe, the Forest of Forgetfulness is growing truffles. We found what we believe to be natural truffles, which I bring here, to the Council of Confectioners, for approval - and to register our school as growers of natural truffles."

The look of surprise and horror on Henry Sorrel's face gave Dr Bakewell a little flutter of satisfaction in his chest, though he kept it to himself and managed not to let it show. 'Take that, Henry' he thought to himself, smugly. He knew Henry Sorrel had been trying to perfect truffle making for years, though still unsuccessfully.

"You have such a truffle with you?" asked Frank Chewdle.

"I do, Confectioner. I have three, one for each of you." He opened his briefcase and took out a little white box, in which he had carefully placed three truffles, each in its own mini paper-case to prevent them from sticking together. He offered the box first to Confectioner Chewdle, then to Tommy Albright and lastly to his nemesis, Henry Sorrel.

The room fell silent as they took a few minutes to inspect the truffles. Just as Professor Drumgoole had done, they sniffed, squeezed, rolled in their hands and eventually ate, while Dr Bakewell sat in his chair, his breathing shallow and quiet as he nervously awaited their comments.

Chapter 36

Dr Bakewell's Blues

Vaughan, Verity and Caroline peered out of the common room window at the stillness outside. The only movement was the fluttering of birds swooping in and out of the grand, conical trees that lined the drive, like soldiers on guard. They seemed to have been staring for ages, muttering between themselves as to what may have happened at Dr Bakewell's meeting, desperate to know the outcome.

"He's here!" squealed Verity, as the little Citroen dolly car spluttered it's way down the drive towards the school. As the car got nearer the school and disappeared out of sight they ran to Ozzy, pulled on the halberd and jumped into the slide to take them into the grand hallway. Flying out at the bottom they were just about to run to Dr Bakewell's Office when a loud voice stopped them.

"Where do you three think you're going?" It was Theo Banks, the Prefect of St Oswald.

"Erm, we need to...." - "We have to see Professor Drumgoole" - "Dr Bakewell needs to see us." The three of them spoke at once.

Theo shook his head. "I don't think so" he said, tapping the Timekeeper's Clock. The three children looked at the clock and realised it was six o'clock - homework time. "There are only two places Dr Bakewell will expect you to be. One - the Library or two, the Study. Unless you have a note?"

Vaughan, Verity and Caroline looked at each other. Of course they didn't have a note - no-one knew anything about the truffles or Dr Bakewell's meeting. Dr Bakewell wouldn't know they'd be waiting for his return, desperate to hear what happened.

"No, we don't have a note, Theo" admitted Vaughan.

"Then you'd better vanish quickly before either of them catch you running around the school instead of studying. Go on, scoot." He said, ushering them away up the staircase to the first floor where the Library was.

"Can you believe that?" moaned Caroline, very put-out.

"Yeah but he's only doing what he's supposed to do" Verity pointed out. "Have you ever heard of anyone going to see Dr Bakewell before? He probably thought we were making it up. Anyway, Dr Bakewell's probably got to talk to Professor Drumgoole about it first. We'll find out later, they'll have to tell us what happened soon." Verity shrugged.

"Yeah, course they will, 'specially since it was Verity that found the truffles." agreed Vaughan.

"S'pose so" Caroline muttered sulkily, "but they'd better tell us soon."

* * *

Dr Bakewell opened the door to his office, hung his bowler hat on the hatstand, put down his briefcase, placed both hands on his hips and let out a long, exhausted sigh. He wearily walked to his desk and flopped into his chair, rubbing his hand across the lower half of his face. He hadn't been there for more than a minute before there was a timid knock on his door.

"Yes?" Dr Bakewell answered. You could hear the tiredness in his voice. His meeting and the journey had taken it's toll and he felt as though would fall asleep if he closed his eyes for just a second. The door by the trophy case was pushed open and Professor Drumgoole's face appeared in the gap.

"You're back then?" he stated, a little timidly.

"Obviously."

The Professor took a moment to study Dr Bakewell before continuing. He knew how heavy a meeting with the Council of

Confectionery could be - so far Dr Bakewell wasn't exactly jumping around with excitement.

"Why do I get the feeling it didn't go very well?" asked Professor Drumgoole gently, both surprised and concerned.

"Because it didn't, Derek." Dr Bakewell breathed out heavily, laid his forearms on the desk and hung his head above them.

"What?"

"I said, it didn't go well. Are you sure those truffles are true truffles?"

"Absolutely" confirmed Professor Drumgoole. "What did they say? Who was on the panel?"

A funny noise escaped Dr Bakewell, a bit like a snort. "Oh you know - Frank Chewdle, obviously. Tommy Albright - he was fair enough. And...Henry Sorrel."

"Henry Sorrel? Surely they wouldn't....."

"Yes, yes he was there too. Whatever my opinions of him may be, at the end of the day he is a Chocolatier, whether I accept it or not."

"And I take it that it was Sorrel that refused to confirm the truffles were genuine?"

"Of course. He said it was possible but highly unlikely and he wouldn't agree due to two reasons. Number one - the texture wasn't quite as smooth nor flavour quite as strong as they should have been and number two - they 'only have my word for it' that they were dug out of the forest floor. He was suggesting I might have been trying to defraud them! Can you believe it? The nerve of that man!"

Professor Drumgoole sank into the chair opposite Dr Bakewell as he thought for a moment.

"What about Chewdle and Albright? What did they say?"

"Frank said he would have been delighted to register them as real, it would have been a great boost to the English

Confectionery Institution, but the whole panel has to be in agreement. Frank was satisfied they were real - as was Tommy Albright. But as Sorrel refused on technical grounds, I can't protest. The truffles can't be registered, we can't harvest them and there's not a thing we can do about it."

"You're not going to just accept that, surely?" Professor Drumgoole leapt to his feet, his face full of defiance. "I'm as good a chocolatier as Henry Sorrel any day and I tell you those are true truffles. 'We can't do anything about it?' Come on George, of course we can. This is the find of the century. Don't take this lying down, fight for it."

"What do you suggest we do then?" asked a very weary Dr Bakewell.

Eyes twinkling with determination, Professor Drumgoole answered him. "Appeal, George. Appeal."

Chapter 37

Letter of Appeal

And so it was done. After two weeks of discussion, suggestions, drafts and re-drafts, the appeal letter was finally ready. Dr Bakewell and Professor Drumgoole sat in the Headmaster's Office as Dr Bakewell read it out loud, one final time.

"I don't think we could have done it any better, George." Professor Drumgoole reassured him, "That contains everything it should and nothing it shouldn't. It's precise, to the point but shows your passion for this school and your work."

"Mmm. Yes, well, it's got to be sent at some point, hasn't it?"

"It certainly has!" exclaimed Professor Drumgoole, "I know I always support COCOA, but this time I'm afraid they've got it wrong and we can't just sit down and accept it. Not without a fight, anyway. And that's what we'll give them. It's ludicrous putting Henry Sorrel on that committee when they know your history."

"Yes, I must admit I was surprised about that too. But then again, me aside of things, the man is a Chocolatier - whatever we think of him."

"For heaven's sake, I'm a Chocolatier - and a better one too I dare say - and I know my truffles. These are real George. I'd stake my reputation on it."

Smiling shrewdly at his colleague Dr Bakewell looked him directly in the eye. "I'm glad to hear that. Because you just have, Derek. You just have."

Dr Bakewell tucked the letter into an envelope, sealed it and wrote the address in red copperplate writing. He sat there for a while looking at it, as he let the ink dry.

Mr. F. Chewdle (Conf)

C.O.C.O.A.

Gingerbread House

2 Pudding Lane

London

SW3 3TS

"You know if they prove us wrong about these truffles we're both ruined, don't you?" Dr Bakewell said seriously to Professor Drumgoole. "Both our reputations will be dashed and there's little doubt the school would be closed for certain then."

"I am aware of that" agreed Professor Drumgoole heavily "but have faith. I know we're right, you know we're right. Heavens, I even think Frank Chewdle knows we're right deep down, he just has to abide by the rules."

"Hmm... so he does" Dr Bakewell said, thoughtfully.

* * *

Although it was now February, Spring was on the horizon and white snowdrops had finally poked their heads through the soil, having been coaxed out by the melting snow and slightly warmer weather. Colour sprinkled the gardens as the snow melted in patches allowing spots of green grass to appear, dotted with occasional clumps of white as the snowdrops burst into bloom, their heads nodding in the ever-present breeze.

Yawning, Vaughan shuffled sleepily into the Refectory where Verity and Caroline were already seated, waiting for him at St Oswald's table.

"What's the matter with you?" Caroline asked briskly.

"Just tired" mumbled Vaughan, running his hand over the back of his head and ruffling his hair, trying to wake himself up.

"Least it's not long 'til Easter, it's early this year, it's in March" Verity reminded them. "I'll be glad when the holidays come - It seems ages since Christmas."

"Not until we've made Easter Eggs!" Caroline panicked, causing Verity and Vaughan to smile, even through his tired state. Caroline was the biggest chocoholic Vaughan had ever known. Easter was still over a month away yet - he was certain Caroline would eat chocolate for breakfast, lunch, dinner and supper if she could. It was a good job the school was very strict about what pupils were allowed to eat, he thought to himself.

Just as he was thinking about how good the food was, Verity ushered them all to the Breakfast Bar to help themselves to breakfast. Reaching into the basket of apples, imagining Caroline eating all types of chocolate, it reminded Vaughan that they hadn't heard anything lately about the truffles Rasher had found. Keeping his voice low so he couldn't be overheard, he mentioned this to Verity.

"Has anything happened about the truffles yet?"

"Not yet" said Verity as she picked an apple from the same basket and slid her tray along to the cereals. Pouring herself a bowl of muesli she added "I heard Dr Bakewell appealed but I don't think he's heard anything back yet. I think he would have told us" she added, pouring on some milk before heading back to their table. Taking their seats, Caroline began picking at the blueberry muffin she had chosen.

"I think it's stupid, this appeal. I mean, Professor Drumgoole's the best Chocolatier around and he said they were real. I mean, it's kind of insulting him, isn't it - not accepting his opinion. It's like saying, 'you may be a chocolatier, you may be a teacher but really, you don't know what you're talking about' " she said in a put-on, authoritative voice. She washed down the muffin with a big gulp of milk, which left a white milky moustache on her top lip. Vaughan giggled at her and she quickly wiped her mouth with the back of her hand.

"But who's the other Chocolatier?" asked Verity. "It's Henry Sorrel, isn't it. He's on the Council, I remember Avery bragging about it last year when he was asked to join. I reckon he's got something to do with this."

The three of them nodded in agreement as they tucked into their breakfasts. Suddenly, Vaughan looked up and nudged Caroline.

"Look" he mumbled, through a mouthful of scrambled egg on toast. Following his gaze the girls looked across the room to the Teacher's Table and saw Mr Soames standing behind Dr Bakewell's chair and hand him an envelope.

* * *

Avery Sorrel sat alongside Percy Snodland at St Wistan's table. "Dad's been rather pleased with himself lately" Avery told him as he settled himself down. "I had a letter from him last week and he asked how Dr Bakewell was. He said he saw him recently and put him in his place again, the daft old fool."

"When did he see him, then?" asked Percy, surprised.

"Tut. I don't know, do I?" Avery snapped. "I know it was something to do with the Council - Father's a chosen Councillor, remember. Anyway, he said Bakewell had some crackpot idea - obviously Dad wouldn't agree to it - and because they rejected him he left the meeting really disappointed. And I mean, really disappointed." He grinned, cruelly. Percy looked thoughtful. "And he didn't say what it was about?"

"Do you not listen or are you just stupid? I told you, didn't I? He went to the council with some daft crackpot idea, that's all. They refused him and burst his bubble so he left all deflated."

"Curious..." pondered Percy, tucking into a big, juicy sausage.

Just then there was a flurry of activity as the Refectory door swung open and Mr Soames bustled in and made a bee-line straight for Dr Bakewell. Percy looked up, chewing his sausage and nudged Avery with his elbow, causing Avery to slip as he cut into his egg on toast. Annoyed, he glared at Percy and was about to give him a piece of his mind but Percy got in first. "Look!" he said as he swallowed his food and nodded towards the Teacher's Table.

Avery looked up and watched as Mr Soames handed Dr Bakewell a large, white envelope, which was tied with a red ribbon. He recognised it at once.

"That's from the Council!" he exclaimed. "The letters Dad gets from them all look like that. What are they writing to him for?"

"Maybe they're just writing to tell him formally his idea was stupid and not to bother again!" suggested Percy, laughing. But Avery wasn't so sure. "Maybe. But I don't like it. Something's going on and I want to know what."

As he spoke, Dr Bakewell wiped his hands and mouth with his napkin and took the envelope from the Butler.

Chapter 38

Breakfast Post

Dr Bakewell took the envelope from Mr Soames, who having fulfilled his duty, nodded acknowledgement of his dismissal and vacated the Refectory. Glancing at Professor Drumgoole who was seated on his left, Dr Bakewell hurriedly untied the ribbon, letting it fall softly to the floor and, using a clean breakfast knife from the table, slit open the envelope.

Fingers trembling, he pulled out the letter contained inside and opened it. He already knew it was from the Council of Confectioners - the red ribbon emblazoned with gold initials C.O.C.O.A. gave that away immediately. He read the sparkly letter, which had been edged in glitter, with a serious face whilst Professor Drumgoole, who was tucking into his breakfast, glanced occasionally across at Dr Bakewell as he read the letter, trying not to look anxious in front of the children. It was obvious that this letter contained the result of their appeal. Not only did the school's future rest on this decision, but so did the livelihoods and reputations of the two greatest confectioners of all time.

Dr Bakewell reached the bottom of the letter, cleared his throat and in silence tucked it back into the envelope. The tiniest of smiles then appeared on his face and he turned to Professor Drumgoole. Very quietly, with an exultant expression he couldn't hide, he spoke the words the Professor so desperately wanted to hear.

"We did it Derek," he whispered as he looked into the face of his trusted colleague and beamed, "we did it!"

* * *

DONG! The school bell suddenly began to peal, telling the children it was now end of breakfast and they had until it's ninth toll to empty the Refectory and be in their classrooms ready to start the day. Just as they were about to leave, Vaughan quickly stopped Verity and Caroline. "Wait" he said as they got up from their seats, "follow me". He quickly ran to the breakfast bar and hid behind one of the stone columns. DONG! "Hide behind one each" he whispered as he gestured to the remaining columns and the girls did as he said. Surprisingly, nobody noticed them, as the teachers and children all hurried immediately to the doors and the Refectory emptied before the third toll of the bell. They waited a few seconds to make absolutely sure everyone had left then crept out of their hiding place.

"What are you doing?" hissed Verity, bewildered.

"Didn't you see that ribbon fall to the floor?" Vaughan asked the girls. "That could be a clue."

"Clue? Never mind looking for clues, we should be out of here by now. We could get caught. We could get detention." Verity panicked, becoming more and more anxious. DONG! The third toll.

"Not if we hurry. Mrs Hilderstone clears away the Refectory, I've seen her and she's a bit slower now since her fall. Anyway, we've got till the ninth bell ring to be in class. Quickly."

Vaughan and the girls ran to the Teacher's Table and had just got there when the Refectory doors opened and in walked Mrs Hilderstone and Mr Soames. "Quick - hide!" whispered Caroline urgently and she dived underneath the Teacher's Table. Following her lead, Vaughan and Verity did the same just in time. As Verity pulled her foot underneath the table, her heel caught the edge of the tablecloth causing it to swing. DONG! The fourth toll. But it wasn't quite quick enough - Mr Soames noticed the movement immediately.

"Hello?" the Butler called out. "Is there anyone there?"

Holding her breath to try to slow down her rapid heartbeat lest it could be heard pounding loudly against her ribs, Verity quickly grabbed hold of the bottom of the tablecloth to steady it. They listened as Mr Soames' footsteps echoed around the room as he walked up to the table, Verity's face developing the pink tinge caused by lack of oxygen. Watching the shadow of his feet coming towards them, the three hiding children ever so quietly crawled in the opposite direction. DONG! The fifth toll pealed just as the Butler lifted up the tablecloth and found nothing. "Must be my imagination" he said as he lowered the cloth and, masked by the peal of the bell, Verity exhaled a much-needed long, slow breath, which enabled the pink tinge in her cheeks to disappear.

Halfway down the table, under Dr Bakewell's seat, Vaughan picked up the ribbon and read it out.

"C-O-C-O-A. Cocoa? What's that?"

"Oh, that's the Council of Confectioners!" Caroline informed them excitedly. "It's not the word cocoa, it's the initials - look." Vaughan and Verity peered closer and noticed there was a tiny full stop in between each letter. "It stands for Council of Confectioners Organisation and Administration."

"Then it must be something to do with Dr Bakewell's appeal" Verity observed cleverly. DONG! The bell sounded it's sixth toll.

"Come on, we know enough for now. We need to get to class pronto" reminded Caroline. Dropping the ribbon onto the floor the three of them crawled towards the doors and stopped. The shadow of two feet were right in front of them, at the far end of the table and stood right between the table and the Refectory doors, blocking their escape route. The three of them looked at each other wondering whatever could they do. They would either get caught being where they shouldn't be, or they would be in trouble for being late for class. As they all silently wondered which would be least trouble to be in, their choice was swiftly taken from them as the tablecloth hiding them was suddenly whipped away, exposing the children.

"Goodness gracious, whatever are you three doing here?" They looked up straight into the bemused face of Mrs Hilderstone.

"Ah...."

"Er...."

"We..."

"Shouldn't you three be in class by now" Mr Soames appeared from nowhere and stood by the side of Mrs Hilderstone. DONG! The seventh toll.

"Please" said Vaughan, "we're trying to help Dr Bakewell. We're not doing anything wrong, I promise, we just needed to see something."

Mr Soames spotted the ribbon on the floor. "I don't suppose it's anything to do with that letter, is it?" he asked, wisely. Surprised, the three children nodded, wide eyed and scared. "It's none of your business, you know. That letter was addressed to Dr Bakewell, not you three. You shouldn't be sneaking around in places you ought not to be in."

"Bert, remember, these are the children that helped me too" Mrs Hilderstone interrupted. "They're good children, not naughty or mischievous. Let them be, they'll be in enough trouble if they're late for class."

This struck a chord with Mr Soames as he did indeed remember Caroline diving underneath Mrs Hilderstone at Christmas, breaking her fall when she toppled off the stepladder. Without Caroline's quick thinking, Mrs Hilderstone could have broken a bone or worse; Mrs Hilderstone was quite right, these were good children, even if they shouldn't be crawling under the Teacher's Table, poking their noses into Dr Bakewell's business.

"Very well" he agreed, "but don't let us catch you in here again unless you're eating. Understand?" DONG! The eighth peal. Time was rapidly running out. Nodding and scrambling to their feet, the children rushed out, calling 'thank you!' over their shoulders as they raced to their next lesson. DONG! As the bell tolled it's ninth peal, they flung open the doors of the bakery and hurled themselves inside, then breathed a sigh of relief. Chef Goodbun, their teacher for this class, wasn't yet in the room. Someone was smiling on them today, they thought. They took their place at the back of the class panting as they waited for their breath to get back to normal and smiled breathlessly at one another. One thing they now knew for sure - Dr Bakewell's appeal was well and truly in motion.

Chapter 39

Bardney Abbey

"It's soooo cold!" Caroline complained, her mouth just peeking above her thick woollen scarf as she strode across the courtyard with Vaughan and Verity, on their way to the Orchard, their breath clearly visible in the bitter cold February air. "Do we have to go now?"

"Stop moaning!" called Verity, leading the way. "It's great when its like this, Vaughan'll love it! The frost sparkles just like diamonds and the trees - oh, it's magical!"

Caroline rolled her eyes at Vaughan. "She loves the Orchard. Yeah, it is really pretty and stuff, I just wish it wasn't so cold!" she said, before blowing into her hands and rubbing them together, to keep them warm. Vaughan smiled at her, took his warm, gloved hand out of his coat pocket and waggled his gloved fingers in front of her face, teasingly. "Should've put your gloves on, Caroline!"

Vaughan quickly dodged a playful push from Caroline in response to his teasing and bumped straight into Theo Banks, who was wrapped up snugly in a thick, padded black jacket and beanie hat. "Watch it!" Theo shouted. Vaughan turned to apologise.

"Sorry, didn't see you th...."

"Vaughan!" Theo smiled, cutting him off mid-sentence. "I've been looking all over for you."

"Me? Why?"

"Dr Crose wants to see you at eleven o'clock. In the Common Room."

"Dr Crose? What for?"

"I don't know. I've been asked to make sure you, Emi and Orla are in the Common Room because she wants to talk to you."

Listening to the conversation, Verity joined in, confused. "Does she want us too? We're his friends."

"No, only Vaughan, Emi and Orla." stated Theo firmly. "Don't be late. See you around" and with that he wandered off back towards the stately school.

"What's that all about?" asked Caroline, who had stopped blowing into her hands and was now looking concerned. Vaughan shrugged. "No idea" he said honestly.

"You, Emi and Orla?" said Verity, thinking out loud. "You don't think they're stopping the scholarship, do you?" she said seriously, a touch of panic in her voice.

Vaughan's stomach lurched. He hadn't even considered that. But that was a good point - Emi, Orla and he were the only scholarship students in St Oswald. Before he could think on this for long, Caroline, the voice of reason, spoke. "That can't be it. They wouldn't set up the scholarships and then get rid of the pupils after a few months. And they wouldn't send Theo to fetch you either, they'd have to call your parents in. Besides, you haven't even taken the end of year exams yet so why would they want to kick you all out? That wouldn't make sense." Caroline's words calmed Vaughan inside and he felt comforted. "So why does she want to see only us?" Caroline looked at him and shrugged. "Only one way to find out, Vaughan. Go to the common room."

* * *

Walking across the grand hallway, Vaughan glanced at the Time-Keeper's Clock. The small spoon hadn't jumped into the eleven o'clock time-slice yet, so he knew he was on time. With him were Verity and Caroline. In silence, they ascended the spiral staircase to Ozzy's Corridor where Vaughan entered the Common Room alone. Looking back at his faithful friends, Verity whispered "we'll be right here." With a small smile of thanks, Vaughan walked in and closed the door behind him.

Dr Crose was seated alongside David, Nicholas and Amy on the soft, comfy pale-blue settee in front of the roaring fire, which instantly warmed Vaughan's near-frozen body and lifted his spirits. She was smiling, so it couldn't be bad news, he reasoned.

"Come in, sit down" she gestured to the seats around her, as Emi and Orla also appeared in the doorway looking equally unsure of themselves. "Look at you all, you look terrified!" she said sweetly, "don't look so scared, there's nothing to be worried about." As she looked at the children she could almost see the worry lift off their shoulders and their faces relaxed instantly. "No, this is exciting! You six are going to go on a little House trip."

It was tradition at Honeycomb Hall that each House celebrated the Feast Day of its founder Saint. The first years would take a trip to the Cathedral which housed the remains of their Saint, to learn about their lives; all other years were given the day off, having already paid their respects to their House Saint in their first year. In the evening the whole school joined in for a celebratory feast in honour of the Saint. Initially, the children from the second-year and upwards were given the day off to remember their pilgrimage and reflect on the lives of their House Saint, and although this was the way the day was always started, inevitably it became a day of fun and relaxation for the House. Dr Crose explained all about St Oswald and that his Feast Day was 29th February. "Usually only the first-years go on the House trip - now, we know you three are in the second-year - Vaughan, Emi, Orla - but this is your first year at Honeycomb. Dr Bakewell has ruled that all scholarship students will join the first years on their trip, so all six of you will go." Feeling so relieved, Vaughan could have flung his arms around her and hugged her. Instead, he breathed a deep sigh of relief and gratitude. "Thanks, Miss!" he grinned.

"I bet you thought you were in trouble, didn't you?" she said, looking from one to the other. To Vaughan's surprise, both Emi and Orla also nodded and were looking equally relieved. He felt less foolish now. "I thought you might! That's why I asked Dr Bakewell if I could tell you - I knew you'd have been really worried if Dr Bakewell asked to see you and I couldn't let that happen, could I?" she said, her friendly smile reappearing. How did she get to read their minds like that, he wondered? She was fast becoming his favourite teacher. "Anyway, I think there are two concerned friends out in the corridor" she said as she looked at Vaughan, "so I'll leave you to it and tell them they're free to come in." She rose up from her seat and walked to the common room door with Emi and Orla. Opening it to see Verity and Caroline trying to listen through the door, she smiled at them. "Everything's fine you two, nothing to worry about. Go on, go on in."

She left the common room and Verity and Caroline ran in, eager to know what it had all been about. Vaughan explained to them about the trip and was pleased to hear the girls confirm that this was indeed true.

"Of course!" said Caroline, slapping her hand on her forehead, "why didn't we think of that? Yes, we went last year. You go to..."

"Bardney Abbey" finished Vaughan proudly.

"Yes, it was an abbey..." Verity agreed. "There's a great story about where he's buried. You'll love it. I can't believe we forgot to tell you about the Feast Day!"

They spent the rest of the break chatting about the Feast Days and the girls told Vaughan when each of the House Feast Day's were - St Oswald was the first of the year, on 29th February; then came St Wistan on 1st June and finally St Swithun on 15th July. The girls told Vaughan all about the types of food they ate on these special days, which then brought them quickly onto the topic of sweets, which led to chocolate which then brought them round to truffles - reminding them that today, Dr Bakewell was absent from school. Today, Dr Bakewell had been to see the Council of Confectioners. Today was the day that everything might change. And only they knew about it. Settling themselves into the window seat of the large window which overlooked the driveway, the three children sat down and eagerly awaited the return of their Headmaster, chattering excitedly about Vaughan's upcoming trip.

Chapter 40

Sorrel's Sabotage

As February progressed it brought with it even colder weather and a second fall of snow and ice. It was almost as if February wanted to remind everyone that Spring hadn't yet arrived and Winter was still very much in charge. All the children complained about being too cold, resulting in poor Mrs Hilderstone having to make sure all the fireplaces in the school were lit, although she found it very difficult to carry anything heavy after her fall and Mr Soames was often seen carrying baskets of firewood and coal through the corridors to help her! But today even the arctic-like weather couldn't dampen Verity's spirits. Today Verity was very excited. In today's Edible Arts lesson, Dr Crose had promised to teach them the art of making sugarcraft flowers. They had seen them before many times, marvelled at how life-like Dr Bakewell and Dr Crose could make these sugary decorations and been amazed at how delicate some of them were. Sometimes it was impossible to distinguish between the sugar flowers and real flowers. But until today, they had not actually made any themselves; during the Christmas preparations they'd concentrated on the more simple designs like holly and ivy leaves, but now they were about to enter the detailed designs.

Sugarcraft was Verity's favourite lesson. She enjoyed the attention to detail it demanded and the incredible results it gave you if you got it right. Caroline enjoyed it but found it frustrating as it was a technique that required practice, practice and patience; Caroline was not the most patient of children and preferred chocolatiering. Vaughan's only experience of sugarcraft was making snowmen and holly leaves at Christmas, so for him it was a mixture of curiosity and excitement.

Since starting at Dr Bakewell's School of Confectionery, Vaughan felt as though he had been given access to a very private club. With every lesson it felt as though a door had opened, allowing him to step through into a room of unseen knowledge - of things he hadn't even realised existed until now. It was as if a whole world was slowly revealing itself to him, beckoning him invitingly into a maze of wonderment, knowledge and skill. And he was loving every single minute of it.

Settling themselves on the pastel-coloured tables of the 'Sugarcraft Kitchen' they waited patiently for Dr Crose to arrive. As their teacher entered the classroom, they respectfully stopped chatting, rose to their feet and greeted their teacher with a cheery "Good Morning Dr Crose," as was their custom.

"Good morning, class" chirruped Dr Crose in reply as she walked through the tables to the far end of the class. She settled herself behind the large white kitchen island at the top of the classroom, which doubled as the teacher's desk. It was the only desk in the room to be bright white and also have it's own sink and silver taps, which sparkled in the light and shone brightly.

The children's desks were simple coloured tables with no gadgets or fixtures; pastel-coloured with shiny silver legs. Two rows of cupboards were positioned along the right hand side of the kitchen, the bottom row on the floor and the top row hovering above them, fixed to the wall. Opposite the cupboards, on the left hand side of the kitchen, were a row of large, white, chunky, square sinks, which Vaughan had heard were called 'Belfast Sinks'. Orla had been very proud when she heard that, because her family originated from Belfast.

The cupboards were also pastel-coloured, matching the children's tables. Baby blue, mint green, lemon, peach and baby pink shades filled the room, giving the kitchen a bright, cheerful, pleasant atmosphere. Just being inside such a colourful classroom made Vaughan think immediately of birthday parties. Pulling a frilly pale-blue apron over her head and tying it behind her back, Dr Crose began the lesson.

"First things first, please all get an apron from the back of class; once you have your apron on, wash your hands at the sinks and return to your tables." Chairs scraped across the astonishingly bright white floor, as students hurried to the back of the room to grab an apron. Unknowingly grabbing hold of the same apron Avery Sorrel was holding, Vaughan winced as Avery immediately snatched it back out of Vaughan's hand, resulting in a small friction burn to Vaughan's finger.

"That's mine" Sorrel hissed, glaring at Vaughan. Vaughan stared blankly back in amazement - there were lots of aprons and technically, it was a school apron, not Avery's apron. But so what, he thought; he was getting the measure of Avery Sorrel by now and decided not to let him wind him up. Vaughan shrugged his shoulders and took another apron before calmly walking to his table, Avery staring after him - not moving, just glowering at Vaughan with disdain.

"Are you joining us, Avery?" Dr Crose called across the kitchen. Avery looked around and realised he had been so busy giving Vaughan daggers that he hadn't noticed the rest of the class were now back at their tables.

"Unfortunately" whispered Verity to herself, under her breath, as Avery returned to his table alongside hers.

Dr Crose lifted two plastic boxes from behind her island-desk and explained to the class what they were going to practice. She also took a pile of plastic document holders, the sort you find in an office and placed them on her desk alongside the boxes.

"As this is the first time you lot have tried making flowers, we'll start with what I think are the easiest flowers to make - the rose. All you will need is fondant icing and a plastic sheet."

Verity spun around to Caroline and Vaughan, who were seated behind her and mouthed 'plastic sheet?' Both Vaughan and Caroline responded with a shrug of the shoulders and subtle shake of their heads, signalling that they didn't know why either. Returning her attention back to her teacher, Verity waited as Dr Crose began distributing the bizarre tools for today's class.

She made her way through the tables, placing a real rose, a small pack of icing and a plastic document wallet on each child's table. When everyone had been given their items, Dr Crose called them all to the front for a demonstration. Curiosity coursing through them, Verity and Vaughan pushed right to the front while Caroline hung a little further back, Vaughan filled with eagerness to see what lay beyond today's door of knowledge that Dr Crose was about to open to them.

* * *

With nimble fingers lightly twizzling and squeezing the icing, Dr Crose expertly demonstrated how to make a sugar rose in less than two minutes. She made two; that was all it took for the class to understand what to do. The children were amazed at how seemingly simple she made it. They returned to their tables and practiced themselves as Dr Crose paraded through the classroom, monitoring and pointing out suggestions to her pupils.

As instructed, Verity sliced off several slices of icing, all the same thickness and rolled them into balls. Then, following Dr Crose's example, she placed the balls in between the sheets of plastic. Using her thumb she then squashed the balls, just as Dr Crose had done.

"Don't forget you don't want little pancakes - flat all over, you need to leave the part that squishes up as it is, so one side of the petal is thicker" Dr Crose advised, as she passed Verity's desk. Verity did so and was relieved to see that the balls of icing now looked a little bit like scattered petals. Then came the tricky bit. She carefully rolled up one 'petal' into itself and it really did look like a rose bud. She was very pleased with herself. After studying the real rose she gradually began to add the sugar petals to the rosebud one by one, just like the real rose, until she had used them all up. She placed it on the table and stepped back to admire it, comparing it to the real rose. There it was, sitting pretty and pink - her very first sugar rose. Then an idea came to her.

"Caroline!" she whispered over her shoulder. "I've got an idea. Let's save these up and use them when we celebrate St Oswald's Feast Day."

"Okay" agreed Caroline, "let's make them all blue and silver. I wonder if Dr Crose has any silver icing?" Just then Dr Crose approached Caroline's desk and she called her teacher over. "Dr Crose, I was just wondering if we can make some sugar flowers and use them for the Feast of St Oswald? It's coming up soon."

"I think that's an excellent idea Caroline, what a lovely thought. Yes, I think that would be perfect - you could use them as decorations over the tables in the Refectory. But you'll have to stick to blue and white though."

"Don't you have any silver colouring?" asked Verity, overhearing the conversation.

"No, we don't. Silver colouring isn't edible. You can eat it in very small amounts but I wouldn't trust any child here not to eat the lot! No, we don't use silver as too much would put you straight into the hospital quarters and I don't think Dr Muller-Weiss would be too impressed with us. You'll have to stick to white, I'm afraid. But by all means use as many shades of blue as you wish, to make it more colourful" and off she moved, checking on other children.

"I never knew that, about silver not being edible" Vaughan whispered to Caroline, as Dr Crose left them to carry on.

"Me neither" admitted Caroline. "How weird, when you can eat gold!"

The children spent the rest of the lesson making blue roses ready to save up for the Feast of St Oswald. Being the twenty-ninth of February of course, they only celebrated it on the actual day every four years and it just so happened that this year was a leap year and they would be able to do just that (when it wasn't a leap year they had to celebrate on the twenty-eighth instead). So they were really looking forward to this year, especially as it was going to be Vaughan's first Feast Day.

By the end of class, between the three of them, they managed to make over a hundred roses - their desks were covered in flowers.

"Tsk. Looks more like a flower shop than a classroom" sniped Avery as he wandered past their tables, looking down his nose at them.

"You're just jealous" Caroline bit back, "'cause we actually put some effort into celebrating our House Saint."

"What - all that's for your Feast Day?" he laughed. "That's over two weeks away. How are going to keep them fresh until then, eh? Didn't think of that, did you, clever clogs Caroline."

Oh no! How were they going to keep them safe for over two weeks? Caroline panicked, she hadn't thought of that, they were just so pleased with them and got carried away. Where can you keep over a hundred, delicate roses, to stop them being damaged or eaten, for two weeks? Looking quickly at Verity and Vaughan, she read their faces - they were as blank as hers. Obviously none of them had thought that far ahead. And Avery had noticed.

"Oh! You don't know do you?" he laughed. "Why don't you just put them in the freezer, ha ha!" and went to walk away, laughing.

"Can you freeze them?" Verity asked him. Avery stopped and turned around. "Yeah course. You can freeze anything" then walked off. Verity looked at Caroline, then Vaughan. "Suppose we'll have to freeze them then. And if they come out all frosty, all the better - they'll look really atmospheric then! Just think, frosty blue roses, how wintry!"

They filled plastic tubs with the roses and stored them safely in the deep-freeze in the classroom storeroom. "That'll keep them safe" said Verity. "Just hope Sorrel doesn't hide them or throw them away. I wouldn't put it past him."

Chapter 41

Feast Day of St Oswald

But Avery didn't throw them away. Or hide them. On the twenty-ninth of February, Vaughan, Verity and Caroline met Dr Crose outside the Sugarcraft Kitchen and asked her to unlock the kitchen as they needed to get something from the classroom for the feast. Entering the storeroom they collected the tubs from the freezer and were pleasantly surprised to see that all the boxes remained, completely untouched. They hadn't told Dr Crose what they were fetching; she knew they had made the roses but didn't know they'd frozen them to keep them fresh and make them look frosty. A cold wintry morning, they would be completely appropriate to celebrate a House who's colours were blue and silver; the children silently congratulating themselves on their ingenuity.

As they placed the tubs on the pastel tables in the kitchen and removed the lids, Dr Crose peered inside, her eyebrows knitting together in a frown. One by one, Vaughan, Verity and Caroline took out the roses and placed them on the tables, smiling and looking at their teacher for praise.

"See miss - frosty roses! Especially for today!" beamed Verity, thrilled. Vaughan however, wondered why Dr Crose didn't look particularly happy. In fact, she looked rather vexed. "You froze them? All of them?" she asked solemnly.

"We did!" said Caroline. "We needed to keep them fresh and safe."

"Caroline, sugar flowers last for months. They dry perfectly well in the air, they don't need to be boxed up in a tub."

"Oh" said a disappointed Caroline. "We thought they'd be safer that way."

"But what about the frosty effect?" prompted Verity, "they look really wintry now with all the ice crystals, don't they?"

"Oh Verity! Why did you freeze them?" she asked again, her face very disappointed.

"Well, to keep them safe. Like Caroline said. We wanted to know what to do with them all and Avery told us we could freeze them." Dr Crose shook her head sadly. "I wish you'd just asked me. I'm your teacher - and your House Master. Oh Verity, sugarcraft doesn't freeze."

"What do you mean?" asked Vaughan, "they've frozen perfectly. Look at them."

"Yes, they are, while they're still frozen. But they'll defrost. What happens to ice cubes when they're taken out of a freezer?"

"They melt" he answered.

"Exactly. And so will the ice crystals that are covering your roses."

"So..?" Vaughan prompted.

"Oh no!" squealed Verity. "Sugar and water...." Caroline gasped as she realised what Dr Crose was driving at.

"Water melts sugar! When they defrost, they'll melt, won't they?"

"Well, not melt completely, but they'll go very soggy yes. And droop. And they wont last until tonight."

The children sat down, Vaughan put his chin on his hand and drummed his fingers, thinking. Verity put her head in her hands and stared at the table, while Caroline put her folded arms on the table and sunk her head onto her wrists. Seeing their dismay, Dr Crose felt she had to do something. She wouldn't put it past Avery Sorrel to have sabotaged them on purpose, but then again, maybe he really was trying to be helpful? She just wasn't sure. After all, sugarcraft will freeze - it just doesn't unfreeze. Maybe he didn't realise that? Or then again, maybe he knew perfectly well?

"I've got an idea" she announced brightly. They slowly raised their heads, exposing their crestfallen faces. "Look, we've all got the day off today. Vaughan, you'll be coming with me to Bardney Abbey..." Vaughan nodded his head eagerly, "but girls, if you want to make some more roses, you can have the kitchen to yourselves and use whatever ingredients you want. Put these roses back in the freezer and when I come back after the trip, we'll give them to Mrs Hilderstone to sprinkle over the table frozen. Hopefully dinner will be over before they start to defrost and turn everything into a soggy blue mess!"

"Be quite funny if they did though, wouldn't it?" grinned Vaughan, cheekily.

And they managed it. Caroline and Verity worked very hard for two hours and managed to make another hundred roses. In fact, along with the frozen ones they'd made in class, they now had twice as many.

* * *

Vaughan, Emi, Orla and the rest of the St Oswald first-years returned from their trip to Bardney Abbey full of excitement, eager to share their adventure with their friends. As they entered the Refectory for dinner, they were amazed how beautiful it was. It had been transformed into a blue grotto in honour of St Oswald. There were blue ribbons twisted around the columns, blue and white streamers hanging from the ceiling, silver candelabra on each table and blue and white roses sprinkled everywhere. The food tables were laden with the traditional Feast Day buffet - smorgasbords of cheese, tuna and cucumber sandwiches, trays of roast chicken drumsticks, warm sausages served in hollowed out bowls of crusty bread, samosas, sliced meat and warm bread for hot sandwiches, pork pies, roast hams, roast pork, nut roasts, spinach roulade, warm salads, eve's pudding, rhubarb crumble and custard, sticky toffee pudding and ice-cream - the children of all houses absolutely loved the Saint's Day's - even when it wasn't their House Saint being honoured!

Mrs Hilderstone had helped Verity and Caroline place the sugar flowers on the tables, giving the effect as though they'd simply fallen of an invisible rose bush in the sky and scattered themselves. Even Dr Bakewell commented on how beautiful it made the room and what a lovely way it was to remember St Oswald. Everyone appreciated their presence, only one person looked stunned to see them everywhere.

At the end of their celebratory dinner as they were about to leave, Verity and Caroline approached Avery on their way out of the hall.

"Thanks for your help today Avery" said Caroline. Perplexed, he looked at her as Percy stared at him in surprise.

"What help?" he sniffed, haughtily.

"Well, you did us a favour" explained Caroline. "If you hadn't told us to freeze those roses - knowing they would go soggy, we would only have had a hundred old ones." "But now" continued Verity, "thanks to you, we have a hundred fresh ones and a hundred frosty, frozen ones. So thanks very much! See ya!" They walked away, leaving Avery muttering to himself, annoyed.

"That felt good!" sighed Verity. "Really good"

"Certainly did" agreed Caroline as they made their way back to the common room. "Anyway, I want to hear all about Vaughan's trip to Bardney."

Chapter 42

Spring Cleaning

After a bitter cold February, March the first finally arrived on a Saturday, when the children were allowed to do as they pleased; the only exceptions were that they must be in the Refectory for breakfast, lunch and dinner at the usual times if they wished to eat. No-one ever missed breakfast and Vaughan, Verity and Caroline were no exception.

After helping themselves to a pancakes, bananas and berries, washed down with a big glass of apple juice, they looked forward to going to visit Farmer Lambrick and seeing Rasher. He'd grown such a lot since the Farmer rescued him, he was now pretty much a fully grown pig and Farmer Lambrick was besotted with him. In fact, the children wondered what on earth the Farmer would do without him, if he was ordered to give him up. So they tried not to think about that and simply enjoyed Rasher while they could - which they hoped would be forever.

As usual they left the Refectory and made their way to the back of the school kitchens, where Verity knocked the door and waited for her father to answer. Almost immediately the door opened and his bulky frame appeared in the doorway.

"Off on your errands, are you?" he asked as he produced four small sackfuls of waste from the kitchen.

"Yep - off to feed Rasher. He's getting really big now" Verity told her father "and he looks forward to seeing us every Saturday."

"Oh, he does, does he?" chuckled her father. "He's a pig Verity, remember. He's not able to 'look forward' to things."

"But he does" Verity insisted, "well, he gets excited when we pour his food in."

"Now that sounds more like it!" he agreed, "pig by name, pig by nature! Alright you three, here you go and mind how you go. Don't want any of you tripping up and having one of these split open on you!"

The children loaded two sacks onto a wheelbarrow and took turns between carrying a sack and pushing the barrow. It was becoming more difficult now that Spring was here - in the Winter it was slippery but the wheelbarrow slid easily over the ice. Now it was spring, the wheel often got caught in muddy patches and clumps of long grass, so they had to stop every couple of minutes to either have a short rest or swap turns. So it took them nearly fifteen minutes to finally reach Farmer Lambrick's little stone farmhouse on the far edge of the school grounds.

* * *

Daffodils had sprung up through the grass and lined the border which ran around the farmhouse, making what had previously looked like a very run down and neglected small house, now a picturesque, rustic cottage. As they knocked the door, they heard the chickens squawking and Rasher grunting. A voice from behind the farmhouse answered.

"Be roight with yer - hang on a mo" which the children knew belonged to Farmer Lambrick.

"T's only us" Caroline called cheerfully and the children left their wheelbarrow full of sacks by the fence and went through the gate to his yard behind.

Farmer Lambrick had obviously been very busy; a greenhouse had appeared on what was before a bare patch of ground and in it were buckets and canes and watering cans. Kneeling in the now empty cabbage patch, sleeves rolled up and trowel in hand, he heard someone approach and turned to greet them. "Oh, it's you three" he said, straightening his back and turning to greet them. He was covered in soil and looked shattered. "Does me no good at all, all this kneeling" he complained as he stood up and stretched, "it's a young man's game this, not an old Farmer loike me."

"What are you doing?" asked Vaughan, curiously.

"It's Spring ain't it?" Farmer replied, looking strangely at him. "Now's the toime to get all the seedlings planted but Oi've got to fertilise the soil first, otherwoise they won't grow so big. So that's what Oi've been doing this morning. Fertiloising."

"What with?" Vaughan asked again. He'd never seen anyone do anything like this before.

"Manure, of course" Farmer Lambrick replied. "Horse, mainly." Noticing Vaughan's blank expression, he clarified. "Horse poo".

"No it's not!" Vaughan said confidently "you don't eat horse poo! What do you really use? My Mum uses some special water from the garden centre on her flowers."

"Well yes, but these aren't fer flowers, these patches are fer vegetables. And Oi'm telling yer the truth - yer use manure. That's poo from either a cow or a horse and it's been used fer centuries. It soaks inter the ground an' the nutrients soak up into the vegetables roots an' help 'em grow bigger, tastier and last longer."

"That's disgusting!" Vaughan said, feeling slightly queasy. "We've been eating that all year."

"Ar, that you 'ave!" chuckled Farmer Lambrick, "An' that yer'll continue ter do, too."

"Actually Vaughan, my Dad says that too" Verity piped up. "He says that before we came to Honeycomb, when he was in the Restaurant, you could always tell the food that had been grown in fertilised soil. He said it was much, much better and that's why Farmer Lambrick fertilises his patches. So we get the best food."

Verity's Dad worked as a cook in the school kitchens but Vaughan hadn't given much thought about it before. "Your Dad worked in a Restaurant before he worked here?" he asked, completely surprised. He noticed Verity's face darken and she seemed to clam up. "Yes, he did. But now he works here." She refused to say any more and Vaughan was sure he saw a faint glisten of tears in her eyes. Ever the protector of Verity, Caroline very swiftly changed the subject. "Rasher's looking amazing" she said, going up to the sty and calling his name. "I think he loves living here."

"Moight be somethin' to do with all the leftovers you three bring 'im every week" Farmer Lambrick agreed. "ooh, the leftovers!" Verity suddenly remembered and dashed to the fence gate. "Come on, I can't carry them all myself" she yelled to Caroline and Vaughan.

The three of them momentarily disappeared from view and returned a few moments later, heaving three sackfuls of food for Rasher. Farmer Lambrick followed and brought the fourth sack himself, having noticed it was considerably larger than the others. Pulling on their wellington boots, Verity and Caroline ventured carefully into the sty and emptied the two smaller sacks into Rasher's trough, while Vaughan picked up the third small sack and followed Farmer Lambrick, who stored the larger sack in a special little bunker. Farmer Lambrick opened the doors and flung in his sack. As he turned to relieve Vaughan of his sack, he said "suppose you've heard about Dr Bakewell's appeal, have you?" Totally taken aback, Vaughan shook his head. "No - well, not really."

"No? Oi 'eard you three got caught sneaking under the Teacher's Table the other day."

"How did you find that out?" asked an astonished Vaughan.

"Mrs Hilderstone" explained the Farmer. "Good friend o' moine she is. An' a good friend o' yours too, Oi daresay. Oi know that you three tried to save 'er from fallin' at Christmas. Very good of yer that was, very good indeed."

"Thanks" mumbled Vaughan, "but what about the appeal? We know he had a letter back from the COCOA but that's all we know." Then a thought occurred to Vaughan. "Do you know something, then?"

Farmer Lambrick looked at Vaughan and gave him that mischievous lop-sided smile of his. "Ar" he said, squinting into the sun. "Oi might do. Oi think you three could do with a good cup o' tea inside, don't you?"

* * *

Farmer Lambrick appeared in the doorway with his round tray laden with four mismatched cups of steaming tea and a plate full of digestive biscuits. He placed the tray on the little rickety coffee table in the middle of the room and sat in his favourite armchair - the soft cosy white one, patterned, with pink roses. The children dived in and helped themselves to a cup of tea and a biscuit each. As soon as they'd settled into their chairs, Farmer Lambrick took a sip of his tea and enlightened them.

"Alroight, so yer know what 'appened when Dr Bakewell went to the Council of Confectioners, don't yer?" To his surprise, all three of them shook their heads, their mouths full of biscuit. "Oh. Roight, Oi'd better explain then. Cut a long story short, to get somethin' agreed by the Council, all members present must be in agreement. One o' the Councillors there refused ter sign ter agree that those truffles we're growin' in that there forest are real. Without the signature of all present, nothing further happens. So, Dr Bakewell left the office downhearted but with two choices. Choice number one - accept it and we carry on loike nothing ever 'appened. The school stays in danger of being shut down, we all lose our jobs, Oi have to get rid of Rasher and you all have to foind new schools. Choice number two - he can appeal to the Council of Confectionery. Depending upon what he says his grounds for appeal are, depend on whether they accept it. They then decide what to do next. The Council of Confectioners are obliged ter notify the Culinary Council of any appeals, so they can make sure everythin's done properly. O' course, Dr Bakewell has a history with the Culinary Council, so although he has two choices, neither of which are particularly appealing to 'im. He'd rather not 'ave to get involved with the Culinary Council again. So, as we grown-ups say, he's caught between a rock an' a hard place."

Vaughan tilted his head slightly and screwed up his nose at Farmer Lambrick. "He's what?" he asked. Understanding Vaughan's twisted expression as that of confusion, he explained the saying. "Yer know - closin' the school is the rock, appealin' and involvin' the Culinary Council is the 'ard place and poor old Dr Bakewell is stuck in the middle. The rock won't move so he can't go that way but the Council moight just be able ter squeeze him through by way of appeal, although that way will be hard and difficult."

"Yeah but at least there's a way through the hard place." said Caroline.

"I bet I know who refused to sign" muttered Verity to Caroline, who nodded in response. "Yeah, I bet it was him too."

Looking blankly at them, the girls turned to Vaughan and explained. "Avery Sorrel's Dad. Henry Sorrel. He's on the Council of Confectioners." Vaughan sighed and shrank back into his chair. What was it with that family, he thought, why did they always want to ruin things? Why did they have to be so spiteful?

"We saw Mr Soames hand Dr Bakewell a letter this week. The letter we saw had a red ribbon around it which Dr Bakewell dropped on the floor. That's why we snuck under the Teacher's Table - to find out what was going on, try to get some clues." Vaughan explained to the Farmer.

"And we found one too. A big one." Caroline added. "The ribbon that was wrapped around the letter had the initials C.O.C.O.A. printed on it."

"The Council of Confectioners" mumbled Farmer Lambrick, thoughtfully.

"Yes, we know that" Caroline interrupted impatiently, "but what did it say?"

"Well, it was hopeful." he told them. "They won't overturn a decision just loike that, yer know. As Oi say, they will have discussed it with the Culinary Council and taken their advice. They made a suggestion to Dr Bakewell; he discussed it with me and we agreed to accept the their offer."

"Will you tell us, please?" begged Verity.

"The Culinary Council stated that Dr Bakewell's claims were extraordinary and if proven, would be of great significance. They were not impressed that Dr Bakewell suggested Henry Sorrel's refusal to sign was personal but nor were they happy that if this was the case, that Henry Sorrel would withhold signing a document on such an important matter just because he and Dr Bakewell don't get along. They said they 'ave a great interest in this matter and insist on bein' involved."

"What did they suggest to Dr Bakewell" asked Vaughan.

"The Council of Confectioners suggested firstly that Henry Sorrel be removed from this matter and he was to have no more involvement. If you ask me, that instruction came from the Culinary Council. So, another member will step into Sorrel's shoes."

Verity smiled. "Serves him right" she grinned.

"One o' the problems was that Dr Bakewell could have gotten the truffles from anywhere, before taking them to COCOA. It's only you that saw Rasher diggin' them up Verity, and as honest as we all know you are, Oi'm afraid COCOA and the Culinary Council won't just take the word of a twelve year old schoolgirl."

Verity looked outraged at this. "It's not that they don't believe you, it's more that they can't. Not without proof, anyway."

Verity wriggled uncomfortably in her seat and folded her arms sulkily, clearly offended by the Council's attitude.

"How do we prove it then?" asked Caroline, feeling annoyed on behalf of Verity.

"COCOA have offered to come to the school with the Culinary Council. They want to venture into the forest themselves, with me and Dr Bakewell o'course, and dig them up themselves. Then they'll 'ave the proof they need that they're from school grounds."

"Then what?" asked Vaughan "What will they do with the truffles once they've dug them up?"

"Oh, then they'll take them inter the school inter one o' the experimental kitchens. They'll do some tests and then finally, 'opefully, they'll confirm they're genuine."

"So until then we just have to wait?" asked Vaughan, completely amazed how awkward and complicated grown-ups could make things.

"No" answered Farmer Lambrick with a cheeky smile slowly spreading across his face "until then we let Rasher out a few more toimes on a 'training exercise', so we see exactly where we need ter take the Council ter foind the truffles!"

Chapter 43

Avery's Shock News

Avery Sorrel and the rest of St Wistan second-years stood in the growing corner of the kitchen garden, with Cuthbert Flowerdew the Gardener and Professor Peach. This morning they were studying Natural Foods and Professor Peach had decided that as Spring was well and truly here, being mid-April, it would be a good idea for them to help Cuthbert prepare the seed beds for the seedlings.

Two children were assigned a seed bed between them and working in pairs, each bed was duly weeded and dug over. Genuinely glad to have their help, Cuthbert pottered about between the beds offering words of encouragement and tips to the children, who in turn were amazed that Cuthbert could do such physical hard work at such an old age. After a short time kneeling and weeding with trowels, the children were told to swap their trowels for spades and 'turn over' the soil by digging as deep and hard as they could; they did as they were told but it didn't take long for them to complain about aching arms, backs and legs. Professor Peach explained that this was good for them and would not only keep them fit but would also enable them to 'appreciate all the work that goes into growing food'. It was 'character building' as Professor Peach referred to it although when Avery wrote home to his parents at the end of the day, he churlishly referred to it as 'child labour'.

When all the seed beds had been dug over and inspected by Cuthbert, the children planted seeds which could be sown outdoors. Apparently, so Professor Peach told them, not all seeds are suitable for planting outdoors, some to be grown undercover, so today they would be planting only three types of seeds - burdock, gooseberry and sorrel.

"Sorrel?" whispered Poppy Quenell to her gardening partner, Oliver Eddington, "who wants to grow another Avery?" Oliver giggled as he took the seeds from Poppy and sprinkled them all over their weed-free seed bed. "Not me - one's enough, thanks!" he said, looking over his shoulder and watching as Avery ordered his partner, Joe, about. "Poor Joe - I'm glad I was paired with you Poppy, just imagine having to work with Avery Sorrel." Poppy shuddered at the thought. "No thanks!" she said.

As they dusted the last of the seeds from their hands Poppy noticed Dr Bakewell stride across the gardens with a stranger, dressed in khaki trousers and a green woolly jumper. "Who's that, Sir? With Dr Bakewell?" she asked Professor Peach as he walked over to inspect their sowings. Looking up in the direction Poppy pointed, he saw the stranger walking across the gardens with Dr Bakewell.

"I've no idea, Poppy. I'm more interested in how my class are doing than what Dr Bakewell is doing. And you and Oliver have done very well indeed. Now, cover up your seeds with this to protect them from the birds." Handing Oliver a bag of something that looked like cat litter, he pottered off to another pair of child-gardeners.

"That told you" said Oliver, as he took a handful of the strange, tiny sticks and began to sprinkle them over the seeds. Poppy stuck her tongue out at him. "What is this stuff anyway?" she asked as she took a handful. Oliver looked at the bag.

"Er... Ver... Vermi... Ver-mi-cu..." he struggled to say the long name printed in large yellow letters on the purple bag.

"Vermiculite?" said Poppy, snatching the bag from him and reading it. "Never heard of it."

"Nor me - I thought it was cat litter!" admitted Oliver.

"I thought it was fish food!" said Poppy and they both laughed.

"Bet Avery pretends to know what it is" said Oliver, as they watched Avery take his bag from Professor Peach. "Even if he hasn't got a clue!"

* * *

Treading carefully across the wet grass, Dr Bakewell escorted his visitor through the gardens, across the school fields towards the Forest of Forgetfulness.

"I'm very grateful to you for coming out here today" he said, as they approached Farmer Lambrick's house.

"Not at all" replied the visitor. "It's a privilege to be invited here. Is this the forest?" he asked, as they approached the border between the forest and the fields, marked with a thin wire fence.

"It is" confirmed Dr Bakewell, as he knocked on the door of Farmer Lambrick's house. "Farmer Lambrick here will escort you inside; it's not called the Forest of Forgetfulness for nothing, you know!" The visitor looked at him and smiled politely, thinking this Bakewell man was a very odd little fellow.

"Alright" he agreed, humouring Dr Bakewell but privately wondering what all the fuss was about. As a ranger from the Forest & Woodland Fellowship , he knew his way around a wood or two and he couldn't imagine that this would be any different to any other forest he'd visited. A few moments later Farmer Lambrick appeared beside him holding a large folded-up map, with Dr Bakewell, harnesses and several ropes in tow.

"Lambrick, this is Paul Oakley from the Forest & Woodland Fellowship. I've asked him to come and take a look in the forest to confirm if the Forest & Woodland Fellowship would class it as ancient woodland." He then introduced Farmer Lambrick to Paul Oakley. "Mr Oakley, this is Farmer Lambrick. He's the only one who can safely find his way around the forest so I advise you to stay close to him at all times." He then beckoned Farmer Lambrick away from Paul Oakley and whispered quietly.

"Don't mention the truffles. All I've asked Mr Oakley to do is confirm the age of the forest. I contacted the Forest & Woodland Fellowship but they said they don't know the age of every forest and they didn't know about this one at all. Apparently they need to see the trees and sent Mr Oakley here to take some samples and photographs. Take him only as far as you need to, I don't want him to get lost."

"Yer can rely on me, Doc" said Farmer Lambrick importantly. "Yer ready Mr Oakley?" Paul Oakley nodded and grabbed the rope that Lambrick threw to him. The two men geared themselves up with harnesses and ropes and stepped over the border into the woodland. "Then welcome, to our Forest of Forgetfulness."

* * *

St Wistan's common room was a hive of activity; it was very similar to St Oswald's common room, albeit it was decorated in shades of green and cream. Georgia Flavell and Daisy Quenell sat on a dark green sofa in front of the empty fire grate, braiding each other's hair, trying to find the best styles to stop their hair from falling out from under their white caps in lessons. Percy Snodland walked through from the corridor and noticing Avery was absent, took a book from the bookshelf opposite and sat in a solitary armchair in front of the window to read. Poppy Quenell and Oliver Eddington had made friends during their earlier lesson and were happily sitting cross-legged on the floor, facing each other, with a tiny table between them, on which they had placed a chess set. They discovered they both loved playing chess and had challenged each other to a game. There was a hubbub of chatter which came from every direction, filling the room, so that no-one could hear anyone else's conversation but their own.

Suddenly the dormitory door next to the fireplace was flung open and banged against the wall, shocking everyone into silence immediately. Avery marched in carrying a piece of paper in his hand, looking angrier than most St Wistan's had ever seen him before. He strode straight over to Percy and shook the letter in front of his face. "Read this" he spat, contempt written across his furious face. Bewildered, Percy looked at his cousin and snatched the letter from him. "Not here..." Avery hissed, "the dormitory. I don't want any..." he turned and looked around him at the other members of his house who were still staring at him, "eavesdroppers." Percy dropped his book on the armchair and the two boys scurried off through the fireplace door to the dormitory, vacating the common room. The common room remained silent in their absence for two seconds, then after a few shrugs and a few comments of 'what was that about, then?' the occupants resumed their earlier activities. Annoyed that the interruption had broken their concentration, Poppy and Oliver resumed their game of chess, managing only to remember it was Oliver's turn, both their game plans forgotten. He made his move on the chessboard but having been distracted, it wasn't the move he had intended earlier and it proved to be the wrong move, allowing Poppy to take one of his knights. He was not best pleased.

In the dormitory Avery sat down on the first bunk. "That's not your bunk, Avery" Percy reminded him. "Oh who cares?" said Avery unconcerned. "just read this." Percy took the letter from him and read it in silence as Avery sat there, grinding his teeth in frustration. As Percy read it, his eyes widened in surprise and his mouth gaped a little. When he reached the bottom he folded it in two and handed it back to Avery.

"Is this true?" he asked incredulously.

"Must be." Avery managed to mutter through clenched teeth. "It's from father himself. My father. Treated like that. It's an outrage."

"It's a mistake, that's what it must be." Percy tried to console Avery but feeling equally angry - Henry Sorrel was his Uncle, after all. His mother's brother. He was a very important man and held a lot of power.

"Doctor...Bakewell..." Avery almost spat out his name with contempt. "It's no mistake, Perce. You read it yourself. My father - your Uncle - a senior member of the Council of Confectioners, has..." he couldn't even manage to get the words out, he was so angry and upset. Percy finished his sentence for him.

"...been suspended from the Council of Confectioners."

Chapter 44

An Historical Day

D r Bakewell's office had been transformed from Headmaster's Office into a scientific laboratory. The experimenting table was covered with flasks and containers of different sizes and shapes, filled with various substances and all sorts of colours. Tubes and glass pipes ran from container to container, looking a bit like a 3d map of the London underground. Some leaned diagonally to the right, some to the left. Some were spiral-shaped and had liquid swirling around, dripping into dishes below. Some jars contained chunks of chocolate; others, gooey caramel or melted jam. A little gas ring was positioned in the centre of the table, blue flames escaping it's base and lapping up around the upside-down lightbulb-shaped glass jar which sat on it; the clear golden liquid contained within bubbled away merrily, the bubbles rising to the surface like hot, golden lemonade, before bursting. Pottering away in front of the experimenting table was Dr Bakewell himself; wearing a white overall and plastic goggles (which had messed his hair up due to him frequently taking them on and off), he looked more like a mad scientist than a respected master baker or Headteacher!

Opposite the experimenting table on the other side of the room stood Dr Bakewell's desk, but today it looked completely different. It was laden with colour and ingredients; chocolate buttons, white chocolate drops, jars of honey, a multitude of dishes containing all sorts of various berries from the garden, a plate of small flowers, jars of jam, bunches of fresh herbs and all Dr Bakewell's utensils. In fact, the only item that remained, reminding you that there was a Headmaster's desk hiding underneath all the confectionery camouflage, was the old-fashioned black telephone that stood proudly in the corner, looking quite out of place today.

Dr Bakewell put on his spotty oven gloves and removed the hot flask with the bubbling golden liquid from the gas burner. As he stretched his arm up high and ever-so-carefully poured some of the liquid into the highest, spiral tube above, allowing it to run down slowly and cool before coating the fresh berries in the dish below, the black telephone unexpectedly sprang to life and rang loudly, causing the receiver to shake violently in its holder. The sudden piercing ring which cut through the silence like a hot knife through butter caused Dr Bakewell to jump, momentarily letting go of the hot lightbulb-shaped flask. The jar dropped onto the experimenting table and shattered instantly; thick, golden, bubbling lava quickly seeping all over his work and carrying sharp glass shards with it as it spread, wider and wider.

"Drat...drat..." he mumbled, not sure what to do first. He quickly threw off his oven mitts and pulled his goggles off, over his shiny bald head, messing his hair up even more. He dropped them to the floor and turned to answer the telephone. He took a quick look at the still-spreading golden liquid and turned back to the experimenting table, eager to stem the flow then realised the telephone was still ringing. For a few seconds he hovered between the two, not wondering which was more important; the telephone, he decided. The liquid will stop in a minute and he can clean up later. No, wait - the liquid. The telephone caller could ring back. No, the telephone. Definitely the telephone.
Diving to his desk he managed to grab the receiver and answer the call just before it rang off.

"Hello?" he wheezed breathlessly, wiping the sweat from his brow with the sleeve of his white overcoat.

"Am I speaking with Dr Bakewell?" came the official voice from the telephone.

"You are" answered Dr Bakewell, equally formally. "Whom may I ask is calling?" his breath slowly began to return to normal pace.

"Paul Oakley. From the Forest & Woodland Fellowship." The Forest & Woodland Fellowship? thought Dr Bakewell. He had presumed they would write to him if they had anything important to tell him, he hadn't expected them to call.

"Ah, yes Mr Oakley. How can I help you?"

"I'll come straight to the point, Dr Bakewell. I have carried out tests taken from samples of the forest and conducted some research going back centuries. That's why it's taken me a while to come back to you. But it was time well spent."

"Oh yes?" urged Dr Bakewell, now completely alert and focused. He could feel his body starting to tremble with nervousness. This news could be fantastic or terrible.

"Oh yes. Dr Bakewell, tests and research confirms that your 'Forest of Forgetfulness' as you call it, contains traces of primeval wildwood."

"It does?" Dr Bakewell had absolutely no idea what on earth primeval wildwood was, but was wasn't about to ask for details. All he wanted to know was if it was an ancient forest or not, not it's geographical make-up. "I see."

Instantly Paul Oakley knew that Dr Bakewell did not see at all. "Dr Bakewell, there are ancient woodlands - which are forests and woods over four hundred years old. And there are primeval wildwoods." Dr Bakewell's heart sank. His forest was primeval then, not ancient after all. If he couldn't prove the forest was ancient, he couldn't prove they were growing true truffles in their own land. And if the Forest & Woodland Fellowship didn't class it as ancient, who else could?

"Oh" he said, crestfallen. "Well, thank you for letting me know. I'm sorry to have wasted your time." He removed the receiver from his ear, about to hang up, when he heard Paul shout down line. "NO - WAIT!"

He put the telephone back to his ear. "I hadn't finished" continued Paul. "I mean, your forest is even more rare. Ancient forests are woods and forests over four hundred years old, but primeval forests covered the land shortly after the ice-age. Until now, there were only three known primeval wildwoods in England. Only three have ever been mapped. Dr Bakewell, you have discovered and introduced us to a fourth, unknown wildwood, right in the grounds of your school! Do you understand what I'm saying? Your forest is more than ancient, Dr Bakewell, it's a piece of living history!"

Chapter 45

The Feast of St Wistan

On the first of May Dr Bakewell received a telephone call in his office. It was a very short call, from Frank Chewdle, the Head Confectioner at C.O.C.O.A. As soon as he placed the receiver safely back in its cradle, Dr Bakewell walked to the door by the trophy case and opened it.

"Derek? Derek! You there?"

"Just a moment" Professor Drumgoole's exasperated voice replied. But Dr Bakewell did not want to wait. He opened the door and marched straight into the Sun Room, where Professor Drumgoole was in the middle of a serious conversation with Cuthbert Flowerdew.

"Sorry to interrupt, but I need to speak to Derek urgently. Do excuse us, won't you Cuthbert?" Dr Bakewell hinted at Cuthbert to leave the room. The old gardener took the hint and understood immediately.

"Righty-ho, Doctor. I'd better be off, anyway" he croaked, "seeds to sow and all that." He nodded courteously at the two men before departing the Sun Room and leaving the Doctor and the Professor to their business. They sat down in the tall, throne-like yellow armchairs either side of the fireplace, the sun's rays streaming in through the windows and shining off the top of Dr Bakewell's balding head. Professor Drumgoole sat back, elbows resting on the arms of the chair and pressed the fingertips of his left and right hand together and pushed them upwards, steeple-like, ready to inform Dr Bakewell of an important staff matter.

"Cuthbert's finding it difficult now, George" Professor Drumgoole began softly, as his steepled hands gave way and his fingers entwined, locking his hands together. "The poor chap's almost eighty and looking after all these grounds, well, it's not easy you know, especially for a man of his years..."

"Yes yes, we'll talk about Cuthbert later." Dr Bakewell signalled a dismissal of Professor Drumgoole's concern with a small waft of his hand. "This is much more urgent. I've had a call from Frank Chewdle." Professor Drumgoole sat bolt upright in his chair; he hadn't expected that. Dr Bakewell had told him all about his call from Paul Oakley at the Forest & Woodland Fellowship and the Professor had been delighted. Together they had composed a letter to Frank Chewdle explaining they had evidence to further support their appeal, but that they were not prepared to discuss it over the telephone.

Dr Bakewell told Professor Drumgoole all about Frank Chewdle's call. It had been very brief, but it was to inform them that on the first of June, Frank Chewdle and members of both C.O.C.O.A and the Culinary Council were going to visit the school and the Forest of Forgetfulness themselves to decide the outcome of the appeal. If they found the appeal successful, then the Culinary Council itself would inform the Government. Hopefully then, the school would be safe.

Professor Drumgoole sat and listened intently, his mind whirring as the enormity of this sunk in. He hadn't expected the Culinary Council to want to be involved, he thought it would go no higher than the National Association of Master Bakers. He knew some of the Association and was on good terms with them; the Culinary Council weren't very warm when it came to Dr Bakewell. They hadn't forgotten the incident of the mice and some of the members just wouldn't let that go. He was recalling this incident when a thought struck him.

"The first of June? That's the Feast Day of St Wistan."

Dr Bakewell nodded. "Indeed."

"We'll have to make sure Chef Goodbun keeps his House away from the Forest and from Lambrick's. The last thing we need is any of this getting through to the Sorrel's. Not until it's all been sorted, anyway."

"I'll speak to him later today." Dr Bakewell said, rubbing his chin with thought. "We'll need Lambrick with us of course. What do you think of bringing Verity along? She was the one that found Rasher. She might be key to him bringing the truffles back."
It was Professor Drumgoole's turn to consider this. Eventually he made a decision.

"I don't think it's wise. I think it's best to leave the children out of this entirely."

* * *

Chef Goodbun was a very clever man. He was a man that followed his own advice - he listened much more than he spoke and he rarely, if ever, raised his voice. If anyone in his class was disruptive or talking too much, he would simply ask them "How many ears do you have?" The bemused child would of course answer "two, sir." "And how many mouths do you have?" would be the Chef's next question. "One, sir" would inevitably be the reply from the chatterbox child. "And that is for a reason." Chef Goodbun would say. "You have twice as many ears because you are meant to listen twice as much as you are meant to talk. And as you have talked for half the lesson so far, it's time to let your ears take over and for you to now be quiet and listen." And it always worked. Any disruptive child would immediately feel embarrassed by their actions and very quickly become silent. And that was how Chef Goodbun himself acted. He was not prone to outbursts or temper tantrums; he listened first and considered matters quietly before saying anything; because of this everyone liked and trusted him.

Dr Bakewell sat with Chef Goodbun at one of the kitchen workstations in the Chef's classroom, discussing matters. After Dr Bakewell explained the truffle situation, Chef Goodbun was initially amazed; truffles were extremely rare and to even think they might have been growing them at their school - without realising - was almost unbelievable. He understood the importance of the events and he also knew all about Dr Bakewell and Henry Sorrel's rivalry; all the teachers knew but out of respect and admiration for Dr Bakewell, no-one ever mentioned it.

The chef assured Dr Bakewell he would think of something to make sure all the students were occupied and that he could leave this with him. Dr Bakewell thanked him and left the classroom, leaving the Chef sitting at the workstation, his chin cupped in the palm of his hand, as he wondered what to do. The Feast Day was supposed to be a day of celebration of their Saint, a day off for the House, so he couldn't exactly keep them in lessons all day. Or could he, he suddenly thought, as an idea sprang to mind?

* * *

That evening after dinner he walked casually into the St Wistan common room. Being almost half past eight, it was the perfect time as all House Members would be in their common rooms before bedtime at nine o'clock. It was, as usual, full of music; children playing board games, reading, chatting and generally relaxing after a hard day's school work. Being the Head of St Wistan it was not unusual for him to appear in the common room so it was a few moments before the children realised his presence and quickly became quiet.

"Evening, Wistans!" he called cheerily as he sauntered to the radio and switched off the music which was filling the room. A few children replied "evening, sir" while others simply smiled at him in reply. He walked to the fireplace and addressed his House.

"As you all know, next week is the Feast Day of St Wistan." A general mumbling of agreement and excitement broke out - the first years excited at the prospect of their forthcoming trip to Evesham Abbey, the others excited about having the day off while the other Houses were in lessons. "As you also know, it is a day of celebration. To celebrate the life and death of our House Saint - our very own Saint Wistan. And I've been thinking about how we can do something different to celebrate this day. Then a thought struck me. Why don't we - together, as a House - come up with food ideas and suggestions for the whole school to eat that day. But there's one point. All food must be in our House Colours! And we, as Saint Wistan's will be the ones to make it! What do you think?" A few people didn't seem too happy about that but most of them thought it was a great idea.

"Yeah - we can tell the other Houses what to eat!"

"Cream and green? How much food is cream and green, though?"

"Dur...ever heard of icing?"

"Yeah dur-brain...and broccoli, spinach, lettuce, cabbage, sea-weed, beans, cucumber - yeah, it's really hard to find green food - not!"

"Whoa - getting Oswald and Swithun to celebrate Wistan's Day? Ace!"

Avery and Percy were unsurprisingly less keen. "We've got kitchen staff to make our food" sniped Avery, "why should we cook for them?"

"I think Saint Wistan would be delighted to see his House celebrating his Feast Day by creating and baking food for the whole school, in his honour." said Chef Goodbun, shrewdly, casting a sideways glance at Avery, who flushed. "If you, his own house won't do it, who will? And one other thing. As I am an Artisan Baker, you will all bake Artisan. There were no mixers or tools in St Wistan's day and this is how we will honour him. It's still your day off, you won't be wearing your uniforms and you will not have me telling you what to do and when to do it. What do you think?"

"I think it's a great idea, sir!"

"Gonna be a lot of work, though."

"Yeah but we're St Wistan's - we can do anything!"

"Yeah, let's do it!"

Feeling relieved that the general response was positive, Chef Goodbun told them all to think about what kinds of food they would like to make and bade them all goodnight. As he left the common room and slid down the slide to the hallway, he congratulated himself on his idea. If they were all baking by hand, for the whole school, it would certainly keep them occupied for the entire day. There was no chance of anyone escaping down to the forest now. Dr Bakewell's mission so far remained safe.

* * *

The children of St Wistan spent the next few days coming up with recipe suggestions which were passed onto Tony Rose, the school chef, to see what he could do. They ranged from the run-of-the-mill ideas, such as cucumber sandwiches and cream cakes to the more bizarre, such as spinach swiss roll and creamed courgettes. They were actually very excited to see what Mr Rose would cook for them. This was the compromise Chef Goodbun had agreed to, Mr Rose would assist with the cooking, just in case!

The first of June arrived and accordance with tradition, the St Wistan first years were taken on a trip to Evesham Abbey, to learn about St Wistan and how he became a saint. Unfortunately as Avery wasn't a scholarship student he wouldn't be allowed on the trip like Vaughan was with the St Oswaldians and so it was up to Chef Goodbun, Head of St Wistan to ensure pupils like Avery and Percy Snodland especially, couldn't creep out and follow them to the forest. Avery's father already knew what Dr Bakewell's intentions were and had already almost thwarted him - Dr Bakewell wanted to give him no second chances by giving his son a chance to sabotage him.

The other years spent the day baking all sorts of puddings and cakes, green and cream of course, for the school to eat that evening. They had a whale of a time and made offerings of mint green profiteroles, green courgette cakes, cucumber smoothies, gooseberry fools, leaf salads, broccoli forest gateaux, runner bean ringlets and watercress jelly, to name but a few. Even Avery Sorrel enjoyed himself, being able to bake without being told how it should be done, but he wasn't about to let on to anyone that he was having fun. So right up until bedtime, all through the laughs and the giggles and the fantastic green feast produced by a very proud Mr Rose, he remained stony-faced and sulked.

Chapter 46

Lady Batternberg

Now that spring had come to an end and summer had just begun, the children had started practising for the most dreaded time of the school year - the end of year exams - which would begin on the first of July as usual. Vaughan was finding it particularly hard, this being his first year at the school but taking second-year exams and so was spending as much time as possible either practising in the kitchen classrooms, or studying in the library. He loved the library, it was his favourite part of the school for it was so stately and traditional-looking. It was two storey's high, with a gallery landing on the first floor with bookshelves which lined the walls on one side, interrupted only by the sash windows which allowed the sunlight to filter through what would be an otherwise dark room. Opposite the bookcases on the other side of the narrow landing was a waist-high wooden balustrade which prevented students from accidentally toppling off the gallery and falling down onto the floor below. On the floor below were the study tables and chairs, all polished cherrywood with golden lamps on each table for reading by. In the centre of the ground floor stood a grand stone fireplace, which, when lit during the cold winter months, gave the library a warm, cosy atmosphere. Vaughan liked to be up in the gallery because he loved being high up and the view from the windows was stunning - he could see far across the school grounds right up to the edge of the forest but he could also peer down onto anyone studying below - it made him feel like a knight, watching over and protecting the school!

This morning the St Oswaldians should have been in Artisan Baking with Chef Goodbun, learning about the different types of sponge cakes (he had already hinted that it might crop up in their exam) but Dr Crose had told them at breakfast that the lesson had been cancelled and instead they had an extra study period. 'To be used for study' she had added, seriously. So immediately, Vaughan decided they should go to the library to revise for their exams and Verity and Caroline agreed. Over the last few weeks it had dawned on him that he must pass the exams in order to be able to move onto the third year. Although he had always known this, now the exams were looming nearer and nearer it became a reality to him how hard he needed to work. Failing was not an option, so he put every available moment into either studying or practising his skills.

Vaughan's talent, it transpired, was flavours and designing cakes. He had, over the last few months, developed a skill in knowing what flavours go well together and what do not. Verity's special skill was showing itself in sugarcraft - she was improving massively in making little figures and animals out of fondant icing. Unsurprisingly, Caroline's forte was chocolatiering; she would often write down ideas for chocolate bars and daydream about making them real one day. They often sat in the library researching baking methods and skills and would discuss what they would do when they eventually left the School of Confectionery, although leaving the school wasn't something they particularly liked to think about very often, for they enjoyed it so much.

It was during this unplanned study period that Vaughan discovered something rather unexpected. He stood at a gallery bookshelf running his fingers over the spines of the books, scanning the titles for books on sponge-cake recipes. He passed by 'Fruit Cakes for Fruitcakes', 'The Rise and Fall of the Sponge' and 'Edible Arts: Decorations for Everyday' when something moving outside caught his eye. He pushed back the Fabulous Flavourings book his finger was hovering over and went to get a better look. It was very unusual to see adults walking through the grounds - he crossed over to the window, put his hands to the glass to shield his eyes from the sun and peered out across the grass - there were definitely adults walking across the fields.

"Verity! Caroline! Come here - quick!" he leaned over the balcony and whisper-called to the girls, who were seated at a study table below, engrossed in the book they were reading together. They looked up at him and stared.

"What?" said Caroline, in a hushed voice.

"Just come here - quick!" Vaughan repeated in an equally hushed tone. The girls looked at each other and raced up the stairs to the upper level where they found Vaughan staring through the window, his hands shielding his eyes.

"What do you make of that?" he stepped aside to allow Verity and Caroline room to see for themselves.

"That's Dr Bakewell - I'd recognise him anywhere, but not the others. Who are they?" asked Caroline, "Where are they going?"

"They're heading towards Farmer Lambrick's place" Verity realised as they watched them move swiftly over the neatly manicured lawns. They thought for a moment, each of them racking their brains. Why would Dr Bakewell take strangers to Farmer Lambrick's farmhouse? Then a thought struck Vaughan like a lightning bolt. "They're not going to Farmer Lambricks. They're going to the Forest."

* * *

"I must say, it's very good of you all to come today" said Dr Bakewell, a little tremor of nervousness in his voice.

"Well, with such an extraordinary claim George, it's only to be expected" replied Frank Chewdle curtly. "One has to be certain of such matters."

"Indeed, an Ancient Forest in school grounds is in itself a remarkable discovery. Worth the trip to see that at least, if nothing else" added a plump, middle-aged woman, who was dressed in a most unsuitable manner for traipsing across fields and forests.

Wearing a smart, navy blue skirt suit and black high heels she tottered and wobbled as her shoes sank into the soft grass as they made their way towards the forest.

"Did she have to come along?" Dr Bakewell whispered discreetly to Professor Drumgoole, as the woman tutted and complained about the walk.

"Considering she's the Chief Chocolatier, I daresay Chewdle had no choice. She's a battleaxe though, you'd better be prepared." Dr Bakewell tutted and rolled his eyes.

They soon reached the farmhouse where Farmer Lambrick was standing outside waiting to greet the visitors, nervously twizzling his tweed cap round in circles as they approached.

"Morning, morning!" he said enthusiastically, shaking the hands of Frank Chewdle, who smiled pleasantly and returned the handshake.

"Good morning." said the plump lady, frostily, rolling back her shoulders.

"Oh, good....good morning, Madam" answered Farmer Lambrick awkwardly. "Where would you..."

"To these so-called truffles of yours. Obviously." Plump lady spoke again not allowing the Farmer to even ask his question.

"Lambrick, this is Lady Batternberg of the Culinary Council. She's Head of Chocolatiering." Professor Drumgoole introduced her. She turned her head so quickly at Professor Drumgoole it almost snapped. "Chief Chocolatier, Drumgoole" she corrected him, unnecessarily. Professor Drumgoole shot a quick look at Dr Bakewell and allowed a small half-smile creep onto his face, to say 'see what I mean?' Dr Bakewell raised an eyebrow in reply, clearly shocked by Lady Batternberg's rudeness. He hadn't met her before and if this encounter was anything to go by, he sincerely hoped he wouldn't meet her again either.

Farmer Lambrick put on a rucksack, got a long leather strap and disappeared for a few seconds. The visitors heard a few grunts, a bit of a cufuffle and then Farmer Lambrick reappeared, complete with Rasher wearing a huge dog collar, which was fixed to the long leather lead held firmly in Farmer Lambrick's hand.

"What on earth!" exclaimed Lady Batternberg.

"Just what's going on here?" asked Frank Chewdle, perplexed.

"This ere's our truffle sniffer" beamed Farmer Lambrick proudly, as Dr Bakewell slapped his hand against his forehead and hung his head. "This is moy..er..this is Rasher."

"And he finds the truffles, does he?" enquired Frank Chewdle, disbelievingly.

"Pigs actually are the best way to locate truffles, Frank" Lady Batternberg whispered snootily to Chewdle, out of earshot of the others. "Personally I think this whole thing is a waste of time. The sooner we get this ridiculous charade over and done with, the better."

"Let's see first" cautioned Chewdle, "we could uncover something truly incredible here."

"Oh hardly. Mark my words, this is one of Bakewell's fanciful ideas. Growing chocolate truffles indeed!"

* * *

Onwards they progressed, deeper into the forest, Lady Batternberg fussing and moaning about her heels sinking in the soft grass. Farmer Lambrick smiled and chuckled to himself, wondering how she would have coped had they visited during the Winter when the ground was pure mud and boggy! At least now that summer was just around the corner, the previously muddy forest floor was now carpeted with lush, green grass. However, this had it's downside - Rasher was having difficulty in finding the truffles underground.

After twenty minutes of Rasher sniffing the tree roots and pawing the ground, they had still found nothing. Dr Bakewell was anxious and beginning to sweat, worried that this might fall apart at the last hurdle.

"Can't you do something? Let him off the lead if you must. Lambrick, this pig has got to find these truffles. I don't need to remind you...." he pleaded, desperately.

"No, yer don't. Sir." added Lambrick hotly. "Last toime there was hardly any grass. Give him toime, he'll find them, Oi know he will."

"Dr Bakewell." Lady Batternberg's haughty voice cut through the air stopping all conversations with its haughty tone. She wobbled towards him and Farmer Lambrick - who was still holding Rasher on his lead - clearly unimpressed. "Congratulations on the certification of your forest. That is a remarkable discovery. However, this is all that has been discovered and I think we have wasted enough time here. Chewdle!" she called over her shoulder, summoning Frank Chewdle who trotted towards her like an obedient labrador. "It's clear there's nothing to find here. We will dismiss the appeal and the findings of the COCOA meeting will stand." Turning towards Dr Bakewell, she began to formally give him the bad news.

"Dr Bakewell. Professor Drumgoole. After visiting your beautiful forest today, I have to inform you - oh! Where have these cats come from?" Wrapping themselves around her ankles were Rhubarb and Custard, rubbing their backs along her legs. Distracted by the cats she momentarily forgot her train of thought. Bending down to fuss them, they started purring contentedly. As they closed their eyes, their purring getting louder, Rashers ears picked up, hearing the mewing of the cats. He sprang forwards and pulled the lead straight out of Farmer Lambrick's fingers. "Rasher! No!" yelled Farmer Lambrick, quickly followed by "oh bloimey!"

Rasher charged towards the cats, egged on by their loud purring. Closer and closer he got, bent his head down and headbutted the large blue blob in front of him, to get to the cats. Unfortunately for Farmer Lambrick, the large blue blob was Lady Batternberg's rather ample bottom. She shrieked in surprise and leapt into the air, rubbing her buttocks as the cats scarpered away from Rasher. They bolted straight for the forest where they began to climb the trees, to get away from the huge pig.

"JUST WHAT'S GOING ON?!" she bellowed. "YOU - FARMER - CONTROL YOUR PIG, OR..." But no-one was paying her any attention. Everyone was running back towards the forest - Farmer Lambrick at the front, quickly followed by Professor Drumgoole, Dr Bakewell and Frank Chewdle. She ran clumsily after them with very un-ladylike strides and followed them back into the forest.

It didn't take long to find Rasher, the grunting and crashing noises and cat-calls made it a great deal easier to find them. As she finally caught up with them, she stopped. All four men were standing in an arc shape around a tree, standing in silence. Farmer Lambrick put his arm out to stop Lady Batternberg from going nearer the tree. For Rasher had found something. Furrowing the ground with his snout, she watched, mesmerised, as Rasher slowly unearthed several balls of dark brown mud. Farmer Lambrick crept towards Rasher, quickly grabbed his lead and lead him away from the tree. Professor Drumgoole gently stepped forwards and collected Rasher's findings. He handed them back to Lady Batternberg and Frank Chewdle who stared at them, before breaking off the outer mud casing. They closed their eyes and sniffed the balls. "Cocoa" murmured Chewdle, before putting one in his mouth. Lady Batternberg quickly followed and tasted one herself. "Well I'll be..." she said softly, "...it's a truffle!"

Chapter 47

Decision Time

On the upper floor of the library, in the gallery, Vaughan, Verity and Caroline peered through the glass into the bright sunshine, squinting to try to get a better view and see what was going on. Unfortunately the adults were just out of sight and they really couldn't see a thing.

"What do you reckon all that's about then?" asked Caroline, who was more nosy than concerned. Lowering his head and his voice, Vaughan whispered a reply.

"It's got to be you-know-what in you-know-where" he said mysteriously.

"What?" Caroline screwed up her nose.

"You know. You-know-what in you-know-where."

"Oh. You mean the tr...."

"TREES! Yes Caroline, they're inspecting the trees" interrupted Verity, nudging Caroline as she did so to stop her blurting it out. There were other children in the library and no-one except the three of them knew anything about the truffles, but Caroline kept forgetting, she was so excited by the thought.

"Oh, oh yes, the trees" Caroline repeated, before they quickly moved downstairs and took a seat at a study table. Once downstairs they huddled around the table to discuss what could be going on.

"There's only two things in the direction they were walking" began Caroline, "Farmer Lambrick's house and the Forest."

"No-one except Lambrick ever goes into the Forest" began Verity "so why would Dr Bakewell take visitors that way unless they were going to go there? They'd need Farmer Lambrick with them - you saw how he was with us when Rasher first escaped, remember? He refused to let us go with him and insisted on going alone."

"Exactly" agreed Caroline, "so why would he now want to take people in there? It doesn't make sense."

"It does if Dr Bakewell's told him to" said Vaughan quietly. The girls looked at him. "Think about it. We know the Council of Confectioners refused to accept the truffles were real - Farmer Lambrick told us. What if Dr Bakewell's desperate enough to want to prove it? Who's the only person, apart from us, that knows where the truffles are?"

"Rasher" stated Caroline, obviously. Vaughan rolled his eyes. "Person, Caroline. They can't ask a pig, can they?" and he smiled at Verity, who smiled shyly back.

"Farmer Lambrick!" answered Verity. "That's it! That's what he's doing - Vaughan, you're a genius! I bet that's exactly it - they must be from the Council and he's taking them to Farmer Lambrick's, getting him to take them into the Forest and then he's going to show them where we found the truffles!"

"Let's hope they're still there then, or Lambrick takes them to the right spot" Vaughan reminded them seriously, "because if they're not there, there's no more chances. If they don't find them for the Councillors, this school might close down."

* * *

Elated but trying desperately hard not to let his excitement and relief show, Dr Bakewell nonchalantly led the visitors back through the grounds and took them into the appropriately named Sun Room. As the sun's rays streamed through the windows, illuminating and warming the room, Dr Bakewell welcomed them warmly, beaming from ear to ear and motioned them to take a seat. He quickly rang a bell to call the Butler, Mr Soames, who arrived within seconds of being summoned. "You rang, sir?" he asked, formally.

"Soames, could you ensure we are not disturbed for the next half an hour please? We have some rather confidential matters to sort."

"Of course, Sir. Will that be all?"

"Oh, yes. Would anyone like a cup of tea or coffee?" he asked the three others. Only Lady Batternberg decided she would like a drink, and requested a cup of tea with three sugars. "Very good, m'lady. Dr Bakewell." said Mr Soames, nodding to the Headmaster before backing out of the Sun Room and leaving them to their business.

"Dr Bakewell" began Lady Batternberg "I am quite surprised. No, I am shocked, I do not mind admitting. When I first heard of your claim, I thought it so ludicrous it must have been a joke of some kind, an April fool. But now I've seen....tasted..." she closed her eyes, as if savouring and remembering the taste of the truffles, "..those delicious truffles, they are most certainly true truffles. This is an extraordinary find, extraordinary" and she re-opened her eyes and watched the Headmaster.

"Thank you, Lady Batternberg" said Dr Bakewell, "I do appreciate your opinion and your honesty. And you, Frank?"
Frank Chewdle looked at him squarely and sighed. "George, I owe you an apology. It shouldn't have gotten to this, we should never have included Sorrel on your hearing. I'm just glad Lady Batternberg was able to come here today, now we have her on side...."

"Oh, I'm on no-one's side, Frank" interjected Lady Batternberg, taking Dr Bakewell and Frank Chewdle by surprise. "I am impartial, remember, I do not take sides." Professor Drumgoole noticed Dr Bakewell's face fall, ever so slightly, and Frank Chewdle looked perplexed. They were hoping beyond hope that Lady Batternberg would be on their side and sign to say the truffles were real.

"And it is exactly because of that impartiality, that Lady Batternberg's opinion is so important." Professor Drumgoole explained. "If she was on our side, then it wouldn't be a fair assessment. It is precisely because she isn't on anyone's side that her decision will be accepted by all the Councils, the National Association and the Government. That is why she is here gentleman, to give an honest, unbiased opinion." Dr Bakewell relaxed; he had to hand it to Professor Drumgoole, he was a shrewd fox when he needed to be. That was why he'd invited her - not because he liked her, but because he didn't - so if she said the truffles were genuine, no-one would object. No-one would argue. No-one would oppose her.

"So, may I ask what your recommendation will be , Lady Batternberg?" asked Dr Bakewell gingerly.

"You may" smiled Lady Batternberg, thawing out of her earlier frostiness. "I will be confirming Honeycomb Hall as a grower of natural truffles and naming you, Dr Bakewell, as the owner of the truffles. I am satisfied they are fit for human consumption and recommend that you harvest these truffles as much as you are able."

Professor Drumgoole and Dr Bakewell burst into huge smiles and thanked Lady Batternberg profusely. A little knock on the door interrupted the expressions of gratitude and Professor Drumgoole opened it to Mr Soames, who stood in the doorway with a silver tray containing a cup of tea and a plate of biscuits.

"Tea, m'lady" said Mr Soames as he handed the cup to Lady Batternberg "and biscuits for you all" before he again backed out of the room.

"Congratulations, Dr Bakewell" said Lady Batternberg, raising her cup. "Here's to your truffles. I trust I may see them on display at your school fete, this year?"

"That you may" smiled Dr Bakewell, nodding at her in reply, "that you may!"

Chapter 48

Return of the Summer Fete

Vaughan awoke with a mix of excitement and sadness. He had to make sure all his drawers were emptied and all his belongings packed away in his suitcase. For today was the thirty-first of July, the last day of the school year.

As he showered and got dressed, he thought back to this time last year, when he was nervously looking forward to the summer fete, desperately hoping his chessboard cake would be enough to win him a scholarship. The chessboard cake! Gosh, he'd learned so much more since then, it made him smile to think of how simple it actually was when at the time he'd thought it had been so complicated! Once he was dressed and had checked his suitcase and drawers one last time, he met Verity and Caroline, who were waiting for him in the common room.

"Morning!" Caroline called cheerfully, as he entered. "Morning" he smiled back.

"You okay?" asked Verity.

"Yeah. Just a bit weird thinking this is our last day. It's going to feel so strange going home for four weeks."

"Oh, you'll soon get used to it" dismissed Caroline. "It's us you'll miss the most!" Vaughan smiled, wondering if she knew just how true that statement really was. Not that he was going to tell them that of course, but he really was going to miss the girls - they were the best friends he had ever made.

Being the thirty-first of July, it was also the day of the summer fete. Since the scholarships had been such a massive success Dr Bakewell had decided it should be an annual event, to welcome new students and also give pupils a great way to end the school year. As soon as breakfast was over, the children were to take their belongings into the common room, where Mr Soames and the House Prefects would look after them, so the students were free to spend the day as they wished.

Vaughan, Verity and Caroline really made the most of the fete and had a lot of fun. "I remember this time last year" said Vaughan as they ran through the Orchard, which was in full bloom. "I was so nervous I couldn't really enjoy myself that much. But I can now!" and laughed as he raced them to the cake-walk ride. This year there were clowns on stilts, walking through the grounds; there were the same tent tables with teachers giving mini-lessons; tables covered with sweets, cakes and chocolate sculptures just like before, and Vaughan noticed the stage had also been set up. He wondered if Cherry Bakewell would be singing again this year.

They went on several rides and ran around for a while until they heard the low rumble of large motor vehicles. Running to the side of the school, they peered around the bushes and watched as the red buses trundled up the driveway, full of this year's hopeful new students. "It seems strange to think that was you last year, Vaughan" said Verity, as the children and their families alighted the buses and gathered before the main entrance to the school. "I know, it seems such a long time ago" agreed Vaughan. "But it was the best thing that I've ever done in my entire life."

The bell pealed ten times and the music was silenced. Vaughan explained to Verity and Caroline what Dr Bakewell and Professor Drumgoole would be telling the visitors, remembering their speeches from last year. When Professor Drumgoole walked towards the tent where they were standing, Vaughan, Verity and Caroline quickly disappeared out of sight, for they knew the hopeful children would be registering their cakes and sweets for the competition, and they didn't want to be seen to be spying.

They spent the morning playing, nibbling treats from the various tables set up in the gardens, and talking to their teachers.

When it came to almost two o'clock, they made their way to the stage.

"Do you think Cherry will be singing again?" Vaughan asked Caroline.

"Probably" she shrugged, "I suppose she'll always come if Dr Bakewell wants her to."

"It's funny though, isn't it?" said Vaughan. "Doesn't Dr Bakewell mind her naming herself after a cake, or is that why he books her? Because of her name?"

"Cherry isn't named after a cake!" laughed Caroline, "why would anyone name themselves after a cake? She could've called herself 'Victoria Sponge' if that was the case, couldn't she?"

Verity put her hand to her mouth in realisation. "Of course, you wouldn't know, would you?" Vaughan looked at her and pulled a quizzical face. "Know what?"

"That's her real name, Vaughan. Dr Bakewell created the Cherry Bakewell cake. She didn't name herself after the cake, he named the cake after her. Cherry is his niece."

"Cherry Bakewell is Dr Bakewell's niece?" repeated Vaughan, completely surprised.

"Yep. Her father is Dr Bakewell's brother. So she is his niece. He hasn't got any children of his own so when she was born he created the cake for her." Verity explained. "She had pale white skin, blonde hair and cherry-red lips. So, he made a cake with a yellow pastry base - her hair; white icing - her skin and a red cherry - her lips and her name. And there you have it. Cherry Bakewell by name, Cherry Bakewell by nature."

"But that's amazing!" exclaimed Vaughan, "how did he ever think of that?"

"Because he's a genius" said Verity, proudly.

"And that's why I expect she'll always sing here when she can" added Caroline. "For her Uncle. He made a cake in her honour, so she'll sing in his honour."

Before they knew it, they heard the school bell peal twice, signalling two o'clock. The three of them stood at the back of the stage and waited expectantly. The music struck up and as expected, to the children's delight, on she walked - the beautiful singing niece of their beloved Headmaster.

She belted out the first song and much like last year, got the crowd singing and dancing along with her. A familiar deep voice spoke from right next to the children. "Enjoying yerselves, are yer?"

"Lambrick!" Vaughan beamed, as the Farmer greeted them. "What are you doing here?"

"T's the last day o' term, isn't it?" answered the Farmer. "Think Oi'd miss out on all the fun? Not on yer nelly! Besides, Dr Bakewell said he'd got a little surprise fer me."

"A surprise? Ooh I wonder what it could be?" said Caroline, joining in. "Maybe it's another pig!"

"Oh-ho, Oi doubt that!" chuckled the Farmer, "though Oi must admit, Oi did ask fer one. Well, either that or a singing Farmer!" He looked towards the stage at Cherry who was still singing her heart out. "But she don't look much loike a Farmer ter me!" and they all chuckled.

They stood there politely as Dr Bakewell appeared on stage after Cherry's performance and announced the names of the ten scholarship children chosen for the next school year. They all clapped enthusiastically as 'Alexander Pink.... Ruby Palmer-Brown... Chelsea Pitt.... Kimi Kemura.... Lenny Richards.... Isla Schirman.... Edward Birch.... Marcus Blythe..... Christopher Wistan and Nicole Hermann' were one by one reunited on stage with their winning entries. Once the applause had died down the children were shown off stage and told to return to their parents. Dr Bakewell then made one more announcement.

"This past year at Honeycomb Hall has been eventful and we made two fantastic discoveries. In recognition of one of our members of staff, Farmer Lambrick..." Farmer Lambrick's jaw dropped open as he stared at the children and they back at him - Dr Bakewell had never referred to him as a member of staff before - "I'm proud to present, for the first time ever at Honeycomb, the one and only 'Singing Farmers'!"

Farmer Lambrick led the cheering and clapped wildly, as to the children's surprise a group of men walked on stage, looking exactly as Dr Bakewell had just described them. Wearing brown corduroy trousers, white cotton shirts, red neckerchiefs and brown floppy hats they really were farmers. The crowd fell silent, the farmers took out their guitars and began to sing.

* * *

To their amazement, the children loved it! The Singing Farmers sang in broad West-Country accents but it only added to their charm! They sang six songs and were surprised to see a lot of the parents and children knowing the words and singing along. They were very different to Cherry, but the crowd loved them just as much and Cherry made a special appearance and joined in with them for the last song, much to Dr Bakewell and Farmer Lambrick's obvious pleasure. When they had finished their set, the crowd rose to their feet and whooped and applauded loudly, calling 'Encore! Encore!' The Singing Farmers departed the stage, the crowd settled back down and Dr Bakewell reappeared once more, calling up the scholarship winners to stand alongside him, centre stage, as he addressed his audience.

"Our scholarship programme this past year has been extremely successful and I am proud to have our next scholarship students standing here beside me, despite some initial objections to us accepting ordinary children into our school. But I tell you this. There is no such thing as an ordinary person, an ordinary child. Each and every child has a talent, a skill. The children here before you have shown great talent in baking, cake decorating and sweet making. As my students, it is my pleasure to harness these talents, develop these skills and help these children become the greatest that they can be. I wish you all a happy holiday and look forward to seeing you all again on the first of September. Please enjoy the rest of the day and once again, let's congratulate our new scholars."

As the crowd once more applauded the ten shy children on the stage, Vaughan looked at Verity and Caroline and they each smiled at each other. It had been a great year. They had become great friends, Vaughan had finally found a school he felt he truly belonged in and between them, they had helped to save the school. Walking towards the red buses which would take them home for the summer, Vaughan paused.

"This has been the best year of my life. Thank you" and he hugged both Verity and Caroline before climbing into bus Number Six and showing his pass to the conductor. Taking a seat by the window, he looked out at Verity and Caroline, who were waving him goodbye. He waved back as the bus began to trundle down the driveway, away from the school. He sat and smiled to himself; for the first time in his life he was already looking forward to the first of September when he would return to Honeycomb Hall and to his friends. As he made his way home he recalled Dr Bakewell's speech. *There is no such thing as an ordinary child. Every child has a talent, a skill.'* Inspired, Vaughan realised Dr Bakewell was right - talents simply lay there hidden in the most unexpected places, waiting to be discovered by the right people, just like the truffles!

Thinking of all that had happened since he started the school, Vaughan smiled to himself. I wonder what next year will bring? he thought to himself. He could hardly wait to find out!

The End

Printed in the USA
CPSIA information can be obtained
at www.ICGtesting.com
LVHW040225120224
771598LV00019B/111

9 781326 444860